More praise for Laurence Shames and *The Naked Detective*

"Like Charles Willeford, Elmore Leonard, and Carl Hiaasen, Laurence Shames is a specialist in tales of low and high jinks in humid places."
—*San Francisco Chronicle*

"With his trademark humor, Shames adds another quirky, fast-paced mystery to his Key West collection."
—*New York Daily News*

"Shames is an engaging storyteller who keeps the action moving and the chuckles coming, adding up to unpretentious but diverting entertainment."
—*The San Diego Union-Tribune*

"Shames is at once literate and accessible, often hilarious, and always on the mark."
—*The Washington Times*

Please turn the page for more reviews. . . .

By Laurence Shames

VIRGIN HEAT
TROPICAL DEPRESSION
SUNBURN
SCAVENGER REEF
FLORIDA STRAITS
MANGROVE SQUEEZE*
WELCOME TO PARADISE*
THE NAKED DETECTIVE*

*Published by The Ballantine Publishing Group

THE
NAKED
DETECTIVE

LAURENCE SHAMES

FAWCETT BOOKS · NEW YORK
The Ballantine Publishing Group

Published by The Ballantine Publishing Group
Copyright © 2000 by Laurence Shames

All rights reserved under International and Pan-American Copyright Conventions. Published in the United States by The Ballantine Publishing Group, a division of Random House, Inc., New York, and simultaneously in Canada by Random House of Canada Limited, Toronto.

Ballantine is a registered trademark and the Ballantine colophon is a trademark of Random House, Inc.

www.randomhouse.com/BB/

Library of Congress Catalog Card Number: 2001116721

ISBN 0-345-43219-3

This edition published by arrangement with Villard Books, a division of Random House, Inc.

Manufactured in the United States of America

First Ballantine Books Edition: June 2001

10 9 8 7 6 5 4 3 2 1

For Marilyn, with more love than I knew I had

Who doth ambition shun,
And loves to live in the sun

—SHAKESPEARE, *As You Like It*

PART ONE

1

I never meant to be a private eye.

The whole thing, in fact, was my accountant's idea. A tax dodge. Half a joke. A few years ago I made some money. Made it the modern American way: by sheer dumb luck, doing work I hated, on a silly product that only made life more trivial and more annoying. I took the dough—not a lot of dough, but enough to live on for the rest of my life if I wasn't an asshole about it—and moved full-time to Key West.

I'd had a funky little house there for years. Wood frame, shady porch, tiny pool that took up most of a backyard choked with thatch and bougainvillea. Vacation house. Daydreaming about that place, the time I'd eventually spend there, got me through a lot of crappy afternoons in my stupid office up in Jersey. Now I wanted to really make it home.

So I told my accountant to free up some cash. "I'm renovating. Building an addition."

"You're putting in an office," he informed me.

"Office? Benny, I'm retired."

3

"Bullshit you're retired. What are you, forty-four?"

"Forty-five."

"Forty-five you don't retire. Forty-five you have a crisis and change careers."

"There's no crisis, Benny. I'm putting in wine storage, a music room, and a hot tub."

He raised his hands to fend off the information. "You never told me that," he said. "It's an office and it'll save you thousands. Tens of thousands. Plus your car becomes deductible."

I made the mistake of keeping silent for a moment. Call me cheap. I shouldn't have even thought about it, but the idea of saving tens of thousands made me pause.

"Become a Realtor," Benny suggested. "Everyone down there becomes a Realtor, right?"

I'd dealt with Realtors in my life. "I'd rather shoot myself," I said.

"Shoot yourself," he muttered, then started free-associating. "Tough guy. Humphrey Bogart. Hey, call yourself a private eye."

"Don't be ridiculous."

He quickly fell in love with his idea. "Ya know," he said, "there's a lot of advantages. Private corporation. One employee: you. You get a gun—"

"Benny, cut it out."

"—get a license—"

"How you get a license?"

"Florida?" he said. "Probably swear you haven't murdered anybody in the last sixty, ninety days."

"Benny, I don't wanna be a private eye."

He paused, blinked, and looked somewhat surprised. "Schmuck! Did I say you have to *be* a private eye? I said we're calling you a private eye. You'll get some business cards, put a listing in the phone book—"

"Commit fraud—"

"What fraud? You're committing failure. Look, the government allows three years' worth of losses. By then we've depreciated the work on the house, the car lease has expired—"

Well, the whole thing was preposterous—and I guess I kind of like preposterous. Having an amusing thing to say at parties, occasionally in bars. Something incongruous and intriguing. So on my tax returns, at least, I became a private eye. Pete Amsterdam, sole proprietor, doing business as Southernmost Detection, Inc.

That was two and a half years ago. I have a license somewhere in a drawer, and a gun I've never fired rusting in a wall safe. Until very recently, thank God, I hadn't had a single client. Three, four times a year someone calls me up, usually on some sordid and depressing matrimonial thing. I lie and say I'm too busy; for some reason the potential client apologizes and quickly gets off the phone, like I'll charge him for my precious time. My only worry has been that the IRS might come snooping around to see if I was legit. This has been a sporadic but uncomfortable concern, since, for me, feeling legit has never come that easy anyway.

But in the meantime the house improvements came out beautiful, suited me to a T. I'm di-

vorced. I live alone. I guess I'm a little eccentric.
Mainly it's that I don't pretend to care about the
things that most people pretend to care about.
The news. What's on television. The outside
world. I have a small, tight core of things that still
can hold my interest; I arrange my life as simply
and neatly as I can around those things, and the
rest just sort of passes me right by. I like wine. I
like music. I like tennis. After that the list grows
pretty short.

Must sound meager to people who live in places
where everyone is busy and engaged and avidly
discusses what's in the theaters or the paper. But
Key West isn't like that. Key West is a place to
withdraw to, a retreat without apology or shame.
And you learn things from the place where you
live. One of the things Key West teaches is that
disappointment and contentment can go together
more easily than you would probably imagine.

So I've been more or less content down here.
Tan, reasonably fit, generally unbothered. I do
what I want and, better still, I don't do what I
don't want. Which includes being a private eye.
In fact, two and a half years into this fraud of a
vocation, I'd practically forgotten I was listed in
the phone book.

Or I had until a few weeks ago, when the client
I'd been dimly dreading came marching into my
unlocked house, stormed past the wine room and
through the music room, out the back door and
around the little pool, to catch me naked in the
hot tub and to turn my whole life upside down.

2

My hot tub is under a poinciana tree—except for the occasional falling pod, a perfect tree to have one's hot tub under. Its branches are bare in the winter, when you want the sun. In late spring it sprouts an astonishing flat-topped canopy of bright red flowers, and in the summer it is mercifully covered with tiny leaves that cast an exquisite dappled shade. Now it was April and the milky buds were just starting to swell and ripen. I looked up at them and thought about my backhand. I'd played tennis that morning and had missed a couple of cross-court passing shots. Probably hadn't dropped my shoulder low enough. I closed my eyes and visualized the perfect motion.

The jets were on, pummeling my lower back. The pump made a sound somewhere between a hiss and a roar. The dreaded client was standing right next to me by the time I heard her say my name.

"Mr. Amsterdam? *Mr. Amsterdam?*"

I opened my eyes. Tiny chlorinated droplets got in them and made me blink. Through the blinking I saw her. A blonde, of course; it's always a blonde, right? Tall. Green-eyed, with a little too much makeup for the daytime. Coral-colored lipstick that was a shade too orange for my taste. The top of a frilly white bra beneath a loosely buttoned lime-green blouse.

Apologetically, the blonde pointed toward the front door of my house. "I rang the bell," she yelled. "I knocked. The door just opened. I really need to talk to someone."

By reflex, I began to say what I always said to the rare misguided souls who tried to hire me. But it was a little hard, while sitting naked in the hot tub in the middle of what, for most people, was a working day, to claim I was too busy. So I said nothing.

"Please," the blonde implored. "A few minutes of your time."

I looked at her. She had a face that held attention. Not delicate but candid and determined, unflinching even in her obvious distress. I felt bad that the noise of the jets was making her yell. On the other hand, the bubbles were the closest thing I had to clothing. I hesitated then figured what the hell and switched the pump off. It was a very Key West way to hold a meeting.

"You're a private detective?" said the blonde. Her voice hadn't quite adjusted to the quiet, and it sounded very loud.

I tried to talk but nothing happened. My balls were half-floating like eggs in a poacher, and it's difficult to lie when naked. I wanted to tell her no, I wasn't a detective, the whole thing was a joke. Then I had an awful thought. Maybe she was from the IRS. Sent to entrap me. They do things like that, let's face it. Feeling ludicrous, I said, "I take on cases now and then."

"But you're new," she said. "Am I right?"

Absurdly, this made me feel defensive. What did I look like, an amateur?

She must have seen the hurt pride in my face. "That's good," she assured me. "This is a tiny town. I need someone who isn't known."

I didn't ask why. I just sat there in the steamy water. There was a silence, and I remember thinking: Now's when she reaches into her purse for a crumbling yellow newspaper clipping. I may not know diddle about being a detective, but I have a certain rudimentary grasp of the detective story. Doesn't everybody? We all grow up with it. It's like the thirty-two-bar jazz tune. We get it without analysis because it's heritage.

And sure enough she reached into her bag. But the clipping she came up with wasn't yellowed, it was mildewed. That's what happens to newsprint in Key West. It sprouts small black fuzzy dots that ripen from the inside out like certain kinds of cheese. Eventually the mold digests the paper and eats the ink and your memories are reduced to wet black dust. She dangled the clipping in front of me. "Are you familiar with this story, Mr. Amsterdam?"

My hands were soaking wet. I shook them off and took the paper.

The headline read APPARENT SUICIDE IN KEY WEST HARBOR, and it so happened it was a story I remembered fairly well. A man had disappeared.

His pants and shirt and wallet and sandals had been found at the water's edge down by the Fort Taylor jetty. He'd left no note. The disappearance had occurred late on a full-moon night, with a strong outgoing tide; the body had never been found. The man's name was Kenny Lukens. He hadn't been in town for long, and little was known about him. He'd lived on his sailboat, which had a broken mast and a torn-up deck and was resting in a cradle on the dry land of Redmond's Boatyard in the Bight. He'd worked as a late-shift bartender at Lefty's, on Duval Street. Seems he'd made no particular impression on his colleagues. Not friendly, not unfriendly. No crazier than most and not obviously despairing. No one knew of drug problems or romantic disappointments. Kenny Lukens just checked out.

This had happened very soon after I'd moved full-time to Florida—which is why I remembered it at all. I'd been feeling both smug and terrified about disappearing to Key West: Was I retiring at a lucky age to paradise, or making the first, half-conscious movement toward oblivion? Kenny Lukens' story had made me wonder what else would have to happen in a person's life so that he'd need to disappear *from* Key West and toward that ultimate retreat.

The blonde's voice pulled me out of my thoughts. "Some people thought the suicide was faked," she said. She said it with a hint of malice, though I couldn't figure who or what the nastiness was aimed at.

"Faked why?"

She looked down at her fingernails, which were the same pink-orange as her lips. Something unpleasantly playful, goading, had come into her manner. "Isn't that the kind of thing detectives figure out, Mr. Amsterdam?"

"Ambitious detectives maybe."

She pouted. She looked let down. I hate letting people down, which is why I don't have that much to do with people. There was a standoff. Finally I caved. "So you think Kenny Lukens is alive?"

She kept on pouting. She was very good at it. Just gazing wistfully between lashes that were lumpy with mascara. The gaze, the sorrow, the needling hope—they all reminded me how much I didn't want to be a private eye.

I dangled the soggy clipping in her direction. "Look, I'm sorry, but it's not the kind of thing I do."

I thought I'd sounded pretty final saying that, but the blonde just stood there over me. This wasn't how it was supposed to play. She was supposed to take the article back, put it in her purse, bite her lip, and maybe start to cry. Except she didn't. A long moment passed. The sun moved behind a poinciana branch and threw me into shade. I made the stupid, fundamental error of getting curious. "Who are you anyway?" I asked. "Ex-wife? Girlfriend? Sister?"

She stared at me. Something vaguely flirtatious happened at the corners of her mouth. She smoothed her skirt across her hips and waved with the muscles of her stomach. Then she

reached up toward her hair. Her polished fingernails slid along her temples, made her shadowed
eyes bend upward at the edges. She pried, apparently, beneath her scalp, then lifted off the wig,
beneath which was some prickly fuzz not much
longer than a crew cut. Tossing the ersatz coif
onto a chaise, she reached into her blouse, probed
past the lace top of her bra, and plucked out two
perfect vinyl tits—which she placed on the damp
edge of the hot tub.

Her voice dropped three-quarters of an octave.
"How rude of me," she said. "I haven't intro-
duced myself."

3

"*So let me* tell you why I had to disappear."

Like a traffic cop I raised a hand. "It's really better if you don't," I said, and tried to figure if I felt more ridiculous sitting naked in the hot tub with a woman I'd never met before standing over me, or a drag queen half undressed.

Kenny Lukens told me anyway, of course. "Someone was threatening to kill me."

I turned away, took a deep breath tart with chlorine. I knew it would come to this. I *knew* it! My asshole accountant. Why hadn't I just paid the fucking tax? Would I have ever missed the measly few grand?

"Kenny, look," I said. "I know jack shit about detective work. I'm not the guy to help you."

He went on like he hadn't heard. "Threatening to kill me, and there was nothing I could do, no one I could tell."

"Ever heard of the police?"

He looked down at my swimming pool, and for an instant I thought maybe he was flirting with suicide again. He would have had a tough time. My pool is four feet deep and not much wider. Without looking up, he said, "This guy owns the police. Besides, I was stealing from him."

Great, I thought. Just great. I'm sitting here braising and this admitted crook has just come swishing through my unlocked house, probably sweeping all my quarters straight into his purse. I have no problem with guys wearing dresses but I guess I'm judgmental about thieves. The disapproval must have shown in my face.

Seeing it, Lukens said, "Mr. Amsterdam, did you ever have a dream?"

A heartbreaking question, asked in a cheap, heartbreaking, Judy Garland tone. Did I ever have a dream? Shit, I've had 'em all. Grow up to be a fireman. Win Wimbledon. Do something grand while my parents were alive, while there was someone to make proud. The usual dreams, the usual unfulfillments. Clichés, in fact. Why did they still have the power to wring a person's guts?

"I had a dream," said Kenny Lukens. He raised his face, and the reflection off the water made him look almost angelic for a moment. "I was going to sail around the world."

I admit this surprised me more than anything so far. Call me conventional—I did not think of drag queens as being avid transoceanic yachtsmen. Those tight skirts and stiletto heels seem so impractical for scuttling across a rolling deck. "Around the world?" I echoed.

"That goal has been my life," he said. "The only thing I've ever worked for. Work awhile, buy a boat, sail New England. Work some more, buy a bigger boat, sail the Caribbean. Luck into a berth, crew across the Atlantic, sail the Med. Everything was leading toward the big one, the circuit."

Lukens fell silent for a moment, his green eyes far away. He was seeing the vast indigo Pacific, I imagine, while I was lounging safe and coddled in my eighty-gallon hot tub. It was humbling, I admit it. Shut me right up.

"Finally I thought I was ready," he went on. "Found a nice ketch in Lauderdale, a Morgan forty-one. Bit of a wreck, of course, or I couldn't have afforded it. So I went back to the old pattern—tending bar to feed the boat. Buying one winch, one shackle at a time. Filling, sanding, painting . . . Spent two years that way. Fiberglass all over me. Band-Aids on every finger. At last the boat was sound. I spent my last paycheck on provisions, did a shakedown cruise to Bimini, then headed out for real. Hit Hawk Channel . . . and made it as far as fucking Sugarloaf—Sugarloaf Key!—before I got dismasted. White squall, freak wind shift. Ripped the shrouds, shredded the main.

"Devastating. One gust and I'm right back where I started. I limped into Key West and got another bar job, raising money for repairs. But the money came too slow. I needed fourteen, sixteen thousand dollars. How many more nights pouring shooters for drunk kids? That's when I started stealing."

He looked at me without a shred of remorse, and I felt a grudging sympathy. The fellowship of disappointment, the brotherhood of frustration. The rare dream that is accomplished sets a person apart; the usual, thwarted dream makes a bond, brings home to us our baleful kinship.

"Bar business," he went on, "everybody steals. Forty, fifty bucks a shift. Pays the rent but it doesn't get you launched around the world. So I got impatient. One night I faked a robbery."

I sloshed in the tub. "Don't tell me," I said. "Please. I don't want to hear it."

"I had the thing thought out," he rambled. "It was a weeknight. After midnight I was on alone. Only got the hard-core regulars then—mostly tough and mumbly guys who talked like they all had different deals going with the owner."

I heard myself say, "Different deals?"

My visitor shrugged. "Who knows? Treasure salvage, gambling—the guy seemed to be involved with lots of stuff. Anyway, the closing routine was simple: Get the assholes out, lock the front door; balance the register, put the cash in one of those bank-deposit pouches; put the pouch in the safe, and leave through the back. So I bagged the money and opened the safe. There was a second pouch in it. That was unusual, but I figured it was the take from the shift before. So much the better. I took both sacks, slipped down the alley to the harbor, got in my dinghy, and sailed across to Tank Island. Buried the two bags, sailed back. Took all of twenty minutes. It was after four A.M. and I don't think anybody saw me.

"I let myself in the back entrance, trashed the office, tore my shirt, called the cops, and made up some bullshit about two strung-out black kids with a gun. As far as I could tell, they bought it."

"They didn't suspect?"

Kenny Lukens sucked his orange lips into a dismissive smirk. "Who knows what they suspected? Who cares? They weren't the problem. The owner was the problem. Lefty Ortega. They phoned him. He came down and right away I knew I'd fucked up big-time. This was not someone you messed with."

"You didn't know that before?" I asked.

"I got hired by a manager. I'd never met the man. I don't think he'd actually worked the bar in years. But now he came in and I was scared from the very first second. His eyes were never still. They flicked around, they jabbed. He had a thick neck with a flat pink scar on it. Hulking shoulders, hairy hands. The cops sucked up to him. He treated them like personal servants. There was some chitchat, then he sent them away, dismissed them.

"Now it was just the two of us," Kenny Lukens continued. "Lefty paced around the office, looked thoughtfully at the empty safe. Very casually he said, 'So, you blamed it on the niggers. Not very original,' he said. 'And not very smart. The niggers don't steal from me. Know how I know that? Three years ago I had a holdup. Couple fucked-up crackheads. Took me a while but I tracked them down. Had their fingers cut off and delivered to people of influence in Bahama Village. Word got out. Don't fuck with Lefty. So I know it wasn't niggers and I know you're full of shit.'

"He kept pacing, but slowly. He wasn't any bigger than me but I knew he could destroy me. He had that kind of violence that just makes you freeze. I said, 'Lefty, I'm telling you the truth!'

"It sounded feeble even to me. He ignored it altogether. He said, 'If it was just that one pouch, we wouldn't have a problem. I'd fire you. A day or two later you'd get beat up. People would hear. That would be enough. But that second pouch, she never should have left it—' "

"She?"

"Hm?"

"You said *she*. Did *he* say *she*?"

Kenny shrugged, let his hands slap down against his thighs. "I said *she*? Jesus, who remembers? What I remember is that then he lunged at me. Grabbed me by my torn-up shirt. My shirt and the skin of my chest. He pulled me close and yelled, 'You piece of shit! Did you look inside that pouch?'

"His breath stank of onions and he was spitting in my face. I couldn't think of anything to say that wouldn't make me sound guiltier. He stared at me then pushed me backward. A desk caught me behind the legs and I sort of half sat down on it.

" 'Listen, scumbag,' he went on. 'Noon tomorrow, you meet me here with that pouch. You don't, you're dead. The bag's been opened, you're dead. You understand? Now get the fuck out of my place.' "

Kenny Lukens paused, and I knew it was my chance to bolt. Spring up naked from the hot tub, dash into my house, find a door with a lock on it, and hide. I'd successfully run away from my own dreams and at least most of my own problems. What sense did it make to become a hostage to some other jerk's? But I didn't bolt. I sat there and kept poaching.

"So I left the office," my visitor resumed, "in a total panic. Tried to think straight. Couldn't. I kept seeing Ortega's eyes, and I just kept thinking, pouch or no pouch, this lunatic is going to have me killed. He can and he will.

"By now it's five A.M. I had an hour of darkness left, and an hour of a good hard tide. Suddenly my mind was made up: Get out, period. I faked the robbery, might as well fake suicide. I loaded some food and water in the dinghy. Sailed around to the Fort Zack jetty and left some things on the beach. Got back in and sailed to the Bahamas."

"In a dinghy?"

"I'm a good sailor, Mr. Amsterdam. And it isn't very hard. People do it all the time in fishing skiffs, inflatables even. Catch the Gulf Stream and away you go. Find an out-island with a quiet harbor, keep a low profile, get another bar gig off the books . . ."

"And the money, the pouches?"

Kenny Lukens looked down and shook his head. By now I was almost accustomed to the crew cut above the lipstick and the made-up eyes. "Left them where they were," he said. "Was afraid I'd miss the tide, get caught by daybreak. All I wanted was to get away."

"And you got away," I said. I shifted in the tub.

Water lapped, the puny waves of a stay-at-home. "So why'd you come back?"

The needling tone crept once again into Kenny Lukens' voice. "Don't you read the paper, Mr. Amsterdam?"

"No," I admitted. "Not anymore. In fact, I don't get why anybody reads the paper. But maybe we'll save that conversation for some time when I'm dry."

"Lefty Ortega's dying," he informed me.

"Ah, so there's a happy ending after all."

"Liver cancer. Going fast."

"This was news in the Bahamas?"

"A friend sent me the *Sentinel*."

I tried not to look surprised that Kenny Lukens had a friend. Not that he didn't have a certain magnetism, even a wacky dignity. But he hadn't been in town that long before he'd disappeared, plus he was such a bundle of competing odd-nesses. Then again, who wasn't? "So you're back to fetch the pouches?"

"*I* can't do it," he said, a little breathlessly. "I'm dead and I'm a thief, remember? Besides, I think I'm being followed."

"Followed? You've been gone two years. You're wearing a dress—"

"Maybe I'm imagining it. My nerves are shot, okay? But look, I can't risk being seen out there. There's people on Tank Island now. Security guards. It's not even Tank Island anymore."

Even I knew that. Marketing maneuver. Typi-cal. Tank Island was a man-made pile of coral and muck that had been spooned up from the shallows when the navy dredged the harbor. In the forties there were oil tanks on it, hence the good blunt name. Abandoned, it had sprouted mangroves and Austrian pines, just like the natural Keys. But by the late nineties the developers had got hold of it. Like shit transformed into Shineola, suddenly Tank Island was reborn as Sunset Key. It had fences on it now, and million-dollar houses, and sand barged in from God knows where, and a beach club complete with striped umbrellas.

"Sure your pouches weren't excavated, built over?"

"I rowed right past last night," he said. "The trees I buried them under are still in place. Eight feet from the high-tide line. Just against the fence."

"Rowed?" I said. "You came back in your dinghy?"

"I worked my way back in a fishing boat. I stole a dinghy."

"Still stealing, Kenny? Even after all this shit?"

He did the Garland shtick again. "I still have my dream, Mr. Amsterdam. Who knows what's in that other pouch? Maybe it's enough to outfit a sailboat, make it up to myself for the time I've lost. Dig it up for me, and I'll give you a third."

I thought about it for some part of a second. Pete Amsterdam, private eye. Specializing in retrieving stolen property for felonious transvestites. "Kenny," I said, "you don't need a detective. You need a child with a yellow pail and shovel."

"I'll make it half," he said.

"It's not about the money. I just don't want to do this."

He bit his orange lip and for a second I thought that he would start to cry. "You're my only chance!" he railed.

"Then you're screwed," I said, and in the next instant regretted being flip. "Look, I hope you get to sail around the world. I really do. But this is not for me."

He stared for one more moment, then finally gave up. Pouting, he retrieved his wig from the chaise; it dangled from his hand like a trophy of some barbaric war. At last he turned to go. He'd made it to the sliding door that led into my house when I once again noticed the falsies on the hot-tub rim. "Hey Kenny, you forgot your tits!"

But my would-be client just kept going.

4

By the time I climbed out of the hot tub, my hands and feet were gray and my private parts resembled something simmered much too long in soup. I lay down on a lounge, draped myself in towels, and waited for my blood pressure to revive.

I tried not to think about Kenny Lukens but I couldn't manage it. What I thought about was his insane and singular allegiance to his dream. After everything he'd bollixed up, after the lost years and the dislocations and the excruciating set-backs, he still keyed his every move to the fantasy of sailing around the world. There was a certain futile grandeur in it that I couldn't help admiring. Most people would have segued into a smaller, safer dream by now, or found a way to live without one. That was maturity. That was realism. Wasn't it?

Pondering that made me very ready for a drink. PI's always have an office bottle, right? Generally some execrable scotch or no-name bourbon that they swig straight from the pint or from smudged and dusty glasses or, God forbid, from paper cups. Well, fuck that. I pulled on a sweatshirt and headed for the wine room—half of the "office" I'd added on back when this detective farce began.

The wine room was a mock cellar in a house that happened to be built on solid coral. It was temperature controlled, humidity controlled, damped against vibration. Built to be perfect for a single, simple purpose, it was one of two rooms in the world I considered wholly satisfactory. Soft lights threw peaceful gleams on patient bottles. A whiff of cedar from the racks prefigured the wood in the wine. I moved to the section where the imported whites were stacked, and grabbed a bottle of Sancerre. Sancerre is perfect for après hot tub. The acidity sizzles on the slightly swollen palate, and the figgy aftertaste sweeps away the lingering smart of vaporized chlorine.

I poured myself a glass and took it to the world's other perfect room, the music room. Key West is not a quiet place. Planes clatter not far above the roofline, drunks and parrots scream, imbeciles on mopeds are always blowing horns. I'd had the music room constructed with a double set of walls and insulation eighteen inches thick. There's a carpet on the floor and felt around the edges of the door. There are two chairs—though admittedly one of them is generally empty. For those rare occasions when I can bring myself to watch a movie, there's a TV set and a VCR. But the room's focus is a vintage set of Dahlquist speakers—still, to my ears, the sweetest ever made.

I went into the music room and tried to decide

what I would listen to. A lot went into the decision. My mood, of course, but also what I was drinking and the time of day. Brahms, for instance, seldom works in daylight and never with white wine. The same may be said of Miles Davis, Thelonius Monk, and Mahler. On the other hand, Mozart and Louis Armstrong, sublime though they are, sometimes fail to fill the hollow of a troubled attitude. Only the absolute greatest of the great are oblivious to the clock and transcend all frames of mind. So I put on Bach. *Art of Fugue*. I settled into my silent chair, sipped my figgy wine, closed my eyes, and let those first eight monumental notes carry me away from the puny screwups, the niggling irritations and distractions life is made of.

If I'd been smart I would have just stayed there in the music room, drinking and listening and tucked away, because this would be my last peaceful, undistracted time for quite a while. That night, scratching in the sand on Sunset Key, Kenny Lukens, the guy who almost became my very first client, was murdered.

I learned of it next morning, bicycling to tennis.

Like I said, I don't read newspapers. But I do check out the headlines in the rank of vending machines in front of Fausto's market. There's something bracingly illicit about a quick, unpaid-for peek at the *Times,* the *Journal, The Miami Herald.* It pleases me, as well, to refresh each morning my profound incuriosity about what lies beneath the fold; let a banner announce the arrival of

Judgment Day, I'll read the first two paragraphs and pedal on.

On this particular morning, however, the head-line on the *Sentinel* grabbed me by the throat, put a burn in my stomach, and sent me scrambling through my tennis bag for quarters. MAN IN WOMAN'S CLOTHING KILLED ON SUNSET KEY.

The article was brief, because the cops knew al-most nothing and the reporter had been squeezed against a deadline. Just after midnight, as the shift was changing for the security guards, a woman had been discovered, crumpled and ap-parently passed out or asleep, against the metal fence that separated the foreshore from the pri-vate property. The patrolling guard, suspecting a homeless person of the type that used to litter Tank Island with soup cans and rusty shopping carts and the remains of campfires, called to the woman, then shook her, then finally realized, when the wig came loose and rolled away, that she was a man, and dead. The police determined that he'd been strangled, then shot in the back, and that he'd been dead about an hour. They had not been able to identify the body. They had no clues and made no surmises about the killing. There were a few details about the crime site: A shallow hole had been dug in the sand, as though someone were burrowing beneath the fence; the victim's arms were stretched out toward the hole; an unregistered dinghy had been pulled up on the beach.

I read this standing on the White Street side-walk, the heightening sun on the back of my neck, my bicycle balanced between my thighs. I read it and felt . . . what? A sharp though more or less impersonal sorrow that Kenny Lukens wouldn't get to sail around the world. That, and—can I admit it?—some whisper of morbid envy that at least he'd gone with his dream apparently intact. But more than either of those things, I just felt strange. Strange that I'd spoken to someone hours before his killing. Strange that I knew more about it than the cops did, more than the newspaper was able to report. It scared me, this knowledge. I had no idea what to do with it.

I put the paper in my tennis bag, and for a while I just stood there, looking at the ground. Sandals scratched past on the sidewalk. People tied up their dogs and went into Fausto's for groceries. At length I continued rather numbly on my way. Life goes on, right? I didn't know what else to do; I followed my routine. Seeking calm and focus in the magnificent geometry of a tennis court, I showed up at Bayview Park and whipped out my racquet and somehow sleepwalked through two badly losing sets.

Afterward, my opponent, Ozzie Kimmel, said to me, with his usual sportsmanship and tact, "You played like a fuckin' spaz today."

I retreated into the shade of the peeling wooden enclosure where the waiting players sat. "Thanks," I said. "Got a lot on my mind."

"You?"

I ignored the sarcasm. I ignored a lot of things about Ozzie Kimmel, which is why we could still play tennis together and, up to a point, be friends. Ozzie was one of those people who'd been in Key West so long—since the early seventies, when he'd drifted in as a drug-taking, tambourine-banging hippie—that he'd become utterly unfit for living anywhere else. For one thing, he lacked the wardrobe. He played tennis shirtless, in a puke-green bathing suit; I'm not sure he owned a real pair of shoes. His manners and his self-control had atrophied; most people considered him an abrasive loudmouth. Most people were right. His natural mode of communication was the profane, relentless tirade, and he didn't care who he offended, if he even noticed. But what can I say?—I liked him. I'd never heard him say a single thing he didn't mean. And he had a beautiful half volley; he invented it each time with a lack of hurry that was pure Zen. Ozzie drove a cab, had for probably close to twenty years. He knew the town as well as anyone who wasn't born there.

I asked him if he knew anything about Lefty Ortega.

"Why?" he asked me back.

The simple question caught me by surprise. I understood at once that I couldn't answer it. Suddenly I had a secret. Suddenly I was supposed to be discreet, on guard. This was new and awkward and I hated it. "Just curious," I said.

"Old Conch family," said Ozzie. That was the local term for Keys natives. It carried great pride or great derision, depending on who was saying it. "Ya gotta love the Conchs," he volunteered.

"All they do is bitch about the island changing, but do they ever miss a chance to get in bed with a developer? I mean, if they hate change so much, why don't they get off their fat ass and get a fuckin' job so they can afford to keep their land?"

"So, the Ortegas . . ." I prompted.

Ozzie reached into his bag and came out with a shredded piece of orange towel. He wiped his neck and lint stuck to his skin. "Right. Came over from Cuba, what?—five, six generations ago. Cigar makers. Stayed on when the industry moved to Tampa. Married with some of the old wrecking families, got political. I think one of the Ortegas was mayor during the thirties. Not that being mayor of this shithole is any great distinction. Buncha fuckin' clowns. Remember the one who water-skied to Cuba? Or how 'bout that midget that was indicted half the time?"

"So anyway, Lefty Ortega—"

"Didn't he just die?"

"Dying's what I heard."

"Dying, dead." Ozzie shrugged off the fine distinction. "He's a prick. Pissy guy trying to act important."

"Is he?"

"Is he what? Important? What the fuck's important in the Keys? Is anything important in the Keys? Papaya truck wanders across the center line and takes out a family of four—is that important? Douchebag from Indiana loses control of his Jet Ski and runs over his wife—is that important? Two lesbians from Windy City—"

"Ozzie, what about Lefty Ortega?"

"Right. That scumbag. Has a bar—"

"That much I know."

"—and controls a lot of real estate. Commercial. I heard he doesn't do leases, only partnerships. So he owns a piece of lots of businesses."

"What kind of businesses?"

He rummaged deeper in his bag and came out with a shirt. It had a faded iguana on it and big holes ringed with yellow in the armpits. Pulling it over his head, he said, "What kinda businesses stay in business in this fuckin' town? T-shirts. Kitschy souvenirs for idiots. Liquor stores."

"All legit?"

Ozzie snorted. "Fuck's legit? Pot, no; tequila, yes? Cubans, yes; Haitians, no? I mean, who the fuck decides—"

I jumped in to forestall another tirade. "I heard he owns the cops."

"The cops!" said Ozzie, managing to invest the word with a detestation that had been fermenting half a lifetime. "Now we're talking assholes. Corrupt or just plain dumb? Remember the one got caught suckin' pussy in the squad car?"

"You think Ortega owns them?"

Ozzie looked at me almost with pity. "Man, are you naive? There's six, eight guys control this town. The guys with the real estate, the tour concessions, the gambling boats. They get what they want. The cops are there to help. . . . Why you so curious all of a sudden?"

I didn't answer. I made a point of getting busy packing up my stuff. It was around eleven-thirty and the courts were emptying. Old doubles players with bent backs and bandaged knees hobbling home for chicken salad in an avocado. I dropped my racquets into my bike basket. "Same time Saturday?" I said, and headed off across the park.

5

Riding home, I was thinking: Why do people get sucked into things that they know, down deep, won't make them happy?

Things like golf. Or volunteering for committees. Or moving to Los Angeles. What is the strange insidious pressure that, every day, persuades large numbers of people to leap headlong into crap like that? Is it just that people are so easily bamboozled? Maybe it's the awful fear of being bored, the belief that being bored is somehow shameful. Better to do *anything,* however dumb, however trivial, than just sit there, quietly and still.

Me, I sort of like being bored, though I admit it's an acquired taste, and difficult to justify to people who live north of, say, Mile Marker 10. Being bored is like drinking tea the exact same temperature as your mouth. You're getting something from it, though it's easy not to notice. And at least, when you're bored, you're not pretending something matters when it doesn't. At least you're not being had.

These thoughts, of course, were a way of as-

suring myself I would get sucked no deeper into
the death of Kenny Lukens. Why should I? I'd
met the guy exactly once. His life had zilch to do
with mine. I owed him nothing. So I rode home,
looking forward to, even craving, a boring afternoon. A good long soak in the hot tub. A bowl of
pasta and a glass of Sangiovese. Some empty time
in which to recover from my shock of the morning and my drubbing on the tennis court.

I climbed off my bike, locked it to the same
palm I always lock it to. Went up the porch steps
and into the house. Dropped my racquets and
stripped, bachelor style, directly into the washing
machine. Grabbed a towel and headed out the
back.

I skirted the pool and was two steps from the
hot tub when I saw them.

I didn't want to see them, but there they were:
Kenny's tits, still perched pink and gleaming on
the apron of the tub, uncanny, accusing, like the
severed body parts of a medieval martyr. I tried
not to look at the tits. I thought of flinging them
like small humped Frisbees over the fence and
into a neighbor's yard. I couldn't do it. I stepped
over them and into the hot tub.

I closed my eyes and sought to calm myself by
picturing the trajectories of tennis balls—the exquisite parabolas of topspin, the floating rise and
steep drop of a slice. Instead I saw Kenny Lukens
with his wig flung off, brow furrowed above his
made-up lashes. I rested my elbow on the lip of
the tub, and at some point my fingers blundered
against a vinyl boob. It was hot from the sun, the

nipple just melted enough to feel tacky to the
touch. I yanked my hand away. And at some
point I understood that I'd be going to the hospital that afternoon. Visiting Lefty Ortega. I didn't
want to do it. It wouldn't make me happy. I was
being had, and I knew that I was being had, getting sucked in deeper to the story of this poor
dead dreamer, and acting as if perhaps his story
mattered, and wondering at every moment if I believed it really did.

I wouldn't go to Key West General with the idea
of getting well, but as a place to die it's probably
as good as any. Better than most, in fact, because
all the rooms have views. One wing, it's true,
looks out at the garbage dump, but another faces
toward the community college. From the third
floor you can gaze across the tops of palms all the
way to the green shimmer of the Gulf. Above the
trees, pelicans swoop; they seem to be bundling
up the world like storks wrap babies, but now
they're carrying it away from you, leaving you
behind as they glide on silent wings.

Lefty Ortega was in Intensive Care. At least
that's what I was told. But when I showed up at
the unit, it seemed they'd lost him. I don't mean
he died; I mean they couldn't find him. Vintage
Key West General.

"How do you lose a person in Intensive Care?"
I asked the duty nurse.

He squirmed a little in his turquoise scrubs,
then picked up the phone. Lefty had been moved
to Critical.

At Critical, the nurse just shook her head.

"He died?"

She looked at me a little funny. I guess she could tell I was hoping that he had. I'd be off the hook then.

"He's been moved to Hospice," she informed me. "Nothing more to be done but keep him comfortable."

So I trudged to yet another wing. By then the stench of the place had gone all through me; I'd forgotten what air smelled like without the adornments of blood and disinfectant.

I found Ortega's room and remembered I was supposed to be a private eye. So I strolled discreetly past, observing. It was a big room, full of flowers; the arrangements were showy, garish, the kind of thing people send when they don't really give a shit, just feel they should be represented. There was a woman at the bedside. I couldn't see her face. She was wearing a scarf; rich, thick hair spilled out beneath it and darkly curled against her slightly downy neck. Her posture was youthful and her legs seemed nervous in shadowy stockings. She was stroking Lefty's forehead.

I moved on to the end of the hallway, biding my time, watching the horribly familiar hospital routines. Where my father died, where my mother died—it was always the same. There was always a guy with a mop, and he was always whistling. There was the woman with the cart of magazines and candy. She was always Filipino, always smiling, always kind. *Ah, you're dying?*

How about an Entertainment Weekly *and a Snickers bar?*

After maybe twenty minutes the woman emerged from Lefty's room. I tried to figure out if she looked devastated, but was distracted by noticing that, all in all, she looked damn good. White blouse tucked snug enough into a straight black skirt to show the salient features of her torso. High Cuban hips that seemed somehow to wiggle when she was standing still. She paused a moment and looked my way; our eyes met for some fraction of a second. Hers were wide-set with a peculiar upturn at the outside edges. As she turned to go I saw a soft and somewhat sallow cheek around the corner from lips that were full and red and bowed. She pivoted on midheel shoes and clicked away.

I watched a little then breathed deep and took my turn at Lefty's bedside.

For a guy whose only care was palliative, he was hooked up to a lot of gizmos. Sensors on his sunken chest led up to a beeping monitor where the weary race of his pulse was run out on a graph. He had a harness like a feed bag on his nose; it squirted oxygen up his nostrils. A chandelier of IV bottles was clustered above him, feeding saline and painkillers through different tubes to various needles taped into his arms and neck.

His cancerous abdomen was huge, bizarrely pregnant-looking; it made a steep egg-shaped hump in the sheet. Like a spider sucking out the innards of a fly, the tumor had drained all the rest of him to feed itself. His cheekbones showed and his collarbones stuck out. The once fearsome shoulders were stringy and pathetic, the arms knobby at the wrists and elbows. The suspicious eyes still darted, just as Kenny Lukens had described, though the whites were yellow now, and it was hard to know what they were seeing. Morphine. My parents had both been on morphine near the ends of their separate lives. My mother had seen square men pouring from the television and dancing down the walls. My father, always fastidious, became deeply troubled by the geometry of the ceiling tiles, and had made me wheel his bed around and around the room until he felt properly aligned.

Why the hell had I come to the hospital?

I swallowed back nausea and said hello to Lefty.

He turned his papery yellow face, looked at me, and promptly went to sleep.

He slept about ten seconds, long enough to snore just once, then blinked himself awake. He raised a finger a few inches off the sheet. Wagging it at me, his voice a slurring rasp, he said, "You fuck my daughter I cut your balls off."

Pleasantly, I said, "Okay, Lefty. Since you feel that strongly about it."

"She got a problem. Don't you take advantage."

"Take advantage? Me?"

He struggled for a breath. His wigged-out yellow

eyes did pinwheels. He dropped his voice a notch. "You find it yet, Bubba?"

I didn't answer right away. I told myself be cagey. "Not yet," I said. "Still looking."

He fell asleep for another snore or two, then woke and gestured weakly toward a corner of the room. "Fuckin' palmetto bugs. Cocksuckers sing to me, ya know. Stand up on their hind legs, put their arms around each other, sing. Antennas waving, won't shut up."

I looked toward the vacant corner. "What do they sing, Lefty?"

He closed his eyes and murmured tunelessly through deeply fissured lips: "When the moon hits your eye like a big pizza pie, that's amore . . ."

"Would kill anybody."

"No shit, Bubba." He laughed, I think. There was some wheezing and his enormous liver shook like half-set Jell-O. Then, to my horror, he reached out and touched my arm. His fingers felt waxy, already dead. He said, "I can't rest, you don't find it. Promise me you'll find it."

Stalling for time, I glanced up at the monitor. Bunch of numbers. When they zeroed out, that was that. I told myself be smart. "I'm working on it, Lefty."

There was a silence. The sick man seemed to settle into it, practicing for the quiet to come.

After a bit I nonchalantly said, "What is it again I'm looking for?"

Lefty's mouth opened. I saw stumps of teeth and a scaly tongue before it closed again. His forehead crawled, his jaundiced eyes narrowed

with a fresh confusion that now took on a tinge
of panic. "You ain't Bubba. Fuck are you?"

"Sure, I'm Bubba," I said, though even as I said
it I felt some echo of the uselessness that Kenny
Lukens had felt in lying to this guy.

"Fuck are you?" he said again. "That fuck
Mickey send you?"

"What fuck Mickey?"

He didn't answer. His eyes slid off me and
strained upward toward a nurse call button on
the wall behind him. His arm slowly lifted, dragging tubes and needles. I blocked it with my body
and leaned down low. Rumor has it that cancer
isn't catching; still, it was creepy bringing my face
close to the foul breath of this dying stranger.
"Okay. I'm a friend of Kenny Lukens, Lefty. Remember Kenny Lukens?"

Ortega's hand dangled in midair. Pulse showed
through the thin skin of his temples. "Cock-
sucker," he whispered.

"He's dead, Lefty. Went to dig up what he stole
from you, got killed."

The dying owe no homage to the dead, and Ortega wasted no sympathy on Kenny's passing. He
just gurgled and scrambled till he was almost sitting up. IV bottles swung like bells and clunked
together. "The pouch? You have it? I pay you."

"Whoever killed him has the fucking pouch."

Ortega just panted through the harness on his
nose, his eyes as wild as the eyes of a cornered
horse.

I suddenly realized I was not only frightened
and appalled, but angry; I still don't know exactly

why. Maybe because any death drags you back to thoughts of every other, all the helplessness and lack of resignation. I grabbed him by the arms. "What the fuck is so important with that pouch that Kenny Lukens died for it?"

Ortega didn't answer.

I think I shook him. "Who's Mickey?"

Nothing.

"Who put the pouch in the safe? Kenny said it was a woman. What woman, Lefty?"

His mouth twitched, his cracked lips quivered and split deeper. Disgusted to find his bony shoulders in my hands, I let them go. He fell back against his pillows. Oxygen was squeaking in his nose; or maybe it was my own breath, coming hard. The graph of his heartbeat was tracing out a jagged range of hills.

His eyes stayed on my face as he reached slowly once again toward the call button. I did nothing to stop him. I was paralyzed. I watched him watching me, and I digested the horror of having touched him. Wheezing, straining, he used up the slack of the tubes in his arms. The button was farther than the tubes would stretch. He kept reaching for it anyway. The tape that held the needles in his veins started pulling back from his purplish-yellow skin; it made a sound like ripping silk and left behind a residue of gummy dots. The needles appeared to be bending in his flesh like spoons in unripe melon. A syringe pulled free with a muffled pop and a small spout of brown- ish blood gushed out of Lefty's forearm.

Dizzy, nauseous, I wheeled out of the room.

The monitor started beeping, screaming at my back. I'd just made it to the elevator when a clot of doctors and nurses went hurrying by in the opposite direction, scrubs and lab coats rustling behind.

6

Back home, I went not for the Sancerre, not for the Vouvray, but straight, and with an unsteady hand, for a jumbo hit of grappa.

Great, I thought—one hour of playing detective and already I'm reaching for the hard stuff in the middle of the afternoon. How much longer before I sank to swilling the crappy bourbon out of paper cups?

I paced awhile, drinking, trying to forget the hospital, trying not to picture the mayhem of the docs convening over Lefty's bedside, stabbing to replace the pulled-out needles, poking to sedate his ravings, hammering his chest to get his insides back on beat. Awful and familiar images of care as violence, violence as procedure.

Desperate for distraction, I went to the music room. I scanned the wall of disks, pondered, hummed, and could find nothing that I felt like listening to, not one symphony or song I believed would succeed in carrying me away.

This happened once or twice a year, and engendered in me a subtle, simmering dread. If al-

42

cohol and music lost their power to soothe me,
what the hell was left, short of really going down
the tubes? What comforts would persuade me
that it was worth even the small trouble I took to
maintain my grip? Here's something that busy
people in busy places tend to spare themselves the
discomfort of noticing: It would be so easy, so
ridiculously easy to let go.

This was not a wholesome line of thought, so I
took my drink and fled to the porch. I love my
porch. It's a haven of passivity, of presence without involvement; a place where worries seem
smaller, diluted by the open air. I have a rocking
chair angled behind a dense, anarchic jasmine
bush. I can look out through the foliage but it's
hard for others to look in. I watch the lime-green
weevils chomping leaves, the lizards puffing out
their ruby throats. I watch the shoeless locals going by, their cracked heels gray and hard against
the pedals of their clunker bikes.

After some porch-sitting and half a glass of
booze, I finally started calming down. Perspective
grew generous; I began to feel, frankly, like I'd
been pretty brave. I'd done the right thing. Con-
fronted Lefty, asked the questions Kenny Lukens
would have wanted me to ask. Thank God I'd
gotten no answers. I had no idea who Lefty
thought I was or what was so important in the
goddamn pouch. Which meant there was no
more I could do. Now I was really finished.
Finito. Case closed. That being so, I may as well
refresh the chill on my warming drink.

I was working up the initiative to fetch the grappa from the freezer, when a woman stopped her bicycle in front of my house.

She was on an old Conch cruiser that had a lot of style: hand-painted fenders, pink and green, a color scheme that continued on the chain guard, which featured a yin-and-yang motif. Wire baskets, front and back. When she stepped down from the seat, I saw that it was covered with what appeared to be a remnant of a blue shag rug.

She headed for my porch stairs and I hunkered lower behind the jasmine, shrinking from some fresh irritation, some new demand. I took a moment to pray she had a wrong address or was selling raffles. Not noticing me in the shadow of the foliage, she moved to the door and peered, a little nosily, I thought, through the screen. I waited for her to raise her hand to knock, then said, "Can I help you?"

She jumped a little as her face turned sideways, a hand went to her midriff. "You scared me."

"Lately visitors scare me too."

"Are you Pete Amsterdam?"

It sounded faintly like an accusation, and I had an impulse to deny it. Instead I only nodded.

"I'm Kenny Lukens' friend," she said. "Maybe he mentioned me."

Nothing clicked at first, and I looked at her harder. She was not your usual-looking woman, but I was pretty sure that she was female. Her hair was reddish—the kind of red that hides inside of brown then flashes forth in certain types of light. Except for feathered sideburns and a fringe at the nape of her neck, it was fitted closely to her scalp, and reminded me a little of the helmet Snoopy wears when playing pilot. Her dress was basically a long black sleeveless T-shirt, and beneath it her unfettered breasts jiggled slightly in a manner that vinyl could not emulate. Her calves were lean and smooth but she had stood firm against the bourgeois impulse to shave her armpits.

"He mentioned a friend," I stammered at last. "But I guess I thought—"

"That it would be a man," she said. "You figured he meant lover and you figured he was gay."

She had me there. Silly Pete, leaping to conclusions just because a fellow wears a frilly bra.

"He wasn't gay," she said. "He cross-dressed now and then. Two very different things. He was a complicated person. A dear person. Can we talk?"

I looked down at a lime-green weevil chomping on a leaf. I didn't feel like talking, not about Kenny Lukens at least, but I was raised to be polite and I didn't see how I could kick this person off my porch. "Listen," I said, "I really don't want—"

"Please," she said, her voice dropping to a companionable whisper. "You and me—you realize we might be the only two who know that it was Kenny out there?" She gestured in the general direction of Tank Island—excuse me, Sunset Key.

"Us," I put in, "and whoever killed him."

She ignored that. "Isn't it weird to be the only ones who know?"

"Yeah. It is. But I still don't see—"

"What we have to talk about? What it would accomplish? It won't accomplish anything. Kenny's gone. It's finished. That's why I feel like talking. Understand?"

I didn't understand. But already I was getting to like this woman's voice. There was something in it that reminded you that it was made of breath. "What's your name?" I asked her.

"Maggie."

"Nice name." I paused and sipped my drink and looked at her some more. She had steady gray eyes, innocent of makeup, and her top lip was prominent, Egyptian almost; the center of it dipped down into a sensuous nub. She had a depth of tan that only locals get, a tan that, like the polish on good marble, seemed to reach a ways beneath the surface; yet her skin looked very supple, faintly moist with herbal things. "Can I tell you something, Maggie? I just got home from Lefty Ortega's bedside, and I'm feeling pretty lousy."

"He talked to you?" She seemed impressed. I guess that was my compensation.

"He raved at me. He's on morphine. I have no idea what any of it meant."

"It's a start."

"It's a finish." I said it more harshly than I'd meant to, and then, of course, I felt bad.

She took it in and nodded gently. She paused then said, "I like grappa too."

"How you know it's grappa?"

All she did was close her eyes and deeply sniff the still and humid space between us. Looking back, I guess that was the moment I began to fall a little bit in love with her. No, wait—that's glib and quick and overly dramatic, exactly the kind of thing a detective story makes a person say. Let's just leave it that I was impressed as hell that she could divine the presence of grappa vapors in the air, and intrigued by the guiltless pleasure in her face as her eyes fell closed.

"Come on inside," I said. "I'll pour you some."

We went into the living room. She claimed a corner of the sofa, sitting diagonal and crossed-legged so that her long dress stretched across her knees and made a basket of her lap. I fetched grappa. We clinked glasses and then I retreated to a chair. She gestured toward the walls, which have some pictures on them. Not museum grade but not crap either, and some care had been taken with the framing.

"Nice place," she said. "You have a trust fund?"

It was such a marvelously gauche question that I snorted. Clearing liquor from my sinuses, I said, "Excuse me?"

"Come on," she said. "No one makes money in this town. You live like this, either you're re-tired or you have a trust fund."

It so happens that my father was a furniture salesman who died broke. I didn't have a trust fund. "Let's leave it at retired."

"What from?"

"Nothing important," I said. The understatement of the year. I sipped my drink and changed the subject instantly. "Where do *you* live?"

For some reason she seemed surprised I didn't know. "That's how I met Kenny. I live in the boatyard."

Brilliantly I asked, "On a boat?"

"Broken-down old trawler," she said. "Cheap and roomy. Propped in a cradle. All the romance of living aboard without the nuisance of actually being in the water."

"Ah," I said.

That seemed to wrap up the discussion of affordable housing, and there was a lapse in the conversation. Lapses are dangerous.

"Pete," Maggie said—it was the first time, except for introductions, that she'd used my name, and she helped herself to it just like she'd claimed the corner of the couch, with an utter lack of formality or self-consciousness—"did Kenny tell you he was being followed?"

I felt my fingers clench around my sweating glass. "Now wait. I thought you said—"

"That it's over. That there's nothing to accomplish." She gave a pained little smile that was not quite an apology. "I know, I know. But it haunts me. . . . Did he say anything to you about it?"

I blew some air between my lips and tried to remember. The effort made me realize that I'd had a lot to drink. "He might have mentioned something," I vaguely said, and drank some more. "I don't think he gave details."

"Well, I'll give you a detail. These people who

he thought were following him—I think they were the same people who came snooping around the boatyard right after he disappeared."

"Two years ago?" I said.

She nodded. "The boatyard's like a little village. Everyone knows everyone. People look out for each other. Someone's there who doesn't belong, it's noticed. Right after Kenny took off, two guys started hanging around. Someone caught them boarding Kenny's boat, called the cops. The cops never showed."

Made sense, I thought, if the intruders had ties to Lefty Ortega.

"And you think these same two guys came back?"

She nodded. Only her head moved; there was a wonderful stillness in her neck and shoulders.

"How did they know Kenny was in town?"

She just looked down at her lap and shook her head.

"Then what makes you think that it's the same two guys?"

"There was something very strange about them," she said, and sipped some grappa. "Strange two years ago. Strange a couple days ago. Too strange to be coincidence."

I leaned forward in my chair and waited for her to tell me what this strange thing was. She shifted her hips. She smoothed her skirt. By now I was leaning so far forward that my shirt pulled away from my chest.

Finally she said, "They were wearing snorkels."

"Snorkels?"

"Snorkels."

I took a moment to process this. Hit men wore trench coats. Bank robbers mashed their faces in stockings. Snorkels I did not know what to make of. "And flippers?" I asked.

"No flippers. Just snorkels and masks. You know, boatyard and all, I guess they figured they'd blend. Lot of people wear snorkels when they're scraping barnacles, brushing off algae."

I rubbed my chin sagaciously. "But isn't that if the boats are in the water?"

"Exactly."

"Exactly what?"

"These guys weren't in the water. That's why they looked strange."

I scratched my ear. "More grappa?"

"I shouldn't. I have a class. Well, maybe just a little."

I got up to fetch the bottle.

As I was tipping it into her glass, she said, "You think about it, it was a pretty good disguise. I mean, everybody looks the same in a snorkel. Have you noticed?"

I refreshed my own drink and conjured images of guys in snorkels. Lips puffed out like clowns' around the chunky mouthpieces. Bundles of salty hair plastered inside foggy masks. Pastel plastic breathing tubes that always went askew while glaciers of snot came oozing from tormented noses. "I've noticed that everyone looks like a horse's ass," I offered. "These guys can't be too bright."

I'd made it to the freezer and was stashing

what was left of the bottle when Maggie said, "So it shouldn't be too hard to find them."

I took a step back toward the living room. "Don't even think about it."

I reclaimed my chair and glass. I took a swig and looked hard at my guest, almost daring her to push me on this one. She didn't, which I found disarming. She just stared gently back. Her un-adorned mouth was calm and still, and at the edge of my vision, though I tried to shut it out, I saw a tuft of tinselly red hair protruding through the cleft between her arm and chest, and I tried not to admit I found it awfully sexy.

Maggie looked past me to the changing light through the window. It's how she told time, I guess. "I have to get to class," she said, and with-out hitch or hurry she was on her feet.

Less gracefully, I rose to walk her to the door. "What kind of class?"

"Yoga," she said. "I teach. At the Leaf Shed. That's what I do."

Aha, I thought. So that explained the exquisite posture and the measured breath. Boy, I was get-ting to be a shrewd observer.

She looked down at my hips as we stood there in the doorway. "You should do some yoga. You walk all stiff."

I didn't see the point of telling her that at that moment I was walking stiff so that I would not fall down.

"Well," she said, "I'm sorry to barge in on you. But I feel better for having talked—don't you?"

I didn't have to think about it long. "No," I said. "I don't."

She just pressed her lips together and moved smoothly down the porch steps. I watched her climb onto her bike with the yin-yang on the chain guard and pedal off.

7

Next morning I got beat again at tennis, this time by an old slicer-and-dicer whose forehand is a tic and whose backhand is a weaselly, contorted little push—a guy I really shouldn't lose to. Not to make excuses, but I had a couple of pretty good ones. For one thing, I was hung over from the grappa. For another, it was sort of on my mind that maybe I was wanted for murder.

On my way to Bayview Park, I'd stopped, as usual, before the rank of newspaper machines in front of Fausto's market. And there, above the fold in the *Sentinel*, was word that Lefty Ortega was no more.

I should not have been surprised—though of course I'd wanted to believe that the docs would get the tough old bastard stabilized, that he'd resume his wigged-out drifting toward the end, and that the crisis precipitated by my visit somehow wouldn't count. So I forced myself to act like I was shocked, riffled quickly through a weak repertoire of amazement—the caught breath, the tsking of the tongue. Then I dug two quarters from the bottom of my tennis bag, and, in what

was quickly turning into an unhappy and life-
draining habit, I bought the goddamn paper and
read it standing on the sidewalk.

The article did not specify the time of Lefty's
death, but said that it was afternoon. This sent me
delving into morbid subtleties. If he was dead by
the time the running medics reached his bedside,
did that mean I killed him? How about if he
jerked and gurgled another twenty minutes? How
about an hour? Did some kind of buzzer go off
when the period of guilt expired? But come on,
the guy was dying anyway. Then again, everybody
murdered is dying anyway. Maybe the miserable
bully had one kind and charitable thought left in
him, one instant of joy, one spoonful of redemp-
tion. When could you say with certainty that
somebody was finished?

This philosophical muddle soon gave way to
practical considerations, in the midst of which I
vaguely realized I was thinking like a criminal.
Who'd seen me at the hospital? I'd asked for
Lefty at Intensive and at Critical. There was a
duty nurse in Hospice who'd probably noticed
me hanging around; there was the smiling woman
with the cart of magazines. And there was Lefty's
daughter—at least I assumed that's who she was.
We'd exchanged a glance when she came out of
the room, and it had seemed to me that her eyes
were dry enough to see through. All these people
were witnesses, potential enemies. I wasn't used
to having enemies. I wasn't used to feeling furtive.
And, now that I thought of it, I'd never regarded

myself as an unhealthy person to be around. Why was everyone I met suddenly dying?

Distractedly scanning the rest of the front page, I noticed a small follow-up item about the killing on Sunset Key. The cops had still not managed to identify the victim. Big surprise. They were asking anyone with information to come forward. Fat chance. No chance now. Let them figure out on their own who Kenny Lukens was, and that these two deaths were, in some murky way, connected.

I threw the paper in the garbage, as if by trashing that one copy I could erase the day's events. A homeless guy came along and plucked it out ten seconds later. I continued on my way to tennis, and of course I played like shit. Who wouldn't have?

But the strangest thing about that tennis game was that I didn't go home afterward. I *always* go straight home from tennis. Get out of my sweaty clothes, have a soak or a swim, analyze, regroup. This, I realize, may seem like just some aimless, trivial routine. To me it's much more serious than that. It's ritual, one of those carefully evolved, scrupulously repeated patterns that define a life, that make it recognizable to the person living it. Violate those rituals, disrupt those private ceremonies, and who knows what else will go ker-blooey?

Still, when I'd packed up my gear and dropped it in the basket of my bike, I just couldn't get the thing to steer toward home. It pointed stubbornly downtown and toward the harbor. Gradually I understood that it was pointing toward

Redmond's Boatyard. I felt I had no choice but to follow it, even though I couldn't tell if it was Kenny Lukens or Maggie the yoga teacher I needed to get closer to.

Redmond's is at the north end of the Bight, at a nick in the shore that not long ago was known as Toxic Triangle. The old electric plant looms over Toxic; the gigantic coast guard pier hems in one side of it. The water part of the Triangle used to be a seedily carefree place where nobody paid rent and hardly anyone had all their teeth. Derelict boats tied lines to tilted pilings or settled gently into dockside muck; their denizens nailed lawn furniture onto splintery decks and lived on six-packs and pork rinds. People slept in hammocks slung from masts, and scruffy dogs ran around with fish heads in their jaws.

Local wisdom had it that Toxic was too funky and too outlaw ever to be gentrified. Ha. It's called North Haven Marina now—another of those places whose former moniker has been officially expunged. Costs two bucks a foot to park your boat there for a night, and dock girls trained to call everybody Captain come running up to pump your gas.

A small irony is that Redmond's dry dock used to be the upscale part of Greater Toxic. People actually paid for space there. There were showers, electricity—it was practically suburban. Now, next to the gleaming new marina, Redmond's seemed a blot and an embarrassment. The yard was dusty and unpaved; the vessels anything but yachty. How long till the city found a way to worm out of the lease?

I pedaled through the rusty street-side gate, clattered over potholes and lumps of coral rock. Boats loomed all around me in untidy rows, propped in cradles, suspended from canvas straps, resting precariously on spindly jacks. Maybe it was just my mood, but I found an awful pathos in those landlocked boats. They seemed defeated, punished with exile for their failures. Paint curled on their desiccated bottoms. Their waterline stripes looked futile in the unbuoyant air. Rudders waved at nothing; keels spiked downward to no effect.

I rode and looked around, and after a couple minutes I found Kenny Lukens' sailboat.

I was sure it was his, though I could not have recognized a Morgan forty-one. It was the name on the transom that made me certain—though Kenny had never mentioned the name. It was stamped in gold block letters framed in navy blue, and the honest truth is that it broke my heart. It was called *Dream Chaser*.

There was a fellow standing by the boat, working on it, fairing the hull with a small hand sander. He was spare and lean and his skin had tanned to a rosewood color; his hair was so blond it was white; it stood straight up. He wore flip-flops and a tiny orange bathing suit flecked with paint. I pedaled up to him and said hello.

"Your boat?" I asked.

"Oh yawh," he said happily. His eyes changed

to slits when he smiled. His sun-bleached eye-
lashes all but disappeared.

"She's beautiful."

He beamed. "Oh yawh."

"Had 'er long?"

"Fife months. Buy her almost soon as I arrife."
There was pride in his voice, wonder on his flat
frank face.

"Where ya from?"

"Riga," he said. "Latvia. Latvian I am. My
name is Andrus."

"I'm Pete. You're a long way from home."

"Denks God. Latvia, your ass it freezes off."

"The boat—you bought it here?"

"Right vere she is sitting," he said. "Good deal
too. Only unpaid bills is vat I'm paying."

I smiled for the Latvian's good luck though
this made me very sad. Why did it always seem
that one guy's bargain was another guy's tragedy? I was suddenly troubled by how little was
left of Kenny Lukens, how little anybody knew
of him, how little it seemed to matter that he'd
passed this way. "Know who owned it before?"
I asked.

"I tink a local couple."

"Why you think that?"

"Clothes they leave behind," he told me.
"Men's clothes, vimmen's clothes."

"Ah. Can I ask you something else? A couple
days ago, were you out here working on the
boat?"

Cheerfully, he said, "Every day I'm vorking on
the boat."

"Did you happen to see a couple of guys hanging around in snorkels?"

"Shnorkels? On the land?"

"Right. Here around the yard."

"Vy shnorkels in the yard?"

"Like, you know, a disguise."

"Ah. Like Halloveen. Pumpkins. Vitches."

"Something like that."

Andrus rubbed the dusty white stubble on his cheek. "No," he murmured. "Shnorkels, no." Then he added, "Vait! Two, three days ago, a couple fellows come racing up on yetskies."

I wondered if he'd noticed that he'd lapsed into his native tongue. "*Yetskies?*"

"Yawh. You know." He made a motion like revving up a motorcycle.

"Oh. Jet Skis."

"Exectly. This is vat I'm saying. On yetskies they come racing up and shnorkels they are vearing. And I remember I am thinking, Vait, either you are going shnorkel or you are going vit the yetski. Vy both?"

"These guys—you remember what they looked like?"

The Latvian bit his lip, shook his head, lovingly patted the Morgan's hull. "I vas vorking," he said. "Making smooth. Really, I don't pay attention."

"You remember what they did?"

"Did? Nothing. Hang around. Look at boats. Then go. Vy you ask?"

I thought of saying that the former owner of *Dream Chaser* was a friend of mine. But that

would lead to way too many questions. So I
moved on to other business. "You know a
woman, Maggie? Teaches yoga?"

The happy fellow smiled yet again. "Nice lady.
Friendly. Nice. Over there she lives."

He pointed across the yard to a beamy trawler
sitting on the ground, its only supports a series of
chocks to hold it level. It looked less like a boat
than like a children's-book rendition of a boat. Its
bottom was painted pink. Its flanks were glossy
burgundy. Blue window boxes had been rigged up
on its gunwales; begonias and geraniums bloomed
in unlikely splendor on its decks. I had to smile
too. And I had to acknowledge a certain school-
boy thrill in learning where Maggie lived; there
was a faint promise of intimacy in seeing her place
as she'd seen mine.

The joyful Latvian had gone back to his sanding. Small knots of muscle stood out in his shoulders as he worked. "Well," I yelled above the
scratching, "nice talking with you. Good luck
with the boat."

"And good luck to you, my friend."

I lifted my butt onto the hot seat of my bike
and began to pedal off. But when I saw the Morgan's transom once again, I felt another pang, another primal wish that Kenny Lukens' vanishing
might not be quite so total. Pointing, I shouted to
the new owner, "You'll keep the name, I hope?"

He looked at me with kind indulgence for my
ignorance of nautical traditions. "Oh yes, of
course. Must always. Is werry bad luck to change
the name."

Q

"Now, on the inhalation, tighten down the anal sphincter. . . . That's right, clamp it down and hold it with the breath. . . . Picture it as a flower closing tightly for the night. . . . This is called the Root Lock pose. If there's any weakness in those muscles, if they start to loosen, just focus your attention on the third-eye center and clamp them down again. . . . Feels strange, I know, but it'll save you problems when you're older. . . . Inhale, squeeze . . . Exhale, release . . . Inhale, *squeeeeeeze . . ."*

Was I really doing this? Sitting painfully cross-legged on a folded towel, eyes closed and hands resting on my knees, trying to locate some mysterious symbolic place between my brows while slamming my asshole shut among a bunch of strangers clamping theirs?

Yes, I really was. Five o'clock yoga at the Leaf Shed, the one-time cigar factory whose pine walls, a century later, were still faintly redolent of the hemplike musk of raw tobacco. A class taught, in a soft and breathy voice, by Maggie, with whom I seemed, quite suddenly, to be a little bit obsessed. But wait—did this fascination really have to do with her, or was it just an aspect of the nagging itch I felt about the unresolved affair of Kenny Lukens? Besides, could you be a little bit obsessed? Wasn't that against the whole concept of obsession? With obsession it was all or nothing, wasn't it?

And weren't these exactly the kinds of nattering, willful things you shouldn't be thinking about in yoga class?

You should be clamping down the butt hole but freeing up the mind. Letting thoughts go. Declining to hold on. Allowing the breath to carry off the poisons of desire and self-consciousness. Not to mention guilt and bafflement and wondering if the police or other friends of Lefty Ortega would soon be coming after me.

So I tried; I really tried. I stretched and grunted to touch my shins while others palmed the floor. I cramped my toes and strained the brittle sinews of my insteps in an earnest effort to do a kneeling back bend. And, at moments, I did, I think, pay a visit to a different realm, transported there by a heady blend of joint pain and humiliation. Not that yoga is competitive. Absolutely not. Still, I could not help noticing when everybody else's forehead was squarely on the ground, while my face jerked and wiggled like that of a blind chicken pecking after unseen feed.

At least, between my travesties of poses, I got to look at Maggie, who, in a simple blue leotard, was grace itself. Her back was amazingly long and straight, as if her torso were exempt from gravity. When she breathed deep, her rib cage swelled and lifted above a plain of lean, lithe middle. Her arms were the slim but sculpted arms of a dancer, and when she raised them in undulating, all-embracing arcs, the untamed hair beneath them glistened slightly in the dusty light. When her arms were at her sides, reddish wisps poked through the dimpled creases between her shoulders and her chest, and looked just like—well, we all know what it looked like. It looked like something you shouldn't be thinking about in yoga class.

Somehow I made it through the ninety minutes. At the end I rolled my towel, retrieved my sneakers, and bided my time. When most of the others had drifted off, I went up to the front of the mirrored studio and suavely said, "Yo, Teach."

Maggie was sitting on the floor, pulling on a pair of baggy drawstring pants, seeming to levitate when she needed to get them past her hips. "So," she said, "you came to class."

"You told me I walk funny, so here I am."

"I didn't say you walk funny. I said you walk stiff."

"I walk stiff because everything hurts. Would you like to have a drink?"

She seemed a little bit uncomfortable with that. She scanned the emptying studio, and, too late, I thought that maybe it was dumb, unfair to ask her here. Her workplace, after all. "Look," she said, "if the only reason you took class—"

"Is to see you? Should I lie?"

"No. But when I'm teaching—"

"It's my turn to need to talk," I said. "It's only fair."

She pulled a rumpled turquoise sweater down over her head. The collar flattened the fringe of hair at the nape of her neck. She reached back and popped it free again. "Okay," she said. "Okay. Anything but grappa."

It was early dusk when we stepped outside the Leaf Shed. The sky was yellow in the west; the last vague purple shadows were stretching toward oblivion on the sidewalk. Palms were softly rustling, and the air seemed strangely mottled, as if light and dark were different-colored marbles being stirred.

"Raul's?" I suggested.

"My favorite," Maggie said, and we climbed onto our bikes.

Suffering back in Jersey all those grim and dreary years, this exact scenario had been a fantasy of mine: heading out for cocktails on a fat-tire, one-speed bicycle. The velvety light, the caressing air, the engaging and exotic woman who was not like everybody else—all this was amazingly close to what I'd daydreamed. In the fantasy, though, my mood was never quite so tangled, my simple, aimless habits never so assaulted by sudden complications. Life, sometimes, is too rich for its own damn good.

Anyway, Raul's was one of those Key West places where you go through the door and, almost instantly, you're back outside again—in this

case, on a trellised patio hung with bougainvillea
and presided over by an ancient mahogany tree
with scarred and mottled bark. We found a table
in a corner and I ordered a bottle of Viognier.
Good aperitif, Viognier. Not sweet but it tastes
like peaches.

We clinked glasses and I told Maggie that I'd
been to Redmond's Boatyard earlier that day. She
seemed surprised.

"I thought you weren't getting any more involved," she said.

"That's what I thought too." I drummed fingers on the table. I knew what I had to say next
but I didn't want to say it. "Ortega died right after I talked to him."

Maggie almost met my eyes, not quite. "I saw
it in the paper."

"I got him real worked up. Agitated. Panting.
The monitor—"

Maggie touched my arm then. Her hand was
very cool. "You're not saying it's your fault? Look,
he was a bad man and he had a terrible disease."

I appreciated that and I liked having her touch
me. There was a sulky silence and I sort of drew
it out. But finally I said, "Ortega dead—that
means we'll probably never know a goddamn
thing about what happened to Kenny. Nothing.
That bother you?"

She took her hand off my arm. I still felt where
her fingers had been. "Doesn't change anything,"
she said. "But—"

"But it stinks. It's incomplete. I guess that's
why I had to go to the boatyard."

The waiter came and poured more wine. I was extremely grateful.

"I saw his boat," I said.

"Dream Chaser," Maggie said wistfully. Could those two wrenching words be said in any other way?

"Spoke to the new owner. Andrus."

"Nice guy, huh? Happy. Gentle."

"He'd seen the guys in snorkels too," I said. "Saw them pulling up on Jet Skis. Remembered zilch except the snorkels."

We drank some wine and briefly looked around the place. At the bar there were a couple of big-haired tourist women getting plastered. A local guy with a parrot was trying to pick them up. He didn't seem to notice that the bird was crapping down his shoulder.

"But here's what I can't figure out," I said. "How did they know Kenny was back? I mean, how long was he in town?"

To my great surprise, Maggie shrugged. "I'm not really sure. Not more than a day or two, I think."

"You *think*?"

Her face got a little bit confused. "Yeah, I think. What's the problem?"

"But he was staying with you, right?" This was not intended as an accusation, though in my own ears it sounded sort of harsh.

"He didn't stay with me. He stayed at a guest house downtown."

Now *my* face got confused. "But wait a sec-

ond. I thought you and Kenny . . . I mean, I
thought the two of you were . . ."

"Lovers?"

The word hung in the air. I couldn't answer it.
I didn't have to.

"Jesus, Pete. You think it all comes down to
sex?"

I might have blushed at that, because the truth
was that's exactly what I thought.

"I told you Kenny wasn't gay," said Maggie. "I
never said he was my lover. We were buddies. We
went for walks. We shopped for clothes. Friends.
Is that so hard to grasp?"

I should have been embarrassed. I *was* embarrassed. But since we're being honest here, let me
admit I was also happy and relieved. Relieved not
to have a rival, even one who was a dead trans-
vestite. I know, I know—this was churlish and ir-
rational. But come on—does anyone really believe
that people are reasonable? Jealousy, desire—
things like that are hardwired into parts of the
brain way too ancient to explain or justify.

"Okay," I said. "I'm sorry for assuming. So
let's back up a step. Kenny stayed at a guest
house. You know which one he stayed at?"

The lissome yoga teacher didn't answer the
question. To my surprise and titillation, *she* was
now the one who kept the conversation mired in
sex. "Me and Kenny lovers?" She exhaled quickly
with just a hint of rueful laugh. "I mean, I liked
him a great deal, but he was a little too strange to
be my lover."

This put me in a dilemma that I guess real detectives must deal with all the time. Should I press
on with details of the murder, or should I quiz her
as to just what kind of lover she was looking for?
Someone, perhaps, with proficiency at tennis and
a passion for good music? What if he had to be
able to touch his toes?

But Maggie changed direction and went on.
"The place he stayed—I think it's called Hibiscus.
On a side street in Bahama Village."

I drank some wine and heard myself say that
I'd go down there tomorrow.

"You will?" said Maggie. There was simple
gratitude in her voice, and when I met her eyes, I
saw that they were opened very wide. She looked
beautiful. Her brow was high and smooth, the
full lips soft and slightly parted. Her expression
was concerned and yet serene, and I could only
wonder at a face capable of conveying both those
things at once.

We looked at each other a little longer than
was polite or safe, and in the stare I figured
something out, or imagined that I did. I thought
I knew now the kind of lover Maggie was looking for. She was looking for someone who would
get involved, someone who would see things
through. Which is to say, exactly the kind of
man I wasn't, and didn't care to be; no—exactly
the kind of man I'd given up on being. But in
that moment, looking at Maggie's open face, I
felt just the faintest quivering of long-dead fan-
tasies of rescue and crusade, chivalry and sacri-

fice. Those quiverings scared the hell out of me
and made me tingle.

I dropped my eyes and reached out for the
Viognier. The bottle was empty. Now how the
hell had that happened? How the hell was any of
this happening?

9

News of the next calamity came not by way of the morning paper—it had occurred too late for deadline—but from the hyperactive mouth of Ozzie Kimmel, when I showed up at the Bayview courts for our customary Saturday game.

"D'ya hear?" he said, as he stepped out of the shadow of the players' shed and yanked off his stretched and faded tank top.

"Hear what?"

He scratched his hairy stomach, tightened the drawstring of his puke-green bathing suit. "Another fuckin' murder."

Instantly I felt a cold spot in my gut, a tightness in my throat. Police-blotter items never used to affect me like that. A murder was too bad for the person murdered. Why should it mean anything to me? "Who?" I said.

"Heard it on the fuckin' radio," said Ozzie. "Ya know what I don't get? The richer and more tarted up this town gets, the safer, cleaner they try to make it look, the more people that get offed."

"Ozzie—who was killed?"

He dived into his ratty bag, came out with a

linty headband. "When I first came here, everyone was broke, everyone was stoned, the town looked like some Caribbean Third World pisshole, everybody lived on cans of beans and bananas off of trees and farted all day long, and nobody got fuckin' murdered. Now and then, okay, someone took bad acid, tried to fly or fell off a boat and drowned. But murdered? No way."

"Ozzie, tell me who was murdered."

He hefted his racquet, took some practice swings, did some torso twists. "What? I can't remember."

"You just heard it on the radio."

"Yeah, but it was some kind of a funny name. Some Polish guy, I think."

"Polish?" I tasted something steely at the back of my throat. "Any chance he was Latvian?"

"Polish, Latvian, who gives a shit? Some poor bastard who just got over here and was fixing up a boat."

"At Redmond's?"

"I think they said Redmond's, yeah. So you heard about it?"

I wiped my forehead and put my racquets back into my bag. "I gotta go."

This flabbergasted Ozzie, cracked a central pillar of his world. "Whaddya mean, you gotta go? It's Saturday. We play on Saturday."

I climbed onto my bike.

Ozzie's amazement turned to indignation. "You can't just go! We're here. We're playing."

I started pedaling away.

To my back, he yelled, "I can't believe this! Wimping out! I'm taking a default!"

A default? The lunatic kept records?

I headed toward the harbor. Key West is a sleep-in town, and at 9:00 A.M. the streets were so quiet that I could hear the suck of my tires on the pavement. Cats slunk silently around garbage cans. Dogs snuggled against the bottom steps of porches. Tin roofs reflected sunlight and threw a silver glow on the undersides of palms.

The quiet was shattered as I neared the boatyard, though it was hard to say by what, exactly. There were no shouts, no sirens or machinery. It was more the nervous buzz of a threatened hive, the indistinctly roiled atmosphere of a place where something violent has happened.

The cops had placed a barricade across the entrance, just some splintery sawhorses whose legs stood uneven in the coral rock. Passersby gawked then moved along. I edged closer. At last, among the chastened hulks in their high, dry cradles, I saw *Dream Chaser,* cordoned off with yellow crime-scene tape.

Old salts will tell you that certain boats are just plain cursed. A virus of disaster inhabits their very decks and fittings, bringing ill winds voyage after voyage, misfortunes season after season, persisting even in the face of changing ports and changing owners. Superstitious nonsense, of course. But looking at *Dream Chaser*—its wrecked rigging still unrepaired, its sanded but as yet unpainted bottom splotched with putty, its last two owners untimely dead—it was hard to feel immune from superstition.

Still on my bike, I rolled up to the cop who was manning the entrance and asked him what had happened.

Gruffly he said, "Nothing I can talk about."

"It's already on the radio," I told him.

"Can't help that."

"Look, can I go in? I have a friend inside." I gestured in the direction of Maggie's trawler with its begonias and geraniums.

"Residents only," he informed me.

"I'm worried about her," I said.

"Lots of people are worried."

"Is everybody else okay?"

"Far's I know," he said, and then we had a little standoff. The cop didn't come right out and tell me to get lost, but his sour, pinched expression behind the Ray-Bans let me know that I was bugging him. He stared at me in the petty, bullying way of certain small-town cops who want to let you know they are memorizing your face, and that some time it will cost you. I stared back for an instant, and wondered if this guy had been a friend of Lefty Ortega's, one of the flunkies whose mission it was to make sure that the guys who ran the town were free to do their business.

But what I was mainly thinking in that moment was what a sorry excuse for a detective I was turning out to be. Real PI's knew how to talk to cops, manly man to man, how to wheedle information. A real PI would have gotten past the barricade, past the crime-scene tape, would have managed to get aboard that cursed boat. A real detective would have smelled the blood and noticed some small but crucial thing that everyone else had overlooked. Instead, I just sat there on my bike, knowing that I seemed to the cop like one more weenie with white shorts and a tennis racquet. Still outside the perimeter of real involvement, I flinched from his belittling stare and pedaled off.

But in no particular direction. I was edgy and nervous and didn't feel like going home. I felt an itch I couldn't place at first. Gradually I recognized it as something that long ago, up north, I used to feel quite often: the itch of purpose, the itch to get something accomplished. But what?

With nothing much in mind, I leaned and swooped through random streets. Not till I'd crossed the ugly clutter of Duval did I realize I was heading to Bahama Village to check out the Hibiscus guest house.

Bahama Village is about the last part of Key West that could really be called a neighborhood. It still features curbside games of dominoes, and corner groceries that compete on the charm of their owners and the coldness of their beer. Generations of families still live together here. Houses are passed on, patched and propped up with cinder blocks and railroad ties; they lean but they endure. Not that the Village is immune from change. Homesteading whites who can't afford the other parts of town are picking up some bargains—you see earnest young white women in torn jeans and bandannas, scraping paint, raking improbable gardens. Gay pride flags hang from porches here and there. But the pace of change is slow for now, as languorous as the streets themselves, and has a human face. It won't stay that way; and as I rode past the rib joints and the fried-fish stands, I vaguely wondered if the hovering developers would let Bahama Village keep its own true name, or if they'd decide that the suggestion of blackness might keep the millionaires away.

On Louisa Street between Emma and Thomas, I stumbled onto the Hibiscus. It had a brightly painted wooden sign out front, and frankly, I found it sooner than I wanted to. I'd been enjoying the feeling of having a project, yet without having to do anything but push the pedals and look around. Now I had to talk. Now I had to play a part.

I locked my bike and went up a set of porch steps that closely resembled my own. All basically alike, these old Conch houses; part of their appeal. This one had been converted so that the small front parlor was now the office. There was a chest-high counter that held a rack filled with the relentless promotional brochures—fishing trips, nightclubs, sunset sails. Potted palms and ficuses brought the outdoors in. A doorway led to the guest rooms that, boardinghouse style, gave onto a common hall. I slapped the little silver bell atop the counter and waited for someone to appear.

After a moment, a woman came bustling along.

She was black, had cornrowed hair, and went about two-forty, with an astonishingly confident smile that seemed to go with someone more conventionally attractive, and that carried all before it. In one breath she said an extravagant hello, told me her name was Vanessa, and asked if she could help me.

"I'm looking for a friend," I said.

"I hope you find one," said Vanessa. She flashed the smile and gave me a mischievous half-wink.

"His name's Kenny Lukens."

She turned her face toward one exorbitantly fleshy shoulder, thought a second. "No one by that name staying here."

"This would have been three, four days ago."

She shook her head, a little quickly for my taste.

I glanced over toward the counter. "Isn't there a register you could check?"

"Hon," she said, "I only got five rooms."

"He might have used a different name."

I thought her face got just a little less friendly then, protective of her clientele. "That makes it tougher, doesn't it?"

"He's about six-foot, white, has green eyes and hair just longer than a crew cut."

"Different name," she said, "maybe he wanted to be left alone."

I ignored that since I had no answer for it. "He might've been in drag."

"You a cop?"

"No."

That wasn't good enough for Vanessa. She fixed

me with big dark steady eyes that coaxed forth
more information.

"I . . . I'm . . . I'm a private investigator."
There, I'd said it. Aloud and of my own free will.
For the first time ever, I believe. I braced myself to
be laughed at and unmasked. I waited for disbe-
lief and mockery. It didn't come. "Name's Pete
Amsterdam."

Vanessa said, "Somebody paying you, Pete Amsterdam?"

"Excuse me?"

"To make trouble."

"I'm not trying to make trouble."

"Then why you looking for him?"

I licked my lips. PI's had to say hard things
sometimes, and they always said them straight.
"Because he's dead."

"Dead?"

"The body they found on Tank Island a couple
nights ago? That was Kenny Lukens. The police
don't seem to know that. They won't learn it from
me. He almost was my client. They don't have to
know that either, okay? Will you help me out?"

Vanessa took a moment to expel a long slow
breath. "Listen, I'm hanging on by a thread here.
I can't afford a mess."

"I understand," I said. "I'm asking you to trust
me."

She looked at me hard. I stared right back. Two
small-timers trying to do the right thing and not
get hurt for doing it. Frankly, I was touched by
the slimness of our respective chances.

Vanessa said at last, "There was a guy who

stayed here that might've been your man. Paid
cash. Called himself Josh." She moved behind the
counter, flipped a page of the register. "Josh
Slocum."

My mouth curled because it so happened that I
recognized that alias. Joshua Slocum, New England sea captain, first man ever to sail alone
around the world. Wrote a book about it.

"That'd be him," I said.

"Nice person," said Vanessa. "Quiet. Consid-
erate. Nervous though."

"Anybody with him? Anybody visit?"

"No," she said. "All by his lonesome. Paid for
three nights, stayed for two. Never came back for
his things."

"You still have them?"

She didn't answer, just squeezed her lips together, paused, then gestured for me to follow
her. She led me down the hall and out the back
door to a courtyard, where a handful of guests
were having breakfast next to a big octagonal hot
tub. Beyond the tub was a small outbuilding, totally swathed in raspberry-colored bougainvillea.
Vanessa's studio apartment. It had African fabrics
and pictures of women embracing on the walls.
There was a small neat kitchen with many jars of
grains and spices.

Vanessa reached into a closet and came out
with a yellow nylon duffel, the kind that's shaped
like a sausage and opens on top. She handed it to
me and I didn't quite know what to do with it; I
couldn't haul it on my bike. "Mind if I look
through it here?" I asked.

She gave an uneasy shrug, and I dumped the contents onto her bedspread. It made for quite a still life, and I tried not to feel like a ghoul or a voyeur riffling through the stuff. Sweat socks and stockings. Jockstraps and bras. Sandals, pumps; sunblock and eyeliner; panties for every mood and occasion. I told myself I was there not to gape at underwear but to look for clues—which made the process not a jot less weird. Five minutes ago I'd finally fessed up to being a private eye, and here I was, sifting through a corpse's personal effects like I knew what I was doing. The power of the things we call ourselves . . .

I tossed aside razors and rouge, foundation and foot powder, looking for something of consequence. A journal would have been nice, but Kenny Lukens didn't seem to have kept a journal. There wasn't even an address book—but then, a person whose past could kill him any day wouldn't have much use for one. I pocketed a handheld compass, which I thought to give to Maggie as a keepsake. And I took a matchbook that intrigued me—there always has to be a matchbook, right? This one was from a place called Freddy's Beachside on Green Turtle Cay, in the Bahamas. But what I found of interest was a phone number scrawled inside that started with the digits 294. That's a Key West exchange.

I raked my fingers one last time through Kenny's things, then turned back toward Vanessa. I thanked her for her time; her eyes asked me once again not to bring down havoc on her little enterprise. We shook hands and I turned to go.

I was halfway to the door when she said to my back, "Just like a man."

I looked across my shoulder to see her beginning to attack the mess I'd left behind. Abashed, I made a move to help repack the duffel. She treated me to a last look at that amazing smile and gestured me away. "Hey," she said, "I'm used to sloppy guests."

10

Back on the street, the world had moved from morning to full day. Houses seemed to stand up straighter, like soldiers at attention, as their shadows were sucked in beneath them. The pavements had spent their nighttime coolness; I felt sharp sunshine through my sneakers and reflected up my legs.

I got back onto my bike and headed home. My mind was cluttered, my routine had been exploded. I needed to retreat.

I didn't get to. Climbing my porch steps, tennis bag in hand, I heard someone suddenly call my name and I did a little sideways jump.

It was Maggie. She was sitting in my favorite rocking chair and, purposely or otherwise, hiding out behind the jasmine bush the same way I was fond of doing. Now she rose without effort, moved toward me in a soundless float as in a painting by Chagall, and for some part of a heartbeat fell into my arms. Backing off immediately, she said, "Something terrible has happened."

"I know," I said. "I tried to visit you at Redmond's."

"You did?"

"Didn't have what it takes to get past the police line. You okay?"

She nodded but her eyes were on the porch planks. I asked her if she'd like some coffee. She said she would, and we went inside.

Fussing in the kitchen, grinding beans and wetting down a filter, it dawned on me, with ineffable regret, that I'd been too distracted and surprised to really feel the hug that Maggie had given me. However fleetingly, her arms had been around my neck, her breasts had been against my ribs. Was it conceivable that I simply hadn't noticed?

We took our coffee and went out back. The pool pump was humming; bits of leaf and some windblown oleander petals were slowly spinning on the surface in a lazy gyre that always missed the skimmer. We had to move our chairs very close directly underneath a palm to be in shade. Something about the hug now came scudding back in memory. Maggie's arms had been very cool against my overheated shoulders; the tiny hairs on her forearms had slightly tickled my neck.

She sipped her java and suddenly said, "The thing about Andrus? He reminded you how lucky you are to be here. He appreciated things. The smell of the air. The fish that hang around the dock. He took none of it for granted."

A eulogy not to be improved on, I thought. So I kept my mouth shut, drank some coffee, and looked down at the pool. In the brief silence I re-

membered something else about the phantom
hug. It had to do with the texture of Maggie's
bosom as it compressed against my chest, and,
while it could be described in terms of cushions,
bread dough, or certain ripening fruits, I don't
think words exist that really nail it. Finally I said,
"You know any more about what happened?"

She lifted her eyes and shrugged. "Supposedly
a robbery. That's the word around the yard, at
least. Andrus caught them at it and they killed
him."

"They?" I said. "Do we know that there was
more than one?"

"No idea. That's just what people say."

I pictured a struggle inside the thin shell of the
Dream Chaser. "Nobody heard a fight?"

"Friday night," said Maggie. "There's a loud
band at the Raw Bar. Plays till two in the morning. You sleep in earplugs or you don't sleep."

I drummed fingers on my chair arm. To the sky
and the overhanging fronds I said, "Why that
boat, of all the boats?"

Maggie looked away. "I've thought about that
too."

"Seen any guys in snorkels lately?"

Maggie didn't answer right away. With her accustomed lack of effort or compunction, she lifted
up her legs and tucked them underneath her. The
motion reminded me that, for one brief instant in
the fleeting hug, the fronts of our thighs had
brushed together. But had they really? Was I remembering or imagining by now, and how much
difference was there anyway?

Finally she said, "So you think—?"

"What I think is that either this is one big bastard of a coincidence, or the people who killed Kenny didn't get their precious pouch and came back to search the boat."

Palms rustled. Water swirled slowly in the pool. I squirmed to where I could reach into my shorts pocket, and pulled out the little flip-top compass. I handed it to Maggie. "Thought you might like to have this. It was Kenny's."

She took it as gently as if it were a baby bird. She looked at me questioningly.

"I went down to the Hibiscus," I explained. "Spoke to the owner. Went through Kenny's things."

"Ah," she said. "Find anything that—?"

"I wish I knew what the hell to look for. I wish I was better at this. I found a matchbook."

I passed it over and something awful happened. For just a fraction of an instant, I thought that maybe I saw something less than altogether candid in Maggie's pretty face. If the guardedness was there at all, it was a tiny thing, a flicker at the corner of the eye, a twitch of some nameless discomfort, and it vanished as fast as it had come. Maybe she had a tickle in her throat, a burp in her gullet, a bug in her ear. I hoped it was something like that, because the possibility, however faint, that my one ally, this woman who had hugged me, was not being perfectly straight gave me a feeling I really couldn't stand.

"Freddy's Beachside," Maggie read. "That's one of the places he worked."

Was it just the pool pump, or did her voice suddenly sound the slightest bit tinny? "Tell me about it," I said.

"He tended bar there. I'm not sure how long. Every time he wrote to me it seemed he had a different job."

"How often did he write?"

"It varied. Two months. Five months. When he got around to it. Every once in a great while he called. Just to chat. No big deal."

I hadn't suggested it was a big deal. Maggie was still holding the matchbook. I asked her to open it. "A Key West number," I said. "Mean anything to you?"

She pursed her lips, a little theatrically, I thought, then shook her head; my suspicion that she was fibbing only deepened. This depressed me. I went into a sulk. I wish I could say it was a fine detectivelike sulk on the details of the case, but it wasn't that at all. I was sulking about the fragility of infatuation, mourning the loss of the first and simplest phase of my happily untested lusting after Maggie. The merest whiff of ambiguity had dulled my fantasy like hot breath dulls a mirror.

The silence dragged on and went sour. Maggie said at last; "You mad at me or something? You seem unfriendly all of a sudden."

Jesus, these yoga teachers see right through you. Was it some catch in my breathing, some slight lifting of my shoulders? Trying to feel friendly again, I sought to recall more aspects of the hug. I couldn't remember a single goddamn piece of it now. But nor did I exactly trust my own mistrust. What started it? A twitch? What if I was wrong? I didn't want to be a moody jerk, and how could I dare accuse this woman of anything? I was flummoxed. Desire mixed in with suspicion might just be the bitterest cocktail you can have.

"Well, I should go," said Maggie, after another pause that I guess was longer than I realized.

She stood up smoothly. I stood up too and walked her through the house and out again onto the porch. Standing there, concern and even affection welled up again, pressed against my faint distrust like a bone chip on a nerve, and I said, "The boatyard—you'll be okay down there?"

She nodded that she would and started down the stairs. Her shoulders stayed level and her neck stayed straight the whole time she was descending, and even as she climbed onto her brightly painted bike.

Back inside, I paced and fretted my way into the music room. I did my riffling-and-deciding thing, then surprised myself by putting on some Monk. Ordinarily, Monk is not someone I would listen to while the sun was in the sky, but this whole day had gotten twisted upside down, and in some cockeyed way I thought that maybe his extraordinary bitterness would cheer me up. I mean, how did you make a melody sarcastic?

Some time later, I remembered the matchbook that was still perched on the arm of what had been Maggie's chair by the pool.

I went out and retrieved it. I carried it around awhile, stalling. I knew I had to call the number scrawled inside, and I knew that calling it would be one more sucker on the octopus, one more tentacle to wrap itself around my life.

I sat down in the living room. Picked up the phone, put it down again, got a drink of water. Finally dialed.

The line was picked up, and before I heard a voice I heard what sounded like an amusement park. Laughing, splashing, brainless little squeals and screams. Finally a rushed but cheery voice said, "Paradise Watersports."

I said, "Um, do you rent Jet Skis?"

"Forty bucks an hour. Hundred, half a day."

I had an inspiration. "Snorkels too?"

"Twenty dollars. Whole outfit, all day long."

"Where you located?"

"Next dock over from the Hyatt. Here till eight. Check out the sunset special. Sixty bucks, two hours."

Sunset on a Jet Ski? Slamming my kidneys and wrenching my spine, when the same time and money could be spent on a Puligny-Montrachet? I didn't think so. "Another day," I told the dock guy, and hung up.

And sat there wondering why Kenny Lukens, having fled to the Bahamas and apparently escaped his very messy past, would keep a number for a Key West Jet Ski outfit in his yellow nylon duffel.

11

If a bike is mainly how you get around, you find yourself passing through the Key West cemetery nearly every day.

The cemetery, maybe five blocks square, is about the only open space in Old Town, the only respite from the grid, the closest thing we have to Central Park. It's a shortcut, a picnic ground, a lovers' lane. And, of course, a tourist attraction. Tourists find dead locals quaint. They love the color photos that the Cubans plaster into head-stones; the plastic flowers left behind in plastic vases; the wry epitaphs that flip the bird at Death. Uncluttered palms grow taller in the graveyard; cypresses like candle flames flicker in its breezes.

The only problem with the Key West cemetery is that you can't actually bury anyone there. Beneath a thin layer of dubious topsoil, the ground is solid coral. You need a jackhammer to break it up, and if you do, an ooze of milky, salty water almost instantly seeps through the fissures.

So corpses are either cemented into toe-stubbing bunkers right at ground level or stacked in family mausoleums resembling vast card cata-

logs. In my thousands of aimless circuits through
the graveyard, I'd casually observed a number of
funerals, but I'd never really thought about the
logistics of these aboveground rites until the day
they "buried" Lefty Ortega.

This was not a funeral I should have gone to.
I'd been in some degree a party to the old bully's
death. If I hadn't actually shoved him into the
abyss, I'd certainly poked and prodded him toward the brink. Why show up now and take a
chance on being recognized as the last visitor to
his hospice room?

Closure, I guess would be the fashionable answer. But I have a deep distrust of fashionable
words like that. They blur specifics, flatten the
wiggy details of real life. Frankly, I don't know
why I went. After my . . . my *what*? Not an argument, not a tiff, not even a misunderstanding. After my moment of doubt with Maggie, I'd had a
troubled evening and a bad night's sleep, and
found myself in that frame of mind where one
loses confidence in the hard clear edges of notions
like free will and conscious choice. It soothes our
pride to imagine that we *decide*. But sometimes it
just doesn't work that way. I showered and found
myself dressing for a funeral.

The real Conchs, having their roots in New
England solemnity and Spanish decorum, are on
special occasions a surprisingly formal people,
even stuffy in a subtropical kind of way. Not
wanting to stand out, I pulled on long pants and a
clean white shirt. Real shoes, with socks. Shoes
feel very hard when you haven't worn them for a

while. Biking in long pants feels funny too, the
way they flap against your calves. I rode down to
the cemetery, locked my bicycle a decent distance
off, and walked toward the assembled crowd before the Ortega mausoleum—a five-story concrete
condo, maybe sixty units in all, with one crypt
winking open on the penthouse floor.

There were a hundred or a hundred-twenty
mourners—a big turnout for Key West, where
people pride themselves on seldom showing up.
The older men wore suits; the women all wore
stockings. It was blisteringly hot. Killer sun is a
constant feature of Key West funerals, as drizzle
can be counted on up north. You stand there and
your neck burns and you sweat. In cases of real
grief, emotion opens pores and you sweat even
more. The priest sweats in his robes; the workers
sweat in their canvas shirts. There is a grim, unspoken worry over putrefaction that tends to
keep the ceremonies brief.

I edged closer and heard part of a speech. The
guy giving it looked vaguely familiar; I think
he was on the city council. He praised Lefty as a
pillar of the community—businessman, family
man—the standard kind of speech. I looked
around. Not that I knew what I was looking for.
Men in snorkels? Guys with blood on their suits?
What I saw was a family—variations on a somber
Spanish face. The men tended toward the craggy,
with bent noses overhanging twitchy lips. The
women had very deep-set eyes and the yellowish
skin that was a class thing back in Cuba; it
seemed to be the chin that determined who would

cross the line into a sullen kind of beauty, and
who would merely look severe. At the front of the
throng I was pretty sure I saw the daughter. Her
hair was pulled up, though little wisps had broken free and by now were plastered against her
damp and reddening neck.

The politician finished and the priest took over.
I looked around some more, concentrating now
on the faces that didn't fit the family mold. A few
big fellows who kept plucking at their jackets—
cops, maybe, uncomfortable out of uniform. Some
men I took to be business associates, who com-
prised a pretty good sampling of South Florida
hustler types—dudes with ponytails and earrings,
pseudo–yacht club guys in blazers, a fat man
sweating grease like a goose and daintily fan-
ning himself like a Japanese lady. The associates
seemed not sorrowful but bothered that they had
to be here, just like they'd been bothered that
they'd had to send showy and expensive flowers
to the hospital. If lack of eye contact was any in-
dication, a lot of these people didn't know one
another. Lefty Ortega, trusting no one, had apparently kept the various aspects of his business as
neatly separate as the mausoleum slots.

The sun beat down. Wet places bloomed on
people's clothes. The priest went from talking to
chanting then suddenly stopped. Two morticians
approached the coffin, which was resting on a
platform that resembled a small painter's scaf-
folding. They fitted cranks to the base, then, with
a medieval literalness, started jacking Lefty up to
heaven. Soon he was above the level of the

mourners' heads; next he pulled even with the lower fronds of the Christmas palms. The mahogany coffin glinted richly in the sunlight; the cranks made a lugubrious and rhythmic squeaking as the struts unfurled and stretched into big X's. Like the last passenger on a balky elevator, the dead man finally reached his floor. One of the morticians fitted his crank into a different socket, and the bed of the platform slid slowly into the open crypt. Lefty was deposited with a chilling thud; the withdrawn platform made a soft ringing scrape, like that of a pizza peel.

A single whimper broke through the steamy motionless air. I guess Lefty had a wife. I guess she was too short to be seen at the front of the group.

The heat-sapped party broke up quickly after that—too quickly for me to slip away ahead of it. The crowd opened so that close family had easy access to the limos waiting in the lane. To my horror, I found myself standing—exposed, conspicuous—squarely on the fault line where the group had split. I tried to shrink back among the other sweaty bodies; short of throwing elbows, there was no way I could retreat. I sidled as far as I could go, and braced for the moment when the dead man's daughter would walk right past. I imagined her meeting my eye, remembering, then pointing, accusing, maybe even screaming. The big men unaccustomed to their suits would lumber through the crowd and grab me. Would they regard me as police business or as an enemy better dealt with privately?

I stood there. Half a dozen very old Ortegas moved past at a pace that was maddeningly sedate. Finally, the daughter, her arm around a tiny woman who must have been her mother, turned to follow. I held my breath. I thought to look away, but realized that such inappropriateness would only be a magnet for attention. I composed my face and fixed my gaze.

And just as I'd feared, Lefty's daughter's eyes clamped on to mine nearly at once. She was wearing a tiny black hat with a veil. I hadn't known that women wore veils anymore, and I'm sure I'd never before been caught in a stare through one. I found it Gothic and riveting. Webby shadows stretched across her brow; her eyes were dark inside of dark, as sexily elusive as nakedness through gauze. Stripped of context, swelling into sunlight, the full red lips were almost lewd. Feeling weird and doomed and dizzy, I thought: If I have to be undone, let it be by such an archaically erotic graveyard stare as this.

But Lefty's daughter didn't flinch, didn't accuse, didn't signal to her father's friends. Instead, she quickly, deftly reached down with the arm that was not around her mother and pressed a scrap of paper into my hot hand.

I swallowed hard and squeezed it tight, and didn't dare even to uncurl my fingers until the crowd had wandered off, and I was safely on my bicycle once more.

I went straight home, peeled off my sodden clothes, and immediately jumped into the pool. I swam a few laps of three or four strokes each, then curled into a ball and let myself sink slowly to the bottom. I liked it down there. There were no sounds, except for a soft hum that you felt more than you heard. Light congealed into a cool thin greenish batter. There was no one there to bother you. I wished I could have stayed there longer.

Surfacing, I did the next best thing—waded to a shady corner and stood there chest-deep in the water. I thought about the note that Lefty's daughter had pressed into my hand. It was a very short note, consisting of nothing more than an address and a time. What intrigued me, though, was the question of when she'd found the opportunity to write it. She could not have noticed me before she was already front row center at her father's funeral. Did she rummage through her purse for pen and paper while the priest was chanting, while the body was ascending?

Another possibility occurred to me—one I didn't like at all. Maybe the note had been written beforehand. Maybe it was part of a stratagem, a trap. The daughter, together with her father's thuggish friends, perhaps, had guessed correctly that the unknown man who'd visited the hospital might also show up at the funeral. But Conch decorum would disallow a violent scene at such a solemn event. Better, then, to lure the poor doomed sucker into an ambush.

One gruesome notion leads to another, and for the first time in the couple of years since I'd stashed it there, I caught myself thinking about the never-fired nine-millimeter in the wall safe.

The mere fact that I was thinking about it made me shiver in the tepid water. Guns really, really scare me; I wished I hadn't let myself be talked into getting one. I'm of the school that basically believes that soft middle-class people like myself should never own a firearm. The first time you whip it out, someone tougher, meaner, and with less to lose takes it away from you and shoots you with it, and you end up with your own bullet stuck in your liver like a garlic clove.

But wait a second. It was the middle of a sunny day and I was standing naked in my bright blue swimming pool. What the hell was I doing, worrying about ambushes and guns, getting myself all jumpy? How had I let things go so far that images of wounds and mortal struggles were poisoning my mind?

Well, however far they'd gone, I could stop them here and now. I knew how. I'd learned the one sure, simple way of avoiding ambushes of all descriptions: Mind your own business and stay the hell at home. That's all it took, and that's what I would do. I just wouldn't go to the address on Lefty's daughter's note. Not at the time she specified, not ever. Done.

As if to lock in my fresh resolve, I took a big deep breath and drifted once again toward the peaceful void at the bottom of the pool. I felt the soft hum of the water, and watched the glinting light, and told myself I wouldn't go, I wouldn't go.

PART TWO

12

I went.

Of course I went. At 7:00 P.M., exactly as instructed. And with my gun still locked up in the wall safe.

I left my house around twenty of. The sun had just set, and layers of pink cloud were stacked up amid slabs of lavender. Heat throbbed off parked cars as the air began slowly to cool. I climbed onto my bike and turned it toward the ocean.

The address on the note was 2000 Atlantic Boulevard. This was Key West's biggest condo, a low waterfront fortress that well-off Conchs just loved. Typical, I guess. Relative newcomers like me were seduced by the charm of the old Conch houses—the grainy, pitted wood; the sloping floors; the bowed, eccentric door frames. Whereas the Conchs themselves couldn't wait to get out of those mildewed, termite-eaten wrecks. If they made a little dough, they blissfully moved to the cinder-block boxes of New Town, or into generic condos that might have been in Fort Myers or Fort Lauderdale. They'd had enough authenticity to last a lifetime. Now they wanted drywall,

Formica, enough amps to run the microwave.
Above all, central air-conditioning. They set the
thermostat at fifty-five, moved the recliner over by
a vent, and sat there basking in the glow of getting over.

It was just before the hour when I reached the
complex, and the truth is, I was pretty nervous.
Felt it behind my knees. I took a quick detour to
look at the water. It was dead flat, as it usually
gets at dusk. It still looked milky green but it was
near the moment when it turned to purple for the
night. This happens with nothing in between, and
it happens in a second. If you blink, you miss it.

The water failed to calm me and I didn't see
that I could stall much longer. I pedaled back toward the condo. I didn't go directly to the entrance but approached in a series of concentric,
leaning arcs while I sort of scoped it out. What
did I expect to see? Men in Ray-Bans hiding in
the oleander bushes? No, if they were going to
jump me, they'd wait until I got inside. I locked
my bike and walked up to the board of names
and doorbells. Ortega, L. was in 4E. I raised my
thumb to ring. I hesitated. Odd-looking thing, a
thumb. I thought about withdrawing it and flee-
ing, no harm done. The thumb jabbed forward
and rang the bell.

In a few seconds the buzzer buzzed. I pushed
through the door and walked under an ugly chandelier throwing bad light on a cheesy mosaic. I
went to the elevator and rode to the top floor. Ascending, I pictured Lefty being cranked up toward his crypt. The image wasn't comforting.

The doors slid open on an endless hallway. Silent. Lit by Deco sconces throwing yellow scallops that folded onto the ceiling. I did the alphabet until I found 4E. I stalled for just a second more, then realized I should look jaunty and assertive, in case I was being examined through the little peephole. So I knocked before I was really ready. I was still clearing my throat and shuffling my feet when the door swung open and Lefty's daughter stood before me.

I sure wasn't ready for the way she looked. She was wearing black silk slacks and a white satin blouse that was open a long way down. There was lace at the edges of her breasts, and a small, embroidered pale blue flower in between them on her bra. Her hair was pinned up, though more loosely than it had been before. Wisps of it escaped at her temples and thinned out into barely visible strands along her jawline. Her eyes were made up, deep-set, and they still seemed somehow veiled. In a musky voice with an edge that might have been ironic, she said, "I wondered if you'd come."

I couldn't immediately get my mouth to work or my eyeballs to stay still. They wanted to look down her shirt but also wanted to check behind the door for people waiting to hurt me. Finally I managed to say, "Why wouldn't I?"

To that she only shrugged. The lace and the little blue flower moved as she did so. She stepped to one side and motioned me into the apartment. My shoulders hunched as I leaned through the doorway. I was ready to be hit or grabbed. Nothing hit me except her perfume. It was too sweet and floral for my taste, but I liked that it was there.

The carpet got thicker as I stepped into the foyer; the living room furniture, in turn, crystallized for me something that I hadn't quite been able to place about her clothes: Both seemed outside of their own time. Not retro-hip, not campy, just intriguingly misplaced. The high life, circa 1961. Pointy bra and sectional sofa. Bad sculptures that were lamps, and black stockings under black silk pants. There was even a wet bar in a tiled and mirrored alcove. It had its own small fridge and a see-through cabinet full of highball glasses and pony glasses and martini glasses. She went to it and offered me a drink.

I felt like pinot noir but doubted I could get it. I asked for scotch and water. She poured me a quadruple and handed it over. Then she retrieved her own glass, which had ice and clear stuff in it. We clinked. We stared briefly at each other as we did so, then she dropped her eyes and I had the distinct impression she was checking out my legs. Have I mentioned I was wearing shorts? I'd put long pants on once that day—that was plenty. Of course, I'd forgotten to figure on the air-conditioning. The apartment was freezing and my leg hairs stood straight up in their follicles. I thought she smiled secretly as she waved me toward the sofa.

She sat down on the edge and used her palms to smooth a space around her. "So, Mr.—"

"Amsterdam. Pete Amsterdam. Pete." I'd staked

out my own section of the sectional, from where I could look at her across a corner of the coffee table.

"I'm Lydia." She sipped her drink and crossed her legs. The silk of her pants made a nice slidey sound and the momentum turned her hips and torso toward me slightly. "What sort of business did you have with my father, Pete?"

"Excuse me?"

She lifted one eyebrow and shot me a gamy, can't-kid-a-kidder sort of look. "Come on," she said. "You went to see him at the hospital. You came to the funeral."

Stalling for time, I thought I'd play it coy. "And this means we had something going on?"

"Pete," she said, "my father kept me in the background, but I know quite a lot about his businesses. I know the men he's in business with." She paused, gave her hair a toss that didn't quite work with the hairpins in. She leaned forward with her chest. "Some of them I know quite well."

Her tone left little doubt as to the sense in which she knew them, and I found it necessary to sip some scotch. I thought back to my deathbed chat with Lefty. Maybe he'd been raving, but he was pretty emphatic about a couple things. One was that his daughter had a problem. The other was that I shouldn't fuck her. I looked at her past the rim of my glass. Her lips were very red and moist. There seemed to be a hint of dampness in her cleavage too, even in the cold apartment. Her thighs wriggled so that fabric squeaked; her tongue didn't seem to rest quite easy in her mouth. Could this be her problem, I wondered—that she was a nymphomaniac? I'd never been quite clear as to whether, in reality, there was such a thing, or if the nympho was a male invention, a figment to whom he could ascribe his own glandular excesses and itchy drawers. And if nymphos really did exist, why hadn't I met one twenty-five years ago, when we could have squared off as more equal contestants and really wrecked a room?

"And now I'll be in charge," Lydia continued. "So there are certain situations I need to . . . get on top of."

With that she drained her glass and got up to refill it. Vodka. Before she turned away from the wet bar, she took a couple hairpins out. "How's your drink?" she asked me.

"Vast."

She came back to the couch and sat this time on my section of the sectional. Perfume wafted. There was a moment of somewhat awkward silence, then she gave a quick giggle and pointed to my naked knee. "You always wear shorts to visit a lady in mourning?" That Conch decorum thing, I guess.

"I guess I didn't think of it as a condolence call," I said.

"No?" she said, and she put her arm up on the back of the couch. It was that symbolic enfolding gesture, the first sly move toward an embrace that men are usually the ones to try. "How *did* you think of it?"

That stumped me for a second. I sucked at my drink. Then I said, "You invited me, remember?"

"That's right. To ask you one simple question that so far you refuse to answer: What was your business with my father?"

I tried to look like I was holding some marvelous and valuable secret. Her reasonable but wrong surmise had given me a handy smoke screen, after all. Only problem was, I had no idea what use to put it to. Finally I said, "You know, it's funny. You assume I had business with your father, and your father assumed I was sent by somebody named Mickey."

"Mickey Veale?" She said it like she'd bit into something rotten.

For the moment I was on a roll. I worked it. "I don't know. Is that his name?"

Instead of answering, she brought her glass up to her lips. She didn't drink from it, though, just slithered her tongue along the rim a couple seconds. Finally she said, "Pete. I ask you a question and all you do is ask a question back. Are you always such a tease?"

Candidly I said, "I don't get to be a tease that often so I try to make the most of it."

She pulled her glass in close to her and touched its frosty base to her chest. "This back and forth, this sparring—you find it sexy?"

I didn't know how to answer that, so I didn't try.

"I do," she went on. "The restraint. The squirming . . . But I still want an answer to my question."

"But then the foreplay would be over," I pointed out.

"And the real thing could begin," she purred.

My throat slammed shut and I drank some scotch to scour it open. I glanced at my hostess's chest. I thought dirty then tried to think practical. I remembered Kenny Lukens' matchbook and took a guess. "Okay. Let's say the business was water sports."

Bad guess. Or rather, a good guess but a bad answer. Lydia didn't like it at all. Her shoulders tightened, her lips flicked back from her teeth, and she said, "So you *are* with Mickey Veale!"

Confused now, I moved to deny it. I didn't deny it fast enough, and Lydia Ortega threw her drink at me.

She didn't throw it at my face. She threw it at my crotch. Iced vodka stung my thighs; I couldn't tell if it was the cold or the alcohol that gave rise to a vivid but not pleasant tingling in my privates. Squirming, slapping ice cubes off my lap, I finally managed to say quite clearly that I didn't even know who Mickey Veale was.

This gave rise to an uneasy silence. Then Lydia laughed. It was not a pretty laugh and I wouldn't swear that it was sane. It was the hard laugh of a mean child, half proud of, half embarrassed by her bad behavior. She cackled for a moment, then bit it off quite suddenly. "My mistake," she said, without remorse. "So tell me, Pete: Just who the hell are you, and what the hell is going on?"

With a lapful of booze it wasn't easy to maintain either the bantering tone or my composure, but some vague and maybe perverse instinct told me not to tip my hand just yet. "Ah," I said, "I've made you curious."

"Yes," she admitted. "But now you're starting to piss me off, and that isn't a good thing to do."

This did not sound coy. There was conviction in it. However tardily, it dawned on me that there was no percentage in playing cute with someone dangerous. Since I didn't know what else to say, I said, "Then I guess I'd better go." I took a last swig of my giant whiskey, then put my glass on the coffee table and started standing up.

I didn't get very far. She shouldered me across the thighs and knocked me backward, then threw herself on top of me and gave me one hard, assaultive kiss, for which I wasn't ready. My lips were locked against my teeth, pinned down as helplessly as a losing wrestler's shoulders, and I could neither kiss back nor escape. Her breasts squeezed down against my shirt; her loins briefly wriggled in my soaking lap. Then she pushed up with a wicked shove against my arms, and suddenly was standing over me.

Her blouse was twisted, her chest heaved, and there was fury in her eyes. In a voice that whistled slightly through bared teeth, she said, "You don't toy with Lydia. Lydia toys with you." Her hand shot forth in an imperious gesture that pointed toward the door. "Now go."

People being animals, I was no longer so sure, after that bizarre and violent kiss, that I wanted to. But the decision had been made. I was being banished. For the best, no doubt, but something nagged at me, something that I couldn't figure out. Through the whole interview with Lefty's daughter, I thought I'd handled myself pretty well. Kept my wits about me, got some information. So was it only my wet, cold shorts that made me feel sheepish and defeated at the end?

Like a woozy fighter, I got up slowly from the couch. I didn't say good night and my hostess didn't move to walk me to the door.

But as I was crossing from the living room to the foyer, she called my name. I stopped and turned to face her. Her hands were on her high Cuban hips. In an age-old combination that everybody knows spells doom and that guys always fall for anyway, her eyes had softened, wide and dreamy, but her lips were curled into a snarling dare. "Come back some time," she said. "When you're feeling less like a tease and more like a man."

13

We've all had evenings when it's 8:30 but feels like 1:00 A.M.

This has to do not with fatigue but with bewilderment, sometimes helped along by a titanic cocktail in place of dinner. At such junctures, it seems that time has hiccuped, that the world is a formerly familiar room in which the furniture's been moved; as with a jazz record started in the middle, you're tantalized but can't quite find the tune. This is how I felt as I dragged my damp ass out the front door of 2000 Atlantic.

What the hell had gone on in there? Lydia had probed me, aroused me, jumped my bones, and ended the performance with a credible attempt to crush my masculinity. Along the way, I'd learned— what? That she was a nympho, maybe, but a tough cookie for sure, and the heir to Lefty's little empire. And that there was a guy named Mickey Veale, presumably involved in water sports, who she didn't like at all.

Fine, but where did it get me? It got me back onto my bicycle, in underpants by Stoli. Underpants that would not dry quickly in the humid

air. At least the evening was warmer than the re-
frigerated condo.

I rode. Gingerly, I addressed the question of
where I was riding to. The sane course, as always,
was retreat. Home to a bathrobe and some music,
some simple food and bed. I knew that but I
didn't go there. Feeling utterly peculiar, smudged
beyond my own outlines, I found myself pedaling
toward Redmond's Boatyard. I needed to see
Maggie.

But wait—*needed* to? Why? I barely knew her.
And the idea of needing someone was as scary as
any of the things I'd fretted about that day. Still,
that's how the thought broke over me: I needed to
see her. You can't undo a thought; once I'd
thought it I was stuck with it.

So I headed from the ocean to the Gulf. It's
a short ride; it reminds you how tiny Key West
is, how comfortingly insignificant. Except this
evening I was having a tough time feeling com-
forted. The notion was scratching at me that
there are things that matter even in places that
don't.

I got to the street-side gate of Redmond's and
saw that the police barricades were already
down; so much for a detailed investigation into
the death of a Latvian. I cruised right in. Residents were strolling here and there among the
cradled vessels, or listening to music, or sitting
on cut-off oil drums and drinking beer. Except
for the yellow crime-scene tape around *Dream
Chaser,* there was no evidence of recent violence,
nearby tragedy. If a pall remained, it was of a

kind that festered underneath the surface and didn't so readily show itself, the kind that went with a forever damaged sense of safety.

I rolled up to Maggie's trawler and, not without difficulty, climbed off my bike. The stars were out; the brighter ones were nested in little puffs of mist that looked like dandelions. I cleared my throat and called her name.

A long moment passed and then she finally appeared on deck. Her boat had a steep shear and high gunwales, and I had to crane my neck way back to see her; it was a little bit like crooning up to someone on a balcony—had that same absurdity and romance. I said hello.

She was wearing another of her T-shirt dresses, all smoothness and ease and unrestricted flow. Her curves were framed in stars. She seemed surprised to see me and didn't answer right away.

I asked her to invite me in.

She pointed toward the stern, then unfurled a rope ladder that clattered against the transom as it fell. I started climbing up. Rope ladders are unstable in the best of times, and this was hardly that. I swung; I wobbled; I felt a little seasick as I swung a leg into the cockpit. Maggie watched me climbing in, and the first thing she said was "Your pants are wet."

This was embarrassing. I wanted to explain it away as fast as possible. I said, "Lefty's daughter."

"Lefty's daughter?"

"She got 'em wet. Can we sit down awhile?"

The yoga teacher stared at me a second, then

turned toward the companionway and led me
down a short and narrow flight of stairs into the
main cabin, which was cozy as a puzzle. Furniture was painted peach and aqua, and everything
fit into something else. The galley counter was
hinged into a table; the back of the settee became
a bookcase. There was about the place the serenity that goes with lack of waste. The lighting
was soft and yellow; there was a restful background noise of water lapping gently at caulked
planks. . . . Then I remembered that the trawler
was on land.

"Am I crazy or do I hear waves?"

"It's a tape," said Maggie. "Soothing, isn't it?"
Then she added, "You have lipstick on your
teeth."

On my *teeth*? Shit. I'd heard of lipstick on the
collar. But the teeth?

"Want some tea?" she asked, lifting a cutting
board to reveal a miniature stove top.

I nodded then sat and took a moment to reflect
on what a fiasco I was making of this visit. I don't
think I seemed drunk, but I couldn't have appeared too sane or sober either. Not with wet
pants and red teeth. Now that I was sitting still, I
thought I detected a trace of Lydia's perfume on
me too. How could I redeem this mess? Drop to
my knees, confess to Maggie that although another woman had gotten me sexed up, it was her
I really wanted? If you thought about it, that was
quite a compliment. But even I understood that
certain compliments were better left unsaid.

Maggie brought the tea. It was herb tea and it

smelled like strawberries. She took hers and sat down smoothly on the companionway stairs. "So," she picked up, "you spoke with Lefty's daughter. Seems to've been a successful interview."

I sipped. It burned my lips but I hoped that it would sear away the lipstick. "I learned a couple things."

"I'll bet you did."

She was probably only ribbing me, but there was something in her tone and in the set of her jaw that allowed me to imagine that maybe, just possibly she was jealous. The idea thrilled me but I didn't have the nerve to test it. I stuck to the detective stuff. "Seems she's running Lefty's businesses now."

"Ah."

For a moment I was stumped as to how to continue. Ocean sounds came through hidden speakers and I had a faint and false sensation of the trawler rocking. Then, suddenly, I knew the real reason I'd needed to come here and what I had to say. I was still casting about for a tactful way to bring it up, when I heard myself blurt out, "Look, since yesterday I've had this shitty feeling that you know more than you're telling me."

Maggie rearranged her legs; her foot bumped against a stair. In anyone else this would have seemed a negligible fidget, barely noticeable, but it was such a violation of the yoga teacher's bodily precision that I found it painful to behold. She looked down at the floor, then up at me again. "You're right."

I blew out some air and leaned forward with my elbows on my knees. "So tell me."

"I'm not sure that I can. Kenny made me promise not to tell anyone."

"Kenny's dead."

"Still, it was a promise." Her calm gray eyes narrowed just a bit; her voice caught and I thought maybe she would start to cry. "A promise to a friend."

Weirdly, my throat closed down in turn. Not in honor of Kenny Lukens or even in sympathy with Maggie's affection for him. No, what put secret tears behind my eyes was something more selfish and helpless and embarrassing to admit. Hurt feelings, pure and simple. "A friend," I echoed. "Very loyal. Very nice. He was a friend. So what am I? Unpaid help? Someone you use to—"

She cut me off, but very quietly. Her lips seemed infinitely careful as they formed the words, "I don't know what you are, Pete. Or what I want you to be. I've been trying for days to figure it out. Can't you see that?"

Some detective. I hadn't seen it, and my lack of seeing now shut my mouth and pinned me where I sat. I stared at Maggie. The light was soft and she was very tan but still I thought I saw her flush. I imagined the warmth climbing up her neck and throbbing at the tender place behind her ears. We were maybe six feet from each other, and I think there was a moment when I might have wafted up from the settee and taken her in my arms and we might have become lovers then and there. But the moment passed before I quite believed in it.

When Maggie spoke again, it was in a tone that was trying real hard to be businesslike. "What I haven't told you," she said, "is that someone found Kenny on Green Turtle Cay. Someone, maybe, from that water sports place."

I sat still and waited for more.

"Small world down here," she said. "Guys get rock fever. They get tired of drinking in Key West, they jump in a skiff and go drinking in the Bahamas. Same life, different island for a while."

"And one of these guys," I said, "just happened to show up at the bar where Kenny was working?"

"Seems that way. Maybe it was just bad luck. More likely he'd been looking for him. Who knows? But it was someone who'd been a regular at Lefty's. He recognized Kenny before Kenny saw him and could bolt."

"They talked?"

"The guy talked at Kenny. He was very drunk. He kept going back and forth between making threats and trying to cut a deal."

"A deal?"

"He told Kenny that Lefty still wanted to have him killed. But he had no loyalty to Lefty. He hated Lefty. He just wanted what was in the pouch. For himself. Said he'd pay ten thousand dollars for it. Said that was way more than it was worth to Kenny anyway."

"And Kenny said?"

"Kenny said nothing. Kenny wouldn't even admit that he was Kenny. He claimed he didn't know what the guy was talking about. Claimed he'd never been in Key West in his life." She shook her head and gave a sad, small laugh. "You know Kenny."

"No," I pointed out, "I don't know Kenny."

"A terrible liar," she said. "But he kept on trying."

"So this guy—"

"Got drunker. Scrawled the Key West number on a matchbook and told Kenny to call and just leave his name when he wanted an easy ten grand. But then he got more threatening, like he'd decided he better take care of Kenny then and there. Kenny was terrified. Went to fetch ice and just kept going. Out the back door, to his dinghy. Sailed off to a different island and never went back."

"But kept the phone number," I said. "Did he ever call this guy?"

"I don't know. He never said."

"Ever mention his name?"

"I don't think he knew it."

"Physical description?"

Maggie shook her head. "Big and drunk is all he said."

I sipped some lukewarm tea and realized that I had a headache. It was too soon for a hangover, so I concluded it was just plain overload. Scotch, foreplay, wet underwear ... Two dead guys, a presumptive nympho whom I did not crave, a demure yoga teacher whom I did. And now clues. It was a lot for one evening. "How long ago was this?" I soldiered on.

Maggie thought a moment. "Three months or so. It was January."

I rubbed my temples. "Ten grand would have gone a long way toward fixing up his boat."

"If he believed he'd really get it," Maggie said. "The whole thing could've been a setup. Lure him with the money, kill him anyway."

I thought back to my one meeting with Kenny Lukens. He was jumpy, all right. Thought he was being followed. Offered me way too good a deal to fetch a pail and shovel and dig the pouches up for him. Or get strangled in his place. "So he passed the setup on to me."

Maggie bit her lip and looked away. "I knew you'd think that. That's partly why I didn't want to tell you. Or even admit to myself that maybe that's what Kenny did. I mean, he lied, he stole— but I don't think he would've knowingly put someone else in danger."

I thought that over, and managed not to take it personally. On paper, at least, I was a private eye. And that's what private eyes did, right? Stood as surrogates for people getting clobbered, threw themselves in front of the onrushing trains of other people's screwups and calamities. Defended and avenged . . . *Me?* It would have been un-seemly to start simpering about it, but Jesus, what a crappy line of work.

Not without dread, I said, "Is there anything else you'd like to tell me?"

She shook her head and took a breath that

didn't come in quite as smoothly as her others. In a soft voice that would have melted tundra, she said, "You still mad at me?"

I didn't answer right away. I couldn't. Not that I had to think very hard about the question. Rather, I had to choke back a reply that was exorbitant, sophomoric, absurd, and dangerous. I had to stop myself from staring into her serene gray eyes and saying that not only was I not angry with her, but that I longed to be her hero. "I'm not mad," I said at last.

I badly wanted to make love to her then, and understood I couldn't. With my preposterous damp shorts and the residue of Lydia still clinging to me, it would have been a desecration. I sighed, and said that I should go.

Maggie didn't beg me to stay. But when I'd risen and was moving, sideways and reluctantly, toward the stairs that were the only exit, she floated up and kissed me quickly on the cheek. I didn't see it coming and I still don't know exactly how she closed the distance between us so smoothly and so silently, and with such precision that nothing touched except her lips brushing light and cool against my face.

I felt their outline as I climbed up to the cockpit then down the rope ladder in the warm and slightly misty night.

14

I've said it before, I'll say it again: I should have gone home. I intended to go home. I was already on my bike and pointing it toward home.

So why didn't I go home?

Near as I can guess, it was some crazy mix of chivalry, testosterone, and simple curiosity. I was wired from lack of food, and sex thwarted by compunction. I wanted Maggie to be proud of me, impressed with my involvement; I wanted to have some accomplishment or at least adventure to lay at her feet.

And Kenny Lukens' boat, the boat where Andrus the happy Latvian had been murdered just two nights before, was right there in my face, fifty, sixty yards away. It was ringed with yellow tape strung between police stanchions but was otherwise unguarded. How could I leave without sneaking aboard and checking it out?

I rolled my bike up closer to *Dream Chaser.* I took a moment to look around. The boatyard was dim and had grown quiet; the few people still at large seemed lost in conversations or millings of their own. I put the bike up on its kickstand

and slipped beneath the crime-scene tape, my sneakers crunching on the limestone gravel.

My heart raced as I stood inside the closed-off circle. Real PI's, of course, commit small illegalities all the time, *big* illegalities now and then. They do so in the honorable confidence that justice lies beyond the law and ranks a million miles above it. Who could disagree? But I have a horror of doing anything unlawful. Far from being proud of this, I think it shows a want of character. The citizen as chicken, still like a quailing high school student, fearing the indelible black mark that will somehow blot his future. What I have felt is a wimpy obedience that justifies the shirking of anything beyond obedience.

But now I stood, dry-throated, where the law said I should not have been. I reached out and touched *Dream Chaser*'s flank; it still held some of the heat of the day, had a temperature like a living thing. I moved to the stern. The cops, apparently, had removed the ladder. I frowned and pawed the gravel and measured distances.

The lip of the transom was level with my eyes. I put my palms flat on it, and jumped, and pushed and pulled and kicked. The process taught me something humbling but useful: Being reasonably fit at forty-seven is only a pale parody of being young and limber. Joints complained at being yanked and then compressed; muscles took offense at all demands beyond the practiced and familiar. But I scrabbled and grunted and clawed, and finally I hauled myself over the transom and fell with a muffled clunk into the vacant cockpit, resting for a moment against the stem that held the wheel.

Lying there beneath the stars, I felt both brave and very silly. The alcohol was wearing off; physical effort had skimmed away the most urgent layer of libido. By the wan light of reawakening reason, this escapade was fucking stupid. But there I was, on board the forbidden boat. I almost giggled at myself. Then I saw a footprint maybe seven inches from my head. It was dark and smeared, like it was left over from wet clay, but after a moment I realized it was made of blood. The giggle died at the back of my throat. I got up onto my hands and knees and crawled toward the companionway.

The hatch had been pulled shut but there was no lock on it. I slid it back and removed the top splashboard from its channel. A meaty smell flew up and made me slightly dizzy. It was a smell of nauseating richness, of salt and iron and fat; a smell of the things we're made of. Trying not to gag, I stepped over the remaining boards and down into the cabin.

By the dim glow that entered through the hatch, I found a light switch, flicked it on, and stared at a scene of random devastation. No, that's not exactly right—it was devastation but there seemed to be a system to it, an appalling kind of thoroughness. Drawers had been pulled out and dumped. Shelves had been swept clean. Floorboards had been lifted so that the bilge could be explored; here and there bulkhead panels had been unscrewed and tossed aside. Presiding over the shambles, like some kind of ghastly, hollow sentry, was the chalked outline of the murdered Latvian. Andrus had come to rest with his body splayed across the navigation table. One arm was raised and it seemed his head had been twisted to expose the jugular. There was a staggering amount of blood. It covered the table, had poured down onto a chair shoved underneath it; it was plentiful enough to pool at low places in the floor. Knots of flies still fed on it; some were stuck where puddles had coagulated around their greedy legs.

I blinked and swallowed and had to remind myself to breathe. Had to remind myself, as well, that I was there not only to confront the dreadful spectacle but to learn from it. But good Christ, where did I start?

I squatted down, began hopelessly riffling through tossed mounds of books and papers and clothing and dishes. Finding nothing that made the slightest bit of sense, I shifted my position, was disgusted to feel my bloodied sneakers sticking to the floor. I started in on another pile of meaningless remains.

That's when I felt the boat move in its cradle.

There was nothing boatlike or watery in the motion; it was more the quick jerk of an earthquake, and it seemed to come an instant before the thumping and scraping that told me *Dream Chaser* was being boarded.

Adrenaline carried panic through my limbs before my mind had quite caught up. I found that I was standing. My eyes darted like those of a cornered rodent, seeking a hole to crawl into, a crevice through which to escape. My breath had become a fast shallow panting; the blood vapors coursed all through me, like I was smelling my own insides. Overhead, footsteps scratched and pounded; the whole cabin seemed to groan with every beat. I shuffled in my sticky shoes, but there was no place to run. I was pinned there, one more victim of the cursed vessel. In desperation, I switched off the light and shrank back in the darkness.

That ploy accomplished nothing except to make me even blinder when the ruthless searchlight came probing through the open hatch. It raked the mess, then nailed me where I stood. In a gesture of great helplessness and pity, I raised my arms, crossed my wrists in front of my face. All I saw was an exploding brightness, and a gun barrel wagging, obscene and without context, a few feet from my head.

Everyone was really friendly at the lockup on Stock Island.

They let me keep my belt and shoelaces, just made me wear an orange jumpsuit over my mildewing shorts. The jumpsuit had neatly pressed lapels, said MONROE COUNTY JAIL in huge white letters on the back, and would have made a magnificent souvenir. The night sergeant took some information from the uniformed cops who'd brought me in, then passed me on to a guard who walked me to the holding tank.

The tank was no Ritz-Carlton—just a jumbo

cell with nasty lighting and a concrete floor—but I was pretty damn happy to be there. I mean, if it had been the guys in snorkels who joined me on the boat, I would probably be dead. As it was, I had a nice cozy jumpsuit and a cot to sit on; amazingly, the jail had been built on waterfront property, and there was even a faint smell of the Gulf to cleanse my blood-filled nostrils.

I settled in and looked around. It was still before midnight on a Sunday; business was slow and the place seemed pretty benign—a time-out place for grown-ups needing to restore their grip. A couple of drunks were talking politics. A homeless guy was bragging to no one in particular about how many cans of tuna he could stuff into his pants. A fellow came over to me and started protesting that the whole thing was bullshit, he hadn't exposed himself, he was only peeing. Then he asked what I was in for. I wanted to sound like one of the guys. Casually, I said, "Ya know, criminal trespass, shit like that."

After about ten minutes the lighting started getting to me, and the novelty of incarceration wore off, and I started wondering just how and when I could get out of there. I didn't have to think about it long. Within the hour a guard came in and told me they were taking me downtown.

I guess I struck them as a bourgeois cream puff, because they didn't even bother cuffing me. Just bundled me into the backseat of a cruiser, and away we went. It was getting on to one o'clock by now. Traffic on the boulevard was very sparse.

All that neon flashing at nothing, all those drive-throughs with no one driving through.

At the rickety old headquarters on Angela Street, my escorts nudged me along the handicap ramp then up a flight of stairs. The stairs were narrow and the whole place smelled of warm copying machines. Pallid light came through door panels of ancient frosted glass. Somewhere, someone was typing; somewhere, someone laughed. The building was a warren of tiny offices and alcoves, and you couldn't tell where sound was coming from.

We stopped in front of a door whose flaking letters said DETECTIVE BUREAU—HOMICIDE DIVISION.

Inside, I was handed over to two plainclothes cops who were sitting at scratched metal desks with name plaques on them: LIEUTENANT CRUZ and LIEUTENANT CORALLO. The desks took up most of the small space that was not already filled by dented file cabinets and a couple of industrial-size oscillating fans that slowly, mournfully turned their faces side to side. Greasy dust clung to the fans; it looked like Spanish moss.

Pretending to be busy with other things, the two detectives studied me obliquely for a moment. Then Cruz stared at me dead on and said, "You look familiar."

He looked familiar to me too. Tall, burly guy with a funny hairline. Looked like his scalp was too small for his skull, and had been stretched into odd configurations like the tongues on a baseball. He had a dimple in his chin that was impossible to shave; short hairs sprouted from it in a whorl. Suddenly I remembered where I'd seen him. Lefty's funeral, a couple of days before. No, wait a second—Lefty's funeral that very morning. Jesus, what a day.

Hoping to distract him from trying too hard to remember where he knew me from, I said, "You're probably thinking of some other guy who wears an orange jumpsuit."

The two cops looked at each other and agreed that they were not amused. The second cop, Corallo, was muscle-bound but quite short; if he was at the funeral too I might have looked right over the top of him. In any case, his arms were so thick that they couldn't hang straight down, but stuck out from his sides like wings on a penguin. His shirt buttons pulled across his chest and he had sweat stains in his armpits. He had an abrupt and high-pitched voice that sounded like a clarinet. He said, "We could yank your license in a minute, funny man."

I may not be tough, but I don't like being threatened, and my first reaction was defiance. "So yank it. I don't drive that much anyway."

The cops looked at each other again. Cruz said, "Not your driver's license, asshole. Your PI license."

Oh, *that*. For a cowardly moment I thought: Great. Terrific. *Please* yank it. Take my license, take my gun, just let me have my life back.

Cruz riffled through some computer printouts on his desk. " 'Pete Amsterdam. Southernmost

Detection, Inc.,' " he read. "In business two and a half years. Surprised we haven't met before."

I thought: Where would we have met? The hot tub? The tennis courts? I didn't see why he had to know this was my debut outing. With quiet assurance I said, "I work clean."

Corallo piped, "Not this time, pal. So why don't you tell us what you were doing on that boat?"

I knew my rights, sort of. Calmly, professionally, even collegially, I said, "Sorry, guys. You know that's privileged."

"Privileged, my ass," Corallo said. "You wanna go to jail?"

"For what?" I said. "A dinky little misdemeanor?"

Cruz folded his thick hands and got judicial. "Criminal trespass is a misdemeanor," he agreed. "Evidence tampering's a felony. One to five."

Weakly, I said, "Years?"

The muscle-bound cop leaned closer and I smelled him. Sweat mixed with deodorant is much worse than sweat alone. "And not in this fucking country club down here," he said. "Upstate." He raised his arm to point. "Where the real criminals go. Rapists. Killers. Lemme ask you something, Amsterdam. You like it up the ass? You fond of sucking big black dicks? Little white wuss like you, you'll be some bad boy's nancy ten minutes after you check in."

I knew they were just trying to scare me. It was working pretty well. I thought about my accountant and his bright ideas. Benny. Smart guy, with his sharpened pencils. Let *him* get cornholed by the chain gang!

I shuffled my feet. I stalled for time. The big old greasy fans turned slowly, their heads shaking in mock sympathy.

Finally, feeling defeated, but feeling too the bleak relief that goes with losing, giving up, I said, "Okay. Let's talk about the boat."

15

Fearing complications, fearing I'm not sure exactly what, I told them as little as I thought I had to. Problem was, that's not the kind of thing I'm good at gauging. Since leaving the world of bosses and meetings, I'd lost the reflex of dishonesty. I could still bullshit when I had to, but now I really had to concentrate. The malarkey no longer flowed by second nature, as it must for people who have jobs.

But I didn't see how I could avoid telling them about Kenny Lukens. About his phony suicide and his intention of reclaiming what he'd stolen from Lefty's bar. About his one visit to my "office." About his murder that same night.

The cops looked at each other. The dimple on Cruz's chin seemed to get deeper; the bristly hairs looked darker. "The stiff from Sunset Key," he said.

"Exactly," I said. They'd let me sit down by now. I went to cross my legs. The bulk of the orange jumpsuit made it a difficult and somewhat clownish maneuver.

"And the second killing," said Corallo, in that

sudden clarinet voice of his, "they're still looking
for what Lukens stole."

A regular Holmes and Watson act. "Seems that
way," I said.

We all took a moment to think. The sound of
obsessive typing still came from some other office. The greasy fans turned slowly side to side.

Cruz leaned closer to me and said, "So wha'd
he steal?"

"Excuse me?"

"What Lukens took," put in Corallo. "What
the murderers are looking for. What is it?"

He was leaning toward me too, his heavy arms
cantilevered into space. All this leaning changed
the geometry of the room in a very unpleasant
way. I said, "I have no idea."

"No idea?" said Cruz. His baseball hairline
moved and I could have sworn that the stubble
on his chin was growing before my eyes.

"Lukens didn't even know," I said. "He just
thought he'd grabbed an extra shift's worth of
cash. Couldn't understand why Lefty cared so
much."

The cops looked at each other and apparently
agreed that they were unconvinced. "Then what
the hell were you looking for on that boat?"
Corallo pressed.

"I don't know what I was looking for."

"Don't know what you were looking for,"
Cruz echoed, giving me a chance, I guess, to hear
how dumb or how improbable I sounded. "Just
casually snooping around."

I managed a moment's feistiness. "Just trying to figure out who killed my client."

"All by yourself," piped Corallo mockingly. The scorn narrowed his eyes and suddenly made his face seem waxy. Steroids probably, all those muscles. "Glory seeker."

Right, I thought. That's me all over.

There was a pause. Some drumming of thick fingers on metal desks. Finally Cruz said, "Wait a second. That's why you look familiar. You were at Ortega's funeral."

I hoped I didn't stiffen when he said that. Prominent among the many things I hadn't told the cops about—my talks with Maggie and with Lydia and with Andrus; the Hibiscus guest house and the matchbook; the men in snorkels and the confrontation on Green Turtle Cay—was my visit with Lefty at the hospital. I sure didn't want to go into it now. "That's right," I said. "I was."

"How come?" said Corallo.

"To see if there was anything to learn."

"Like?" said Cruz.

I shrugged. "Like—who knows? Just to get a sense of who his friends were, how he operated."

"And wha'd ya figure out?" Corallo pressed.

"I figured out about that thingie they use to cram the coffins into the high-up crypts."

Corallo shot a disgusted look at Cruz. Cruz rubbed his eyes. I yawned. This was not calculated nonchalance, just plain exhaustion. After a moment, Cruz said, "Why the hell didn't you come to us? From the start?"

"Come on," I said. "What kind of private eye does that?"

They looked at me with a grudging respect then. No—I just wanted to imagine that they did. What they looked at me with was boredom and annoyance and fatigue.

Cruz said, "Listen, Amsterdam, no offense, but you're a fuckin' amateur. You want to be a PI in this town, get yourself a long lens and go stake out motel rooms. This is police business. Your client's dead. Your job's finished. Stay the hell out of it and we'll forget about tonight. Okay?"

I stared at the floor and made a point of looking like I was carefully weighing the proposition.

But the weird part is that I *was* weighing it. I should have been the happiest man alive. Absolved of my first felony, and unequivocally ordered to give up the fumbling crusade that was wrecking my small contentment. It was the perfect out, and yet it didn't set right. I felt like something of value was being wrested from me, even if it was a thing that made me miserable. And I found to my amazement that I wasn't ready to pledge to give it up. As if a promise still mattered in this world, I searched for a way to avoid giving my word. I said, "Will you let me keep the jumpsuit?"

It was way too late for anyone to see the humor. Cruz frowned so that his hairline moved. Corallo puffed up his barrel chest and said, "Take the fuckin' thing off. And go the hell home."

16

I crashed immediately and slept till ten.

I would have slept still later, except for a loud, insistent hammering on my front door. It went on awhile, stopped, then started in again; it got louder, then switched over to a tapping on the window. At length I gave up on going back to sleep, pulled on a robe, and went downstairs.

I opened the front door and saw Ozzie Kimmel. This was not a great start to the day. He was wearing a tank top that had once been red. Now it had faded to a splotched and hideous orangey pink, with armholes so stretched that they hung down nearly to the waist. He was holding a newspaper, slapping it from time to time, and laughing maniacally. "Awright, Pete!" he yelled between cackles. "Popped your cherry, guy! You're a real local now! A regular Bubba. Right in there with the other deadbeat fall-down perverts! Yes!"

Beyond Ozzie, the morning was very bright. I narrowed my eyes, and wished I could have narrowed my ears. "What are you talking about?" I wearily asked.

He brayed in my face and slapped the paper again. "Page two! Police blotter, man! The locals' honor roll! The cavalcade of assholes! You made it! Right up there with the lunatics shooting BB guns at chickens and the crazy lezzies fighting over strap-on dildos. Congratulations, Bubba!"

"Let me see that," I said, and reached out for the paper. Sure enough, there I was. By name, in a bland little six-line item. Local detective arrested at murder site. Held for questioning at county jail.

Ozzie said, "You don't look happy."

I gave him his paper back. I didn't answer.

"Great publicity," he said. "You can't buy publicity like that."

"I need some coffee."

Ozzie seemed to think that meant I was inviting him in for some. But he was wrong. I started closing the door on him.

He was used to that kind of thing and didn't take offense. Through the narrowing aperture, he said, "Come on, let's play some tennis."

Tennis? Did I play tennis? It had only been a few days since my routine had been annihilated, but already the aimless, peaceful life I lived before was starting to seem as distant as a half-remembered dream. So I told myself: Play tennis. Start doing normal things again, and maybe you'll feel normal. I told Ozzie I'd meet him in an hour.

"I'll kick your ass," he said, and turned to go. "Here, I'm done with this." He handed me his paper.

I threw it in the garbage and made myself some breakfast.

Sometime between finishing my granola and pulling on my sneakers, I remembered that my bicycle was not locked to its accustomed palm.

It had been left behind, unchained, at Redmond's Boatyard when I got arrested. Which no doubt meant that it was gone by now—bicycle theft being Key West's crime of choice. Call me petty, but this bothered me a lot. It's depressing to lose a bike. It pulls you back to all the little heartaches of childhood, all the things that seemed wildly unjust and made you want to cry. Toys that broke the first time you played with them. Ice cream cones that tumbled to the ground. Things that grown-ups took away from you because they imagined you'd outgrown them. Oh well. I tried to shrug it off. I'd walk to tennis. No big deal.

Except I didn't get to walk to tennis.

With a towel around my neck and my racquets slung jauntily across my shoulder, I came out of my house to find two enormous fellows loitering at the base of the porch steps. They were wearing dark and shiny pants that strained across their meaty thighs, and big loose shirts such as one might wear a holster under. They might have been brothers, or salt-and-pepper shakers; they looked that much alike.

I gave them a friendly smile and tried to walk around them. They didn't let me.

"Lydia Ortega wants to see you," said one of them. He said it with a heavy Conch accent, in which taut New England vowels are stretched like taffy by a Southern languor and made lilting by a hint of Spanish singsong. He sucked his teeth right after he said it. His top lip crawled around on his gums.

"Ah," I said. "And how is Lydia? Tell her I'll stop by later."

"She wants to see you now," said the other goon.

Like his partner, he had a piggy nose and the ungenerous expression of someone whose features were squeezed too close together. I tried to figure if these were faces belonging to the Ortega clan. A degenerate branch, maybe. I also could not help wondering how these two guys would look in snorkels.

Showing them my racquets, I said, "I'm sorry, but I have a tennis game right now."

The first goon said, "Welluh, I think you're gonna miss it."

"I can't miss it. It's against a guy who takes defaults."

To this the large men were insensitive. They stepped in a little closer; their shadows fell across me like a mildewed blanket. I shuffled my feet but didn't move. I was pleased with myself for not being more afraid, but I knew down deep that this wasn't courage, just befuddlement. I'd never been abducted before, and I didn't know how to act. Should I scream for help? Should I fight? Pummel them with slashing backhands?

Frankly, my chances of winning by force just didn't seem that good. I let out a long slow disappointed sigh, and vaguely wondered how I all of a sudden had got so popular, and why every confrontation seemed to end with me throwing up my hands and caving.

"Okay," I said at last. "Let's go talk to Lydia."

17

Driving crosstown with the finger-breakers, I really wished that I was on my bike.

On a bike you can smell what's blooming, yard by yard. You can feel when a puff of breeze starts up from nowhere, and when it fades away, dropping one by one the fronds it had lifted. I missed my bicycle pretty badly.

We reached the giant condo and took the elevator up.

Lydia met us at her door. If she'd ever been in mourning for her father, she was out of it already. She was wearing tight cream-colored pants and a red blouse that draped in some places and clung in others. I wanted to look more closely at the clingy parts, but sandwiched as I was between her goons, I felt a little shy about it. Lydia herself seemed to feel no such hesitation. She looked me up and down, then down and up, lingering, I thought, on the zone between my sweat socks and my shorts. The examination made me feel a little cheap, but I must admit I kind of liked it. With a nod toward my racquets and my towel, she said, "Ah, it's Mr. Casual."

Frankly, I thought it was a pretty good description and I had no comeback for it.

We went into the living room. The AC was blasting, of course, and my thighs were cold. Lydia motioned for me to sit. I avoided the sectional. I was afraid it might still be damp from last night's vodka, and besides, I wanted some space of my own. I settled gingerly into an armchair. The two goons stood on either side of me like giant bookends in the shape of snarling dogs.

Lydia sat opposite me and crossed her knees with a flourish. "So," she began. "You didn't tell me you're a private eye."

Reasonably, I said, "Wouldn't be very private if I told everyone."

"But now it's in the paper," she pointed out.

"Yes," I said. "Ironic, isn't it?"

She frowned and looked down at her lap. "Drink?"

It was something after eleven in the morning. I shook my head. She looked a little disappointed. There went her chance to have one.

She got over it. She even smiled. "Pete," she said, "I'm going to ask you some questions. And today you're going to answer them."

I waited. At the edges of my vision, I could see the knobby asses and thick arms of the men who'd brought me here. Their scarred fingers and hairy knuckles struck me as pretty good reasons to cooperate. Yet from the start the interview did not go well.

"Who's your client?" Lydia began.

"I don't have a client."

This happened to be an honest answer but it clearly didn't satisfy.

"Don't bullshit me," she said. "You working for Mickey Veale?"

"Him again," I said. "Why would I be working for him?"

"And don't start that question-with-a-question crap. What were you doing on that boat?"

"Looking for something. Next you're going to ask me what, and I'm going to tell you I don't know."

Lydia exhaled; her breath whistled slightly. She looked sideways at her flunkies and they squeezed in closer next to me. They didn't hit me, didn't touch me, and yet I had a certain airless feeling, like when you flatten the last bubble in a Ziploc bag.

With fraying patience, Lefty's daughter said, "Okay, let's start again. Tell me who you're working for."

I tried to clarify; I really did. "I'm working for myself," I said. "I almost had a client but he died. Okay?"

"And who was he?" she pressed.

I thought it should be obvious. "The guy whose boat I got arrested on."

Lydia looked a little bit confused. "The Polish guy?"

"He was Latvian."

Her face revealed a profound lack of interest in fine distinctions among the Baltic nations.

"But that isn't who I mean," I said. "I mean the

first guy who owned the boat. The guy who robbed your father's place a couple years ago."

"That bartender? He's dead?"

I leaned very slowly forward in my chair. The goons, who might very well have been the killers, after all, leaned very slowly forward with me, like we were somehow glued together. I could not hold back from saying, "You want me to believe you didn't know?"

Time got very viscous when I said that. Expressions chased one another across Lydia Ortega's face. She looked surprised, or tried to. Then she seemed angry, cornered, and I thought she'd sic the thugs on me. The anger simmered down to what might almost have been hurt; the real or fake offense then girded itself with haughtiness, a brittle resolve to seize control again.

Which she did in an instant, simply by seeming to ignore the question altogether.

"Dead," she said. "Too bad . . . So. You know he robbed my father. What else do you know about it?"

I wasn't ready for the way time revved back to normal speed, for the pace of her recovery. I felt a beat behind, and spoke too fast, trying to catch up. "I know your father was pissed off enough to have him killed," I said. "I know that, on his deathbed, he was still obsessed with getting back whatever it was that was stolen."

Smugly, but not without, I thought, a certain nervousness, Lydia said, "But you don't know what that was."

"No," I admitted, "I don't. All I know is that it was in a bank-deposit pouch. As for what's inside . . . maybe you could tell me."

She smiled at me sweetly, then sat up straighter and snugged her blouse so that the cloth went translucent against her bra. "You're pressing your luck, Pete Amsterdam."

To that I had nothing to say. A moment passed. Lydia crossed her legs the other way. Her slacks rustled and I watched the creases rise and fall along her thighs. In a tone suddenly executive and brisk, she said, "Well, then I guess you'll work for me."

"Excuse me?"

"You have no client. You understand the importance of the pouch—"

"I don't want to work for you."

She balled her fists, pressed them down into her restless hips, and looked insulted. "And why not?"

The question boggled tact. Could I tell her that I didn't care to work for lunatics, or nymphos, or front-running suspects? "I just don't."

Ignoring that, she said, "What's your usual fee?"

In spite of everything, I almost laughed. My usual fee? My usual fee was *bupkis*.

Lydia said, "Two thousand a week okay?"

"It's not about the money."

She laughed. Her red mouth got very wide and strands of sinew rose up in her neck. Even the matched goons smiled. Why did people always find this such an uproarious remark?

While everyone was feeling blithe and cheery, I said lightly, "It was a woman who put the pouch into the safe. Your father said that himself. Can you think of who that woman might've been?"

Lydia's spasm of merriment stopped on a dime. There was something unwholesome in how quickly it ended, how radically it changed. She shot me a look that almost seemed to hiss.

The look was scary, but suddenly I knew what a real detective would say right at this moment, and I did my best to say it with firmness and certainty. "Come on now, Lydia, if you want us to work together, you have to be straight with me."

With utter finality, she said, "No, I don't."

So much for that.

"That's why I'm paying you," she went on. "So I can make the rules."

"And that's why I'm declining."

Your basic standoff. We allowed it a moment to sink in. Then Lydia settled back into flirty mode and gave her hair a winsome shake. She leaned far forward and did some slick maneuver that made her boobs swell. At the same moment, her goons put their huge hairy hands on the arms of my chair. A pretty graphic carrot and stick. "Pete," she purred, "it's so much better we stay friends."

Friends? She had me abducted when she felt like chatting and wiggled her backside when she wanted information. This was not my idea of friendship. Then again, with the rank warmth of the thugs pulsing on both sides of me, I had to acknowledge it was better than some other arrangements I could think of. "Friends," I echoed. "Believe me, I agree. So don't hire me. Please. Let's just keep it . . ." Keep it what? Weird? Insane? Finally I had the word for how we'd keep it. I gestured down at my tennis outfit and my chilly legs. "Let's just keep it casual."

She looked at my crotch, I swear she did. "Casual. Okay. But let me give you one piece of advice. Check out Mickey Veale. Paradise Watersports."

"Why?"

"Because he's a scumbag and a liar and a sneak."

"Your father was in business with him," I pointed out.

"So am I," she said. "What of it?"

18

I'm not the kind of person who believes in miracles.

Miracles, angels, affirmations, apparitions—all that muzzy-headed New Age shit. I mean, come *on*.

But let me confess that, when Lydia's goons finally drove me home and I climbed from their car with my racquets and towel, I beheld something that partook of the miraculous: My bicycle was there, chained to the palm I always chain it to.

As if doubting its reality, I went over and touched it. The fenders were dented, and rust lived in the dents. The handlebars were rough with tiny bubbles of corrosion and not quite aligned with the tires. It was mine, all right. The only thing foreign was the lock. But I knew where that had come from; it could only have been Maggie.

I imagined her roused from sleep as the cops clambered aboard *Dream Chaser*. Drowsily coming up her companionway, perhaps, in time to see me carted off. And caring enough to climb down into the night to rescue my abandoned bike, to keep it safe. I pictured her rolling it over the gravel toward her trawler, locking it, with a mute nuzzling intimacy, to her own; and my throat closed down with gratitude. It was a small thing, maybe—but what was devotion if not the habit and the piling up of small considerations?

I went into the house. As I stepped across the threshold I saw a key and a brief note that had been slid under the door. The note said, *Hope you're okay. Teaching at noon. Home after that. Please come see me when you can. M.*

A flattering invitation, if less emphatic than sending bruisers to kidnap me. I stepped into the kitchen to check the clock. Just after twelve-thirty. This meant that if I stalled, say, another ten or fifteen minutes, I could show up just in time to miss the more humbling exertions—the contorting and the coiling, the straining up and the clamping down—and to join in as the class was moving into its deep-relaxation phase. Dessert without the bother of the meal. Why not? I walked around in circles for a little while, then traded in my tennis towel for one big enough to lie down on, and headed out again.

It was great being reunited with my bike. I rode slowly, savoring. A few houses down from mine, jasmine was in bloom. Half a block beyond, the sweeter, pinker smell of frangipani overwhelmed it. A midday heaviness was in the air. Cats didn't wander; bugs didn't fly. Lizards stood on top of rocks, and blinked, and puffed their throats out. The asphalt had softened enough so that I could feel the slightest sexy yielding underneath my tires.

I locked up outside the Leaf Shed, took my sneakers off on the porch, and tiptoed toward the studio. Inside, ten or twelve people with assorted bandannas and tattoos and eyebrow studs and nose rings were standing on their heads; it was one of those moments when you can't help wondering: What if a Martian spaceship landed right outside and this was the first thing that the little green men saw? The more advanced practitioners shot their legs straight up in open air; a couple of beginners in red leotards used the mirrored wall to support their inverted asses. The mirror doubled the already ample volumes, and the reflected image suggested something grossly floral—Georgia O'Keeffe on a very bad day. At the front of the room, Maggie was as graceful upside down as right-side up. Her back was long and it seemed to cost her nothing to hold her hips aloft. Her gray tights traced out the muscles in her thighs; her taut calves reminded me of full-to-bursting wineskins.

I spread my towel on the floor and lay down on it. Suddenly I was sort of sleepy. No way was I going to launch myself into a shoulder stand. I rested.

I rested on a freelance basis until the class came down off its shoulders, and then I rested as part of the group, as Maggie eased into deep relaxation. Padding silently amid the prone bodies, her voice a mesmerizing purr, she urged us to let our weight settle into the earth, our eyeballs to float lightly in their sockets, our tongues to be soft in our mouths. Above all, our minds should be still.

If thoughts came, they should not be held but allowed to pass like breeze through a wide-open room, neither possessing nor possessed.

This was the part that gave me trouble.

I could soften my feet and let my ankles flop as well as the next guy, but, lying there, eyes closed amid the hot smells of ancient tobacco and baking limestone, I couldn't stem the restless flow of thoughts. Thoughts came, and when they came, they stuck, attached by burrs of suspicion.

Around the time I should have been relaxing my liver and my pancreas, I became preoccupied with recollections of last night's interview with the homicide detectives. While it was happening, it had seemed rigorous and long, but now suddenly I wondered if maybe they'd let me off too easily and too abruptly. They'd been nasty and intimidating—and then they gave me the merest wrist slap and sent me on my way. Why? Was there some deal implicit in their clemency? Were they as nervous as I was about what else might come out if the meeting continued . . . ?

By the time I'd let these thoughts pass through, I'd lost the opportunity to ease my diaphragm and the little muscles between my ribs.

I groped for serenity, and was finally settling down to releasing the sinews of my collarbone and throat, when once again my mind was shanghaied. This time it was Lydia. Her off-the-wall idea of hiring me. Her overly generous offer of pay. Was it a fee or a bribe? And then there was this near obsession with Mickey Veale. Was this a festering vendetta between the two of them, or just a way for Lydia to divert attention from herself? Then again, Veale was more than a convenient beard. He was also, apparently, a principal in Paradise Watersports, which trafficked in Jet Skis and snorkels. . . .

"Let go of any tension in the jaw," Maggie was cooing.

Yeah, right.

"The forehead is soft, unlined, unworried. The skin at the hairline is supple. . . ."

The skin at *my* hairline was crawly, and it itched. Afraid of letting down my teacher, I didn't allow myself to scratch. I breathed deep and got through to the end of class.

When it was over, people rearranged their bandannas, found their sandals, and started leaving. I stood up and bided my time. Maggie came over and stood close to me. But we both felt shy, I guess; we didn't touch.

"Thanks for the bike," I said.

She said, "I'm glad you're okay. What happened?"

"Got arrested." To myself I sounded awfully blasé. Like I got arrested every other week.

"That's terrible. Your forehead looks all tense."

"No big deal. I'd never seen the inside of a jail before."

Her gray eyes got wide and maybe a little moist with sympathy. "I feel like it's my fault."

"It isn't."

"I feel terrible. It must have been awful."

"Not really. A little sordid, maybe."

"The way I kept pushing you, trying to convince—"

I badly wanted her to stop blaming herself, and I finally stumbled upon an awkward but effective way of getting her to. I closed the narrow space between us, wrapped my arms around her back, and kissed her. It was not the seamless, dewy, wholehearted kiss that maybe it should have been. There was some fear in it, some hesitation, and since her lips were moving as I zeroed in on them, we didn't quite connect dead center. Still, it was enough of a kiss so that I could feel the tiny nub of flesh in the middle of her upper lip, and would remember forever that her mouth tasted of raspberries.

Then I pulled away. We stared at each other. There's a look that two people share when it is inevitable that they're becoming lovers; that they've become lovers, in spirit if not yet in deed. The look is the bond that sex confirms. I think that was the look we shared, though of course you're never really sure till after.

The moment went on a long time. At some point I had to speak. Anything I said would have seemed clumsy and irrelevant. But what I did say was especially ridiculous. "Have you ever ridden a Jet Ski?"

Maggie's eyelids quivered as her mind traced out the preposterous segue. After a beat, she said, "I hate Jet Skis."

"So do I. They're noisy, vulgar, infuriating, and generally run by trailer-trash morons. I thought we'd go out for sunset."

She studied me for telltale signs of whimsy. "You're serious?"

"Paradise Watersports," I said. "I'd like to get to know them."

"Ah," she said, and dropped her eyes. "So, you're still—?"

In spite of myself, I nodded that I was. "Listen, if you'd rather not—"

"No," she said. "I'd love to come along."

We looked at each other again. There followed one of those delicious and excruciating silences through which a torrent of possibility noiselessly roars. Finally I braced myself and said, "Got plans for the afternoon?"

Maggie gave a little shrug and said, "Not really."

"I'm going home for a glass of wine and a long soak in the hot tub. Want to join me?"

She blinked, and pursed her lips, and said, "I don't have a bathing suit here."

Not grinning then was one of the hardest things I have ever had to do. I summoned up the decades of relative maturity and used their gathered gravity to clamp down every muscle in my face. My cheeks got so tight that my eyes watered and I heard a ringing in my ears. I like to think I kept the grin to a worldly little curl at the corners of my mouth.

Maggie stared at me and finally answered with the tiniest lift of an eyebrow. We left the studio together.

19

Flinty, dry rosés get no respect in this benighted country, though there is no finer accompaniment for, say, cold poached salmon—or for getting naked with a new lover in the middle of a weekday afternoon. So I went into the wine room and grabbed a good Bandol.

Opening it, icing it, my hands felt blockish, awkward. I was nervous—I admit it. I tried to figure out if Maggie was too. It didn't show in her posture or her movements. Unrushed, smooth as ever. With her usual lack of ceremony she opened up the fridge, found some cheese and olives, put them on a tray. Then she asked me if I had an extra robe.

Robes! Why hadn't I thought of that? Terry cloth, shawl collar—very elegant, very Hepburn-Tracy. I ran up to my bedroom and grabbed a couple.

Maggie slipped into the bathroom to put hers on. I tried to feel suave and cool about this; I failed. She was in my house and removing all her clothing. This was an amazing concept. Her breasts would press against the inside of a gar-

ment that I myself had worn; her nipples would
touch the very same terry cloth loops. Her freed
loins would be barely hidden by curtains of cloth
that would shift and flutter and separate with
every breeze and every motion. Nakedness as
close as a loosely tied belt. . . . Forget about who-
dunit and what was in the goddamn pouch—*this*
was suspense.

She came out of the bathroom. Small faint
freckles ran down her chest and underneath her
collar. There was intimacy in the way she'd
folded up the sleeves. I could manage nothing
better than a tight congested smile. I stepped inside to change.

The panels of my robe would not lie flat. For
some reason I thought of that old saw about hiding one's light beneath a bushel basket. Okay, let's
not exaggerate—a half bushel would work. I
arranged myself as best I could and went back
into the kitchen.

Maggie had taken the food and wine and
moved out by the pool. I joined her at a little
table in the shade. Fronds were lightly rustling
and rattling; they were silver from reflections off
the water and they sounded like maracas. The air
smelled faintly of chlorine, more faintly of iodine
wafting off the ocean. We clinked glasses, though
didn't toast to anything in particular. Arousal was
making it hard for me to talk. We sipped some
Bandol and nibbled some olives. After a while I
reached across the table and gently seized her collar. I held the bunched cloth as though it were her
flesh, and pulled her softly toward me. We kissed.

Her mouth was cool from the wine and salty from the olives.

I asked if I could see a little more of her. She answered with her eyes, and I coaxed apart the panels of her robe; I felt the friction as the nubby cloth slid against her belt. I saw that the faint freckles stopped at the tops of her breasts. The skin between them was very pale but had a russet cast. There was a beautiful rounded chevron at the place where her last rib arched above her midriff. I reached once again for my wine with a hand that was trembling slightly.

That's when the knock came at the door.

It was a loud indignant knock. Maggie pulled away by reflex and snugged her robe around her throat. I gulped some rosé and muttered a curse and gnawed my lip. "It'll stop," I said, though in my heart I knew it wouldn't.

And I was right. The knock intensified, became a hammering, took on a rhythm, the whole routine. I sighed and got up from the table. "This won't take long."

I barreled through the house, smoothing my robe as I went. Ozzie Kimmel was peering in my window, crouching down for a better angle, shading his eyes to cancel the glare. I opened the front door and he pivoted to face me.

His tennis bag was at his feet, and he was wearing the same hideous tank top he'd been wearing that morning, but now sweat had turned the ugly orange pink back to a parody of its former red. Rivulets started in his armpits and ran all down his sides. Without a hello, he said,

"What the hell is it with you these days? Last time you just walk out. Today you don't show up—"

"So this means you peek in my windows?"

But Ozzie knew he had the higher ground and didn't give it up. "I hadda play doubles 'cause of you. I *hate* doubles! Lob, dink. Dink, slice. Fetch, fetch. Then your fuckin' partner misses. I hate it! What's so important you couldn't show up?"

I tapped my foot and told the truth. "I got kidnapped, okay?"

"Kidnapped!" said Ozzie. He mugged, and shuffled, and briefly seemed impressed. "Police blotter. Kidnapped." He looked me up and down. Then he pointed and said, "Hey, you got a boner!"

Other people, maybe, might have noticed this. Ozzie was that rare individual past the age of twelve who would comment on it. I did a little dance and shrank behind the door. He looked around and his shrewd eyes settled on the two bicycles locked up together, flank to flank, like tired horses. "You got a woman in there?"

"None of your business."

"Kidnapped," he scoffed. "Pussynapped!"

"Now you're being a jerk."

He didn't take offense. If he took offense every time someone told him off, he'd have no time for anything else. "Who is she?"

"Forget it, Ozzie. Go away."

"When we gonna play?"

"Soon. I'll see you in the park. We'll make a date. Goo'bye."

He gave me a last reproachful, houndlike look and turned to go. When he'd reached the bottom of the stairs I said, "Hey, you know anything about a guy named Mickey Veale?"

"Yeah."

"Well, what?"

"He's fat."

"Fat?"

"Fat slob. New in town."

"How new?"

"Who keeps track of time?" he said. "Couple years, something like that. Curly greasy hair. Owns the gambling boat."

"I thought he had water sports."

"That too, probably. Fat pig. Owns a lotta stuff. Came from Vegas. One of these assholes, thinks he can just cruise in from some bigger place and right away become a big shot here."

"Sounds like he is."

"That's the bitch of it," said Ozzie. "We're so fuckin' easy to outclass."

He climbed onto his bike. As he started rolling, he shook his head and said, "Doubles. I hope you're hosin' her at least."

I closed the door, and locked it, and pulled the curtains so there were no gaps between the panels.

I took a deep slow breath then resettled my robe and marched back toward the pool. I stepped outside to find that Maggie wasn't there. This threw me, but only for a second; I realized that she must have slipped into the bathroom while I was busy getting rid of Ozzie. I reclaimed my chair and my rosé. The sun had warmed my glass; without the chill, the wine had a slightly bitter aftertaste of burned marshmallow. It was strange but not unpleasant. I considered it and waited for my new lover to return.

She soon appeared in the doorway, and I understood at once that a calamity had taken place: She'd put her leotard back on. It blurred her breasts and locked away her loins. It even changed her face. Before, her face had seemed somehow to be everywhere expanding—eyes widening, lips parting, the planes of her cheeks growing more lavish as they flushed. Now her features compressed into a look that was a little guarded, a little sheepish. She moved toward me and touched my hair.

"You know what, Pete?" she said. "I'm sorry but I'm just not ready."

I tried to speak. I couldn't.

She sat down where she'd sat before. "I realized it when we got interrupted. It's not the right time yet. That friend of yours, he did us a favor."

Some favor, I thought. I'll kill him.

"I mean," she went on, "are you even all that sure *you're* ready?"

Let's face it—sometimes men and women just don't understand each other. If I was any readier, my prostate gland would have exploded. But I couldn't very well say that. The grace of the true gallant may be beyond the reach of most of us, but there's no excuse not to be a sport, at least. "Hey," I managed, "if it doesn't feel right—"

"It was feeling wonderful," she said. "That's what makes this difficult. You mad?"

I shook my head. I wasn't mad. Devastated maybe, but not mad.

But not inclined toward chitchat either. By reflex I ate an olive. There was a sulky silence, then Maggie announced that she should go. I didn't try to talk her out of it.

"Can we see each other soon?" she said.

"I guess," I said. I didn't mean for it to sound churlish. No—that's a lie. Of course I meant it to sound churlish.

She left.

Alone, I ate more olives, put on the wry, self-deprecating expression I imagined a man should wear in this sort of circumstance, and poured myself more wine. After a time, I took off my robe and, glass in hand, I walked into the pool. For the first time in my life I wished the water was a whole lot colder.

20

I finished the bottle, then had a nap on a pool-side lounge.

I woke up groggy and grumpy an hour later, as the air was changing from the spiky white heat of high afternoon to the even yellow warmth that carried through to sunset. I yawned and remembered my resolve to check out Paradise Watersports. Nothing else this day had gone the way I'd planned; maybe that at least could still be salvaged. I rolled off the lounge chair and into the water. The dunk dispelled the grogginess. The grumpiness stayed with me.

I only got grumpier when I arrived downtown and was accosted, halfway down the busy dock next to the Hyatt, by a hyperactive goofy kid with a lanyard around his neck. "How ya doin'?" he chirped. "Gettin' out on the water today? Best way to see the island. *Only* way, ya want the truth. Gonna be a gorgeous sunset. Postcard city. Fix y'up with a Jet Ski?"

His tone was double-dipped in the ersatz heartiness of tourist towns, the rote and grating gusto that waiters and concierges use to mask deep boredom and a nagging impulse to abuse and mock the customers. I told him, yeah, I'd take a Jet Ski.

He seemed put out that I didn't say it with more frenzied enthusiasm. He reached deep for another hit of friendliness. "Where ya from?"

They always ask this. I don't know why. No one cares about the answer. I almost told him I was local, just so he'd ease off on the bullshit. Then again, being taken for a tourist is a pretty good guarantee that you'll be forgotten at once. "Jersey."

I could see in his face then that he was trying not to laugh. It was amazing, really. Jersey. Laughingstock of the union, the nexus of all disdain. Just say the word, and people thousands of miles away would double over with contemptuous glee.

"Ever been on a Jet Ski before?" he asked.

"No."

"It's easy."

I looked around at the other knuckleheads and defectives who were renting them. "It must be."

The kid walked me to a small booth to do the paperwork, then down to the floating platform where the Jet Skis were tied. I was given instructions. "Here's the throttle. The key hooks to your vest, so if you fall off, the ski doesn't wind up in Cuba. Any questions?"

I pointed my chin toward the bustling harbor. "Who has the right-of-way out there?"

Judging by the kid's reaction, this was the funniest thing I'd said since admitting I'm from Jersey. "Whoever has the least to lose," he said. "Take big wakes head-on. Have fun."

Fun. Right. I started the engine. Puffs of exhaust shot forth and stank up the water. I eased out from the dock and, feeling like a horse's ass, I was on my way.

The time just before sunset is rush hour in Key West Harbor. The fishing boats are plowing in, the cocktail cruises are barreling out. The sun is a low fireball frying everybody's retinas. Glutting up the basin, huge catamarans and refurbished schooners perform the ancient mayhem of raising sail, booms swinging and canvas snapping. Now and then a shrimp boat lumbers through, outriggers poised like a bully's fists to mow down pleasure craft.

Into this bedlam, like a skunk blundering onto an interstate, I steered my little plastic toy at idle speed. Charter boats, their captains cranky from their clients and the glare, slammed across my path. Flats skiffs up on plane whistled past me in a blur. The water was everywhere scarred with foamy wakes that spread like opening zippers; it rose up in jellied lumps then dropped me into seams whose sides were steep as fresh-dug ditches. I started feeling queasy, and imagined that more speed would make the ride less nauseating. I hit the throttle. My neck snapped back, my arms twanged in their sockets, and I almost ran into a ridiculous pontoon boat whose deck was covered in Astroturf.

But I was through the worst of it. The main channel was behind me; up ahead was the shal-

low anchorage just inside Christmas Tree Island.
I paused there long enough to let the blood flow
back into my knuckles, then continued past the
islet to the vast green flat that stretches north and
westward to the drop-off of the Gulf.

Out here—certainly less than a mile from
where I'd started—the nerve-racking ride seemed
suddenly worthwhile. Out here it was spectacu-
lar, serene, already a different world. The clear
unroiled water was maybe two feet deep; below
it, gray-green turtle grass swayed against a sandy
bottom shaped into tiny dunes by the accidents of
current. See-through shrimp drifted here and
there among the tufts; needle-nosed fish smaller
than a pinky darted in battalions. The sun hov-
ered very close to the horizon. It had turned more
pink than orange and was mercifully shrouded in
a silvery haze. I turned my engine off to watch it
vanish.

When it had sliced through the surface of the
Gulf, its reflection sprang up to join it, and it became not a sphere but a cylinder, a fat candle
quickly burning down. I squinted, and in the
melancholy of sunset I guess it was inevitable that
I thought of Maggie and of the sex that hadn't
happened. I pictured her in my bathrobe. Saw the
freckles at the tops of her breasts and the russet
paleness in between them. Tasted the olive-tinged
kisses and wondered what went wrong.

I thought about it and an awful thing began to
happen: I started to get suspicious of Maggie
once again, started to wonder if there was some-

thing more than sexual bashfulness in the way
she was stringing me along.

I mean, okay, a woman was entitled not to
sleep with me. But our foreplay had been tender,
unhurried, marvelous. There'd been no sign of
unease or hesitation before her abrupt and total
change of heart. Could there have been something calculated about the whole performance?
Sex me up and lead me by the gonads. Keep tabs
on me by keeping me aroused. Why not? Lydia
sent thugs, Maggie sent mixed signals. Either had
the power to control a man, to make him captive.

But why? I watched the sun's fire melt into a
copper slick that spread across the water, and
tried to figure if Maggie had a reason for wanting
to confuse me. The fact was, she knew more
about Kenny than anyone, and she'd hid things
from me once already. Supposedly she'd come
clean. But coming halfway clean was a time-
honored way of continuing to lie. What else
might she be hiding?

I thought it over and stared at the sky. A broad
band of yellow rolled up from the western horizon like an enormous bolster. At its upper edge it
phased into a peculiar acid green that I've never
seen anywhere but in the Keys. I stared, and a
new misgiving tweaked me. Kenny Lukens had
told me that he never even peeked inside the second pouch. But why should I believe that?
Wouldn't it be more in line with human nature to
check out what one had pilfered?

And if Kenny *had* looked in the pouch, and *did*

know what was in it, and just had to tell *some-body* about it, who would he have told? His only Key West friend. His one true confidante. My supposed ally and almost my lover: Maggie.

I thought about that and my queasiness returned, but now it wasn't the waves that were giving me a bellyache. Now it was the possibility that Maggie knew exactly what was in that pouch, and wanted it, and, like her pal Kenny before her, was setting me up to run some potentially fatal errand to retrieve it.

The sky dimmed. So did my mood. By now I was taking something almost like pleasure in my mounting paranoia, and I probed an even creepier idea: How did I know for sure that Maggie had in fact been Kenny Lukens' friend? I had only her account of it. He hadn't mentioned her. It was she who'd prompted me again and again to imagine them as bosom buddies. But what proof did I have? She claimed he called her from the Bahamas; how did I know that was true? She said he'd sent letters; I'd never seen them. True, she had a story that neatly explained the matchbook from Green Turtle Cay—but that story didn't have to come from Kenny. It could just as easily have come from the person in pursuit of Kenny—someone with whom Maggie was in cahoots.

I shivered. There was moisture underneath my life vest and the air was gradually cooling, but that's not why I got goose bumps. I got goose bumps because I was weirding myself out, big-time. I felt by now that I had come this close to shtupping a murderess, commingling my seed with that of a monster. Then I thought: Pete, for God's sake get a grip. The woman teaches yoga. She drinks herb tea. Who ever heard of a killer teaching yoga? You can't send her to the Chair just because she put her leotard back on.

I frowned up at the heavens. The acid green had dulled to a lusterless silver. Looking back across my shoulder, I saw that the first stars were just emerging in the east. I took a long slow breath, then started up my Jet Ski. The engine noise was ugly but I was glad to have it drowning out my thoughts.

The harbor traffic had thinned to almost nothing as I headed in; the chop had all gone flat. Reggae wafted from the wharfside bars. Lights spilled from the honky-tonks and tiki huts and made the water underneath me look magenta.

I was more than halfway home when the contraption I was riding took a sudden right-hand turn and carried me out again toward Sunset Key.

21

Back when it was still Tank Island, Sunset Key belonged to everyone and no one; it was one of those unofficial public parks that often get more use than designated ones. On the side that faced Key West, rocks and current made it difficult to land, but on the Gulf side there was placid water and tiny crescent beaches where people dragged their boats and laid out picnics and indulged in semipublic nudity. Dogs had adventures in the underbrush and came back with sandy snouts.

Now the current had been tamed by jetties, and there was a spiffy new dock that only the official launch was allowed to use. The underbrush had been cleaned out; No Trespassing signs had sprouted in its place. A metal fence ringed the island, as near to the high-tide line as the developers could sink their pilings.

In the gathering dusk, I edged closer to the shore and saw a classic image of half-finished Florida—fancy houses waiting for their grass to grow; others that were mere skeletons of two-by-fours. Promising graciousness, there was a clubhouse with a striped canopy; ersatz palapas lined a glowing pool. All very cozy.

But I was looking for a murder site, not a real estate investment—and some not quite reasonable hunch made me confident that I would find it. It would be away from lights and homes. At a spot where palms survived just outside the fence. A small dinghy could scrape ashore there, and there would be a nameless residue of something dreadful having happened.

I idled, traced out scallops of the coastline, and at length became certain that I'd reached the place. A tongue of sand led to a shadowed scrap of beach. I ran the Jet Ski onto it, thinking: another day, another trespass, another crime scene violated. Yet I felt oddly calm, calmer than when my thoughts had still been stuck on Maggie. I climbed off the Ski and walked the foreshore till it rose up steeply in a kind of terrace. There, squeezed right up against the fence, were a pair of palms bent parallel as dancers.

Between them, there was a slight depression in the sand. Unreasonably but firmly, I became convinced that this had to be the hole that Kenny Lukens was digging when he died. The depression was very shallow, practically filled in already, and it made me very sad. We all know that everything passes. All human effort gets erased. But on a beach it happens with dizzy and humiliating speed. Wind and tide flatten and sculpt. Crabs and ants launch tiny avalanches of tumbling grains. Past configurations count for nothing; the people who were there yesterday might never have been born.

I squatted down next to the disappearing hole. I don't know why, but it seemed important to me to touch the sand. I dug my hands in.

The sand still held late sunshine, was much warmer than the evening air. It was powdery on top, but underneath it caked around palm roots that were as hard as collarbones. I kneaded the sand, sifted it, turned it over. Then my fingers found something that wasn't beach. It was slender and smooth but had at one end a jagged, splintered point. I dug it out, examined it in the dying light. It seemed to be a broken plastic swizzle stick. Of course—there always had to be a matchbook and there always had to be a swizzle stick. This one had two flat squares at the top, overlapping each other on the diagonal.

I put it in the pocket of my life vest, then like a terrier I flicked some sand back onto the secret place I'd messed with. As I did so, I came abruptly to the end of my fragile and probably phony calm. I ran back to the Jet Ski, pushed it out into the water, and got the hell out of there.

"Did ya love it?" asked the goofy kid with the lanyard around his neck.

I slid off the Jet Ski and onto the dock. "Fabulous," I said. "Terrific."

I fished the swizzle stick out of my pocket and examined it under the humming lights. It was translucent red, and the flat squares turned out to be dice. A three and a four. Tiny depressions had been stamped in; they still held faint flecks of white paint, the rest having been scoured by the sand. I showed it to the kid. "Any idea where this is from?"

He studied it like it was an artifact from Troy. At last he said, "Looks like one of ours. Want a discount coupon?"

"Excuse me?"

"Discount coupon for the gambling boat. The *Lucky Duck*. I'm not supposed to give a coupon if you already got the sunset special, but what the hell."

Everybody loves a bargain, right? "Sure," I said. "I'll take a coupon."

I gave him back the life vest and we went up to the kiosk where he'd done the paperwork. He handed me a fake ten-dollar bill. It took a moment before I realized that in the oval where U. S. Grant should have been, there was a picture of a guy who looked a lot like Nero. Slick curly hair surmounted a broad and loose and sensual face, which rested in turn on a bed of rippling chins. He smiled like a rich cheese was tickling his gums. He looked familiar, and after a moment I remembered him from Lefty's funeral. The man with the Japanese fan.

"Mickey Veale?" I guessed.

"You know Mickey?" asked the kid.

"Only heard of him. What's he like?"

"He's a pisser. Good boss. First-name kind of guy. Not a suit, ya know?"

I looked again at the satyr who'd put himself on money. I could see him in a toga way easier than I could see him in a suit. "I heard he came from Vegas."

"Yup. Vegas got too wholesome for him. 'Least that's what he says. They put in kiddie rides, he was out of there."

I thought: Gee, if it turns out that he's not a murderer, chances are I could have a few laughs with this guy. "He go out on the boat?"

"Keeps an office on it," said the kid. "Some nights he goes out, some nights he doesn't."

"I need a reservation?"

"Just show up at a quarter of eleven. North Haven Marina. It's over—"

"Next to Redmond's," I put in. "Toxic Triangle."

The kid looked at me a little funny. "You're not really from New Jersey, are you?"

I took it as a compliment but insisted that I was. I said good night and went to fetch my bike.

22

And then I actually got to spend a couple hours at home.

Frankly, this was heaven—a heaven of the simplest things. A hot shower. A plate of scrambled eggs. A glass of young and cedary Côtes-du-Rhône and some music on the stereo. Bill Evans playing live stuff from the fifties, early sixties. Getting amazing precision out of crappy road pianos, with no chance for a second take. No one's ever done it better.

I made coffee. In years long past I wouldn't have bothered, but it so happened that the boat sailed at what had become my usual bedtime, and it would have been embarrassing to fall asleep amid the revelry and on the job. Around ten-thirty I got back on my bike and headed toward the harbor once again.

I skirted Redmond's, skirted thoughts of Maggie, and at the far end of a brand-new pier I found the *Lucky Duck*. It could not have been mistaken for, say, the *QE2*. It was smallish—a hundred ten, a hundred twenty feet. Its paint was lumpy and its fittings were scratched and tarnished. But it would not be fair to say it was a tub. It was just old, and obsolete, degraded like a pushed-aside executive by a succession of ever-lower uses. It had a nice line to it, and in its heyday—probably the twenties—it had likely been a helluva private yacht. The rails were gullied now but teak; the main cabin was sided with mahogany and the cleats that held the dock lines were solid brass.

I lined up at the bottom of the gangplank. The boat, I guessed, could take around a hundred fifty people, but this was a Monday toward the end of April, and there weren't more than sixty in the line. Every one of us cheapskates had a discount coupon with Mickey Veale's portrait on it.

After a while we paid our $19.95 and boarded. I made a quick tour of the ship. In what had once been the wheelhouse, there was a small bar and three poker tables. The room smelled of cigars and whiskey spilled on felt that never quite dried. A sort of breezeway led back to the main saloon, which was a complete casino in miniature. Slot machines lined the portholed walls; a craps table and a roulette wheel took up two corners. A second bar shared the aft bulkhead with a bleak buffet that looked like something from a chain motel close by to an interstate. Between the cold cuts and the booze was a narrow stairway that led down to the heads and, I imagined, to the boss's shipboard office.

The engines started, the gangplank was raised, and the crowd fell on the cubes of Swiss cheese and the little tubes of turkey like they were going to the gallows in the morning.

I stepped outside to watch our progress
through the harbor. We passed buoys that, up
close, were gigantic, then rounded the jetty at
Fort Zack and headed out to sea. A late moon
was rising, sluggish, pink and dusty; waves of
phosphorescence spread out from our bow. I took
a deep breath that smelled of iodine and fish, and
realized rather suddenly that I had no plan. What
exactly was I doing here? I hated buffets and I
didn't like to gamble. Why squander adrenaline
that could be saved for less contrived emergen-
cies? I hoped, of course, to study Mickey Veale.
But if he wasn't aboard, it would be a long and
wasted night.

Then a subversive little question started prick-
ing me: Wasted as compared with what?

I kicked that one aside and watched the stars.
In another fifteen minutes or so, just inside the
reef, we crossed the three-mile limit. I felt the
boat slip into neutral, heard the grinding fall of
the anchor chain. The hook was set with a slow
jolt in reverse, then someone rang a bell and it
was time for the gaming to begin.

I enjoyed a last calm moment and stepped into
the casino. After the clean tang of the ocean, the
cabin seemed very smoky, and held another smell
I dimly remembered from, like, junior high school
dances—the soupy smell of nervous desire, of libido twisted up like breath in a trombone. Cards
were being shuffled. There was the dry click of
chips being stacked, the muted ring of coins. I
picked my way over to the bar. There were seven
or eight stools, most of which were empty. It

seemed a time and place for bourbon. I ordered one and reached for my wallet.

"It's free," the bartender advised, "if we bring it to you while you're playing."

"Thanks," I said. "I'll pay for it."

He looked at me as though I were some grand eccentric, then went on to other business. I drank. I watched. There was a blackjack player with a dreadful tic, a cocktail waitress whose gender was in doubt. Bored, I drank too fast. Then Mickey Veale appeared in the stairway not ten feet from where I sat.

He was even heavier than his picture made him look, a bloated product of late empire. He wore an enormous mint-green guayabera that hung down far below his middle; even so, you could tell that the waistband of his pants had been exiled to some damp place beneath the epic belly. His swelling arms seemed attached as though by webbing to his flanks; his neck was crinkled like a dryer hose.

He lumbered up the steps, pushing weightily on the brass banister, eyes raking the tables and gauging the action at the slots. He began to work the room. A handshake here, a backslap there. His smile was wide and flubbery and his eyes squeezed shut when he laughed—by all appearances, your basic gregarious and jolly fat man. Lydia Ortega had said he was a sneak. He didn't look sneaky to me. Unless he was the type who distracted by sheer mass and flamboyance, who used an excess of impressions to hide the real goods underneath.

He kibitzed roulette awhile, spent some time overlooking blackjack. Finally he worked his way back toward the little bar. At one end was a couple whose life seemed to be falling quietly apart and who clearly wanted to be left alone. At the other end was me. Mickey Veale and I made some cautious eye contact. He gestured vaguely toward the gambling floor and saved me the trouble of trying to start a conversation. "Not running lucky?" he asked.

"Haven't put it to the test," I said. "Mainly just out for a boat ride."

He gave me a nod that was full of understanding, like I was one more lonely insomniac of a kind he'd met before.

I smiled wanly and realized I was out of things to say. I paused for a breath and smelled the big man's aftershave. Clove. Nice, not too sweet. I heard myself continue: "So—I understand you came from Vegas?"

He seemed neither surprised nor suspicious that I knew this. In fact, it seemed to give him pleasure. He liked it that he was known, talked about, a character. He extended a pillowy hand and told me his name. I told him mine and we shook. Then he went on, "Getting out of Vegas— best goddamn thing I ever did."

"How come?"

"Vegas is finished." He looked down at my nearly empty glass. "Buy you a drink?"

I nodded that he could. He lifted several chins to the bartender. Two jumbos quickly appeared.

"Cheers," he said. He perched largely on a

stool and slurped his drink. "Vegas, the Indians
are kicking their ass. On the gaming side, I mean.
They're getting murdered. So wha' does Vegas
do? They go all soft and family. Disneyland with
chips. Floor shows with cartoon characters. From
G-strings to G ratings." He leaned a little closer
and went on confidentially, "Day care. Fuckin'
day care! In Vegas? It's sickening. When the
hookers started doing story hour, I knew it was
time to get out."

"So how'd you pick Key West?" I asked him.

He loudly chewed an ice cube before he answered. "Lemme tell ya somethin'. Key West is
the best town in America. The last grown-up,
raunchy, sleazy place. God bless it! Ya know
when I realized this? When they had that court
case about what was naked and what was not.
Remember?"

It so happened that I did remember. It had to
do with Fantasy Fest, two, three years ago. Some
killjoys were alleging that it was illegal for people
to parade naked and simulate sex acts in front of
thousands of onlookers on Duval Street. Several
arrests were made.

"The hearings made the news," Mickey Veale
went on. "National. One woman said, 'I wasn't
naked, I was wearing body paint.' Another woman
said, 'I wasn't naked, I had glitter on.' And I
thought, Yes! A town where painted titties count
as clothes, where sparkles in the pubic hair count
as underpants, this is a town for me! So I closed up
shop in Vegas, and here I am." He finished off the
rest of his drink in one heroic swallow and ges-

tured for another. "And what brings you here? Vacation?"

I didn't answer right away. I was still sorting through my first impressions of Mickey Veale. So far he struck me as crude, profane, and in-your-face; which is to say I liked him pretty well. But now that it was my turn to talk, I wasn't sure how to begin. Caginess did not seem suited to the time or place; Veale's at least seeming unguardedness called for a response in kind. So I thought the hell with it and blurted, "I came to Key West because my life kind of sucked, and I came to your boat because of a couple of murders."

Mickey Veale said, "What?"

He was looking at me like I was a nut, and I wished that I could start again, could swim upward through the empty air and regain the comfort of the diving board. My throat closing down around the word, I said again, "Murders."

He squinted at me and said with certainty, "You're not a cop."

With considerably less certainty, I said, "I'm a detective."

He looked me up and down. "You don't look like a detective."

Was this getting personal? A two-bit gambling boat in a two-bit town—what was he expecting, Robert Mitchum? I shrugged and stared at him. His big face had changed and was changing some more. Gone was the shmoozing-with-customers smile. His eyes had turned cautious and he seemed beset. He might have even flinched. But of course there are a lot of different kinds of flinches. Guilty ones; affronted ones; ones that mean nothing and only have to do with gas.

After a moment, he shot a nervous look across his shoulder at the sluggish action on his gambling floor and said, "Look, I'm running a business here. Let's not have any trouble."

I put my glass down on the bar and suavely dried my hand on my shorts. "Then maybe there's someplace quiet we could talk."

23

Veale led me down the narrow flight of stairs. Even before the door to his office was fully opened, I received a very unpleasant surprise.

Sitting at a desk, playing solitaire in a pool of greenish light, was one of the last people in the world I hoped to see: Officer Cruz. One of the homicide cops who'd interrogated me the other night. Who'd ordered me to drop this thing. Who'd threatened me with evidence tampering and warned me of the erotic horrors that would befall me in the pen. He looked up at me and the skin tightened at his improbable hairline. "Fuck you doing here?" he said.

At that, Mickey Veale brightened somewhat, seemed to get his balance back. He even managed to get a little playfulness into his tone. "Ah," he said, "you gentlemen know each other."

"We've met," said Cruz, and he continued turning cards. "Amsterdam likes to poke around crime scenes."

His dismissive tone annoyed me. I paid taxes. I had rights. I said, "Somebody has to. I mean, if the cops are playing solitaire on gambling boats . . ."

Cruz bristled but Veale seemed to enjoy the repartee. Smiling once again, he said, "Officer Cruz does security for me. So does his partner, Officer Corallo. On their own time. Perfectly legit. Have a seat."

Sitting, I thought, Security, right. A do-nothing job for very good pay; a vaguely lawful kind of bribery. Ozzie Kimmel had nailed it—the cops were in the pocket of the handful of players who ran the town. Why was I surprised?

I must have been brooding on this, because Mickey Veale, seated opposite me by now, said, "So, Pete, you wanted to talk?"

I cleared my throat, said, "Right." Then I remembered a familiar dream, probably one of those that everybody has: You're in a play. Maybe you're the lead. And as the curtain lifts you suddenly realize that you've never seen a script. . . . I started anyway. "Lefty Ortega—I believe you knew him?"

"We had some business together," said Veale.

"What kind of business?"

"Water sports. A concession over by the Hyatt."

"Paradise," I said.

"That's right."

"So now you're in business with Lydia?"

"Seems that way," said Veale. "I mean, Christ, Lefty's barely cold."

"Lydia thinks I shouldn't trust you. Why would that be, Mickey?"

Veale shrugged affably, indifferently. "Lydia's a whore."

"You like whores," I reminded him.

"Some," he admitted, and left it at that.

I drummed fingers on the desk. Thinking aloud, I said, "She hates you. You hate her. Why would people who hate each other's guts be partners in a business?"

"You think that's unusual?" said Veale.

He had me there.

He paused a moment, then continued rather condescendingly, rubbing my face in my naivete. "Pete," he said, "have you ever done business in a foreign country? That's what it's like down here. You need a local partner to get you in. You don't have to like them. You have to give them a piece of something, in exchange for which they grease the wheels for you."

At this I could not help glancing at the moonlighting homicide detective, sulking over his now suspended game of cards. "Like what wheels do they grease?" I asked.

Casually, Mickey Veale said, "Licenses, permits, variances. Boring municipal crap."

I expected it got more exciting than permits but I let it slide. "Okay," I said. "So you gave the Ortegas a piece of the water-sports business. What else?"

The big man slowly folded his pudgy hands. "Sorry, that isn't public information."

In semiconscious mimicry, I folded my hands too. Leaning forward I said, "That's okay. I'm not a public eye."

I thought that was rather clever. No one else did. There was an awkward moment that turned out to serve a useful purpose. A failed joke creates embarrassment, and embarrassment breeds hostility, and I'd badly needed something to get my juices flowing. More aggressive now, I said, "Look, two people have been killed—"

I got loudly interrupted at that point. Officer Cruz had been sitting there as taut as a chained-up dog. Now he jumped in so fast that it was clear he'd just been waiting for me to cross a certain line, *hoping* I'd cross a certain line. "I told you to stay away from—"

I surprised myself by pointing a finger and shouting him down in turn. "Are you off duty? Then back off and let me talk."

Cruz was halfway out of his chair by now. I was about one-tenth out of mine, when it dawned on me, to my horror and amazement, that I was close to striking a fighting pose. This was preposterous. I remembered reading, as a kid, that the person who threw the first punch was the one who'd run out of ideas. This notion had struck me as pretty wise but now I saw it was baloney. Who threw the first punch was the guy who believed he could score a quick knockout and not get hit back. By increments I hoped would be invisible, I started lowering my cowardly ass back into the seat.

Luckily for me, Mickey Veale decided to play peacemaker. "Gents," he said, "let's not get all excited. I've got nothing to hide. Go ahead and ask your questions."

Easy for him to say. By now my heart was in my

mouth. I took a long, slow breath and tried to re-member what my questions ought to be. "Okay, okay," I said. "Let's start with the first guy who was killed. Kenny Lukens. Worked at Lefty's bar. A couple of years ago he faked a robbery and ended up with something Lefty wanted pretty badly."

"What?" said Mickey Veale.

"He doesn't know!" said Cruz.

"You don't know?" said Veale.

"I don't know."

"That's peculiar," said Veale.

"Yeah, it is."

"I mean, it's weird."

"Yes," I said. "It's peculiar and weird. Can we move on?"

I noticed then that Officer Cruz was shaking his head and smirking. I knew this was a com-ment on my interrogating skills and I confess it rattled me. I felt like an intern hacking off his first appendix with the master surgeon looking on. I bit my lip and blundered ahead. "Lukens bolted. Went to the Bahamas. Some time there-after, a Key West guy showed up and threatened him."

I was studying Veale, trying to gauge how much of this tale he already knew. His fat face had the elastic puffiness of rising dough, and about as much expression. "I'm not sure I follow you," he said.

"This guy," I said, "was a regular at Lefty's. I think maybe he worked for you at Paradise."

Veale poked a finger in his cheek. It sank in knuckle deep. "And what makes you think that?"

I'd already started pushing breath when I realized that I couldn't tell him. If I told him about finding the matchbook, I'd have to mention the Hibiscus guest house in front of Cruz, and that might make trouble for Vanessa, which I'd promised that I wouldn't do. Worse, how would I know any of this except through a confidante of Kenny's?—and the thought of implicating Maggie made me feel ill. Some interrogator. I'm getting one-word answers or no answers at all, and had come a hairbreadth from spilling everything I knew. I sucked back whatever it was I'd started to say, and said instead, "Sorry—that isn't public information either."

Veale turned his palms up, gave a little shrug, and looked at Cruz. Cruz shot him a disgusted glance then smirked again at me. I tried to sit tight but I squirmed. Squirmed, and tried to figure out what my next gambit ought to be. I felt outflanked, outclassed, and lousy.

But it so happened that I'd brought with me a trump card. I hadn't decided if I would play it or save it; its mere possession was delectable. It should not, I knew, be played in desperation; but this was a rather desperate moment, and playing it was the only thing I could think of to do. So, with a gesture I envisioned as a compact yet dramatic flourish, I reached into a pocket of my shorts and produced the broken swizzle stick I'd dug up on Sunset Key. Slowly and portentously I placed it on the desk in front of Veale and Cruz.

They looked at it and blinked.

Speaking barely above a whisper, I said, "I found this right where Kenny Lukens was killed."

A pregnant silence followed. I didn't actually expect a breakdown, tears, a spontaneous confession, but stranger things have happened. I leaned slightly forward in my chair.

At last Cruz said, "Ah. Exhibit A. A piece of flotsam. You're pathetic, Amsterdam."

I was less hurt by this than dazed. I eased back in my chair, crossed my arms in self-defense.

"You know how much crap washes up on that beach?" the cop went on. "We've got twenty things like this already in the lab. Cigarette packs, sunblock tubes, plastic hotel keys. They mean nothing. Get a job, Amsterdam. Get a life."

A life. For a while there I'd thought I had one. Now I shrank inside myself and pouted.

The boat rocked. With malice posing as indifference, I watched as Cruz's fingers moved lazily, disdainfully toward my swizzle stick. I let the fingers get close enough that I could see the texture of their cuticles and discern the whorls on their tips, and then I snatched the stick away and returned it to my pocket. This was childish, I admit. But he'd insulted my find, my one and only piece of evidence, laughed it off as flotsam. I wasn't about to let him play with it, still less have it.

A ridiculous standoff ensued—Cruz's empty fingers dangling in space, me sulking like a brat. Mickey Veale loomed larger than ever on the far side of the desk, seemed actually to swell into the

role of grown-up referee in a scrap between
ragged boys. He smiled in mock benignity and
said, "Any more questions, Mr. Amsterdam?"

I sulked and squirmed and could think of only
one. "When the hell can I get off this boat?"

24

The answer, to my sorrow, was 6:00 A.M.

I went back upstairs to the small hell of the casino and watched people die by the increments of a quarter or a buck. Around four o'clock a breeze came up, and things got really strange. The people playing slots were sitting in tall chairs with casters on the legs. When they pulled the handle, their momentum, added to the rocking of the boat, sent them rolling downhill through the haze of cigarettes to the far side of the cabin. Sometimes they slammed into a bulkhead. When the boat tipped back the other way, they hurtled once again toward their machine to see that they had lost. Now and then a slot spit forth a rain of coins at a trajectory like someone throwing up.

I stepped outside to get some air. The moon was near the zenith, but the sky was soggy and there was a lack of conviction in the way it shone. Something awfully melancholy too—the humble sorrow of the perennial warm-up act, doing its best but doomed to be outdone, erased, by the gaudier talents of the headliner, the sun. Still, I

watched awhile. The wind raised a light chop on
the sea; moonlight put a milky gleam in the top-
most curls of the wavelets. Now and then a
green-gold arc of phosphorescence tracked the
passing of an unseen ray. The drone of the casino
was muted by the walls and windows and scattered by the breeze, spread thin till it could almost pass for quiet.

Or it could until a different sound intruded.
The sound was far away, and hard to locate in the
wind, but it gradually resolved into the high nattering buzz of small engines—more than one of
them, I thought. Early fishermen, probably, drinking coffee from thermoses and staking out their
portions of the reef for dawn. I scanned the horizon but saw nothing. The engine sounds got
closer, now taking on the rise and drop in pitch
that went with little bounces in the chop. And finally, maybe a mile off and faintly mauve in the
listless moonlight, I thought I saw a pair of misty
rooster tails of the kind that were shot skyward
not by boats but Jet Skis. I squinted toward these
phantoms, trying to assure myself that they were
really there, that they really were connected to the
engine sounds.

Then another detail barged in on the night. A
cone of light flashed forth on the water underneath me. I couldn't see the source of the light,
but it could only have come from our boat. It
stayed on for some fraction of a second, switched
off, and then switched on again.

When the former dimness had returned, the
motor sounds no longer seemed to be getting

closer. I squinted toward where I thought I'd seen
the rooster tails but saw only a featureless swath
of predawn ocean. Gradually, the whine of engines fell away, restoring the flawed quiet of the
background hum. The breeze dropped, the surface of the water healed itself; it was as if nothing
whatsoever had occurred.

Perplexed, exhausted, doubting my eyes, I tried
and failed to make some sense of the dim vague
episode. Then my brain shut down and, passive
as a plant, I waited for first light.

It came at last as an undramatic paling of the
eastern sky, a lazy snuffing out of stars, then exploded in yellow slashes that sliced through
lavender slabs of cloud, and seared the retina,
and briefly made the ocean red as blood before
turning it turquoise.

It was already hot when the *Lucky Duck*
groaned against its pilings and was made fast to
the dock. I didn't see Veale or Cruz before I dis-
embarked.

In principle, I'm all for decadence. Crazy hours;
riotous drinking; the edgy desperate drive that
peels the skin off life and pushes your face into
the tart and pulpy stuff inside—why the hell not?

I just don't seem to have the constitution for it.
Up all night, I felt like shit. I'd never quite gotten
drunk and I didn't have a hangover. I just felt dull
and itchy and disoriented. The morning sunshine
embarrassed me; I saw myself as an affront to the
day. I craved sleep, but when I'd reclaimed my bicycle from its lockup near the dock, the moving

air slapped some semblance of alertness into me
and I wasn't sleepy anymore.

Suddenly I wanted pancakes.

Don't ask me why; I don't even like pancakes.
But I rode downtown through empty streets and
went to a place that opened early and served ba-
nana pancakes in an open courtyard full of cats
and chickens. Drinking coffee, mopping syrup,
glancing around at the other grubby souls who
hadn't been to bed yet and whose tortured shirt-
tails had long ago given up on staying in their
pants, I wondered, with only minor anxiety, if
this was what a nervous breakdown would be
like: You still had a self, you still went through
the motions of a life, but the life you were living
no longer seemed congruent with the person living it. At forty-seven I knew who I was. I was a
guy who hit the sack around eleven and woke up
to an austere and wholesome bowl of cereal and
fruit, a bonanza of vitamins and fiber. So who
was this unshaven red-eyed impostor poking sodden pancakes with a slightly trembling fork?

I started getting worried. A little angry too.
That bastard Cruz was right—I ought to get a
life, or at least preserve the little life I had. Why
was I letting it go down the tubes? Well, I
wouldn't let it, not without a fight. I would grab
a piece of it and hold on, do something wherein
I'd recognize myself. I slurped down the last of
my coffee and decided, exhausted or otherwise, I
would go and play some tennis.

So I rode home, threw cold water on my face,
tucked myself into my jock. By the time I made it

to the park, it was around eight-thirty and the usual idiots were assembling. Including, of course, Ozzie Kimmel. He was holding forth in the shade of the players' enclosure, and when he saw me he sang out, "Aha! He's here! . . . You've been dodging me."

I loved this about Ozzie. A more marginal person could hardly be imagined, and yet he kept right on believing that everything referred to him. "Don't be ridiculous," I said.

"Come on," he said. "You stiff me, what, like three, four times already, then you show up on a day I drive. I'm usually not here."

This reminded me that I no longer knew what day it was, still less what days Ozzie Kimmel worked. Vaguely I said, "So where's the cab?"

"Fuck the cab. I didn't wanna. You got a game?"

"No," I said. "I don't."

At that he brightened, but cautiously. He'd been kicked before. But he couldn't quite keep his tail from wagging at the prospect of a ball to fetch. "We gonna play?"

"Come on," I said. "Let's do it."

So we played a set, and, boy, did I stink up the court. Served like hell, volleyed worse, and couldn't find my forehand. This was humbling but salubrious. Reminded me that leisure too was serious, required discipline, even passion. Do it half-ass and it was a thinner, poorer thing by far.

Ozzie picked up the ball after my final errant shot and said, "Another set?"

Slow and hangdog, I walked toward the net. "Oz," I whined, "I haven't slept, I got pancakes churning in my stomach like cement, and I think I'm gonna barf."

"Excuses, excuses. What kinda weenie plays one set?"

I put my racquet in its case.

Ozzie still didn't believe I was quitting. "One more lousy set. You're nauseous, I won't use the drop shot."

I draped a towel over my shoulder and started walking off the court.

In a tone of compromise, he said, "Okay. Three games."

Still moving away, I half turned to look at him. "Oz, you know anything about smuggling?"

He didn't miss a beat, and of course he referred the question to himself. "I've done a little of it. Why?"

"You've done a little of it?" I echoed stupidly.

"In the seventies. Sure. Everybody did. Marijuana from Jamaica, Mexico, Belize. Came in in bales. Mother ships brought 'em almost to the reef, transferred 'em onto fishing boats. Which is where I worked. Sometimes bales fell overboard. Or guys got paranoid and ditched 'em. People found 'em on the beach. Called 'em square grouper. It was good. Everybody made some money."

Seeking shade, I continued walking off the court. And tried to hide that I was slightly shocked. Was I Key West's last puritan, the last bourgeois? Here I was, supposedly hard-boiled and all that stuff, and everybody but me seemed so cool and so blasé about the various and sundry crimes they had committed.

Ozzie might have read some disapproval in my posture. Or more likely he just felt like talking. "Hey," he went on, "smuggling is the whole story of this town. Rum-running, drugs—I mean, what's the point of living on a dinky island at the edge of nowhere if you're not gonna smuggle shit in?"

Some assertions are simply too peculiar to argue against. So I just said, "And it still goes on?"

"What are you, a newcomer? 'Course it does."

"What gets smuggled now?"

Ozzie blew a dismissive, farting sound between his lips. "Aah, it isn't what it was. No demand for reefer. Hard shit's all moved up to Miami. What's left? Haitians? Cuban cigars? I don't really know."

We reached the peeling wood enclosure. Ozzie produced a frayed rag with which he began to dry his hairy chest.

"Well, let me ask you this," I said. "Other than smuggling, can you imagine why a pair of Jet Skis would approach an anchored boat at four A.M.?"

"You saw this?" he said. "Jet Skis at four in the morning?"

"Let's just keep it hypothetical."

He didn't answer right away. He daintily picked lint from the rim of his navel, then gave in and really reamed the thing. "Jet Skis. That's interesting."

"Why?"

"No real room to stash stuff on a Jet Ski. What they're smuggling would have to be something really small."

The power of suggestion instantly kicked in. I pursed my lips and pictured emeralds. I pictured pearls. I pictured superfast computer chips. Then I said, "Wait a second. I have no idea if they were really smuggling."

Ozzie snickered as he reached into his bag for one of his appalling tank tops. "Okay," he said, "they weren't smuggling. They just felt like going for a little ride at four A.M. What were you, born yesterday?"

The question hung there as Ozzie's head briefly disappeared into his torn and faded shirt. I had a moment blurrily to reflect on all the things that had surprised me lately, all my recent blindsidings by the unwholesome and illicit moves that people made. "You know," I said, "sometimes I think I was."

25

Finally I got to go to sleep, and you can bet I made the most of it.

I didn't toss. I didn't dream. I stayed down till 3:00 P.M., by which time the full heat of the day had collected and compressed in my upstairs bedroom, and I woke at last, as puffy and moist as a dumpling in a steamer. The pillow was wet beneath my head. The sheet was wet on top of me. This might sound gross but it felt totally wonderful. It was a jungle feeling, generative and raw. It suggested vines and parrots and lovemaking on piles of hot leaves.

I lay there awhile, savoring, then threw off the sheet and rolled over to a dry part of the bed. A new batch of sensations followed, no less delicious than the first. Evaporation cooled me; I tingled at the collarbones and hairline. I felt moisture wicking off my back, the skin shrinking ever so slightly as dampness was coaxed from it. Truth was, I could have been perfectly content for several hours, just lolling there, rolling, folding arms and legs in different combinations, trying out various configurations of sheets and pillows. Why

not? Out in the world, things were befuddling
and frustrating and complicated. Here, all was
simplicity and peace. What's wrong with avoiding aggravation?

But finally, reluctantly, I rose from bed. I
headed for the shower, then decided, no, I'd start
off with a cool plunge in the pool. I grabbed a
towel and went downstairs. Padded through the
kitchen and out the sliding door to the sun-baked
deck.

But I never made it into the water. I looked
down and saw a pair of dead rats floating there,
spinning lazily on the current from the pump.

They were palm rats—smaller and less filthy
than their urban cousins, but rats nonetheless,
and plenty unappetizing. They were just beginning to bloat. Their sparse fur had corkscrewed
into tufts between which were lewd bare patches
of stretched skin whose color was an ugly pinkish
taupe. Their eyes were closed but the lids were an
appalling red; their ears seemed to have grown
soggy, and futile whiskers floated on the surface.
Their tails had been tied together.

With a disgusted fascination, I watched awhile
as the rats spun in their morbid circuit, and tried
to figure out the meaning of this. Why *two* rats?
Why tied together? Did they symbolize the
two murdered men? Lefty and Lydia Ortega? I
watched them and pondered. Sometimes their
tails stretched out full length, then twanged back,
pulling the corpses close together as in a dance
routine. Maybe I was reading too much into this.
There were two to make it twice as nasty. They

were tied together so that I would know a human hand had intervened, that these were not simply unfortunate or klutzy rats that had fallen from a tree. They were supposed to scare me.

They did scare me, but in a delayed-reaction kind of way. I was still too groggy to get frightened all at once. Besides, I had practical matters to deal with. I had to get the rats out of the pool before they decomposed and gummed up the works.

I went over to the shrubbery and started looking for a stick. Call me squeamish—I don't like to touch dead things. If this is a superstition, it's a pretty primal one, I'd bet, based on the notion of death itself as a contagious particle, the mother of all germs. In any case, I found a fallen frond with a good hard spine, then waited for the rats to do a final do-si-do over to my side of the pool. I scooped them by the knot in their tails; they hung down like a pair of sausages; water dribbled from their mouths. I flung them back into the bushes. They spun slowly like the weighted snare that cowboys from the pampas use, then crashed through leaves and twigs and came to rest somewhere out of sight.

I shuddered and tossed away the frond. I looked down at the pool but there was no way I was getting in it so soon after death had visited. It occurred to me to put an extra chlorine tablet in the bobber. Then I sat down in a lounge chair, and finally the fear caught up with me, slow and whispering at first, then clamorous and strangling.

I'd just been put on notice that someone capable of killing was extremely pissed off at me. And all at once it seemed that, in everything I'd done so far, I'd been stupidly cavalier, careless and unserious. My approach had been pure Key West. Which is to say I'd been blundering along through a haze of heat and goofiness as though the standards of the outside world did not apply, as if doing things smilingly half-ass was good enough, because the whole thing was basically one big joke. To an extent that seemed suddenly incredible, I'd overlooked the simple facts that violence was violence, and murder was murder, and death was death, wherever you happened to be.

I sat there for a while. Bugs buzzed; lizards posed on rocks. Then, spinning off my fear, a strange thing happened: Even though I absolutely knew I hadn't touched the rats, I became obsessed with the worry that I had rat on my hands. I splayed my fingers and held them out in front of me so that I wouldn't accidentally touch my mouth or eyes. Then I stood, and used an elbow to slide the screen door open, and moved in a quiet panic to the kitchen sink.

Using lots of dish detergent, I washed my hands over and over again. Scrubbing, wringing, I suddenly understood something that I hadn't grasped before: that there is no paranoia quite like island paranoia. Here I was, stuck on a flat, bare hunk of rock four miles long by two miles wide, with a deadly enemy who knew exactly where I lived. I'm no crusader. I'm a guy who's largely given up on the world. How in Jesus had I done this to myself?

I rinsed my hands and went to dry them. But then I was unsure I'd scrubbed them thoroughly enough, that I'd gotten to the tiny webs deep down at the bases of my fingers. I soaped them once again. And told myself I'd been a fool from the beginning for imagining that I could dip into this business, play detective for a while, then pull away whenever I decided that I'd had enough. Life and death were a shade more serious than that, even in Key West.

Naked at the sink, I turned the water off at last. Reached out for a dish towel and dried my hands. Dried them vigorously, roughly, to hide from myself the fact that they were shaking.

PART THREE

26

Say this for Lefty Ortega's daughter—the woman had some outfits.

I went to see her soon after pulling the dead rats from the pool. I'd finished washing my hands, then gone upstairs for a shower and washed them some more. Dressed, I choked down some toast against a faint but lingering nausea. Then I hopped onto my bike and rode through the stagnant heat of late afternoon to the giant oceanside condo.

I reached her door and rang the bell. A moment passed, then I heard the little shutter open on the peephole. The deadbolt slid free. The door swung open and there she was.

She was wearing backless, high-heeled silver slippers whose open toes framed ranks of bright red toenails. Her hair was a little bit askew; her lipstick overreached the boundaries of her lips and was just slightly faded. Covering her body, sort of, was a pink though mostly see-through tunic over tiny patches of polka-dotted undies. "Ah," she said, "it's my little private eye."

Sometimes diminutives suggest affection. Other

times they're just . . . diminutives. I didn't feel like
I was being complimented. But I didn't take time
to brood about the slight. Still standing in the
doorway, I said, "Lydia, we have to talk."

She looked at me harder then. "You seem
pale."

I couldn't be sure, but I had the vague impression that she took a certain mean pleasure from
the fact that I seemed pale, as if my being shaken
vindicated her somehow.

"Have a scotch?" she asked.

I realized that, having once asked Lydia for
scotch, I was doomed to drinking scotch with her
forever. On the other hand, scotch at that moment did not seem like a bad idea at all. I nodded,
and she led me toward the living room, regal on
her silver slippers.

On the way, apropos of nothing, she said, "I'm
just up from the pool."

"Ah," I said. Ridiculously, I was both deflated
and relieved to gather that her polka-dotted
undies were in fact a bathing suit. What the hell
difference did it make? Then again, it made a difference.

She glided to the wet bar and started making
drinks. I sat down in the armchair that was far-
thest from the AC vent. After a moment she delivered another of her heroic highballs. We clinked
glasses and she folded herself down onto the sectional.

Once she'd settled into a pose of suitable languor, she said, "So. You're checking in. Like a
good little detective."

The bantering tone again. The banter, the scotch—Lydia got cozy with a pattern and there she wanted to stay. Except the banter wasn't working for me now, had become an irritating habit I was bent on breaking. I leaned forward with my elbows on my knees. "Lydia, listen. You haven't hired me. I'm not working for you. I'm here to ask some questions. You're going to answer them."

She sipped her vodka and shot me a subtly infuriating look, the mock-impressed look that a woman gives a cocky boy when pretending to take him seriously. She wiggled her ass against the couch. "Ooh," she said, "we're masterful today."

I left that alone. "Someone's harassing me," I said. "Telling me to get lost. Which I would gladly do, except there's no place I can go. So I need to get this settled. What's in the pouch, Lydia?"

She shot me another of her coy and cool and goading looks, but this time I thought I saw just the narrowest little crack in it. Behind the courtesan's blitheness I sensed a hint of vacant desperation, a patch of something as dark and empty as a starless swath of midnight sky. She tried to cover it over with cuteness. "I thought it's the detective's job—"

I cut her off and sought to pry open that little chink I'd seen. "Your father was still fretting about it on his deathbed. That mean anything to you?"

Her only answer to that was a look that seemed intended to slice off the top of my head.

I went on. "So I doubt that it was only money. Dying people don't need cash. It was something more important than that. More important to a number of people. A woman put it in the safe. I'm betting that woman could only have been you. What was so important, Lydia?"

She held my gaze a moment, then dropped her eyes and rattled the ice cubes in her drink. For an instant this seemed a species of surrender, but quickly her face turned petulant, impatient, as though she were trying to convince us both that none of this was of real consequence; it was just a petty annoyance, hardly worth discussing. Then, into a scene that was already excruciating, she injected a note of the surreal. She gave her shoulders a bothered lift and said, "This top's a little damp. Excuse me."

She set down her vodka, leaned slightly forward, and with an impressive elasticity of limb, she reached behind herself, underneath her tunic, and undid the clasps of her strapless bra. Tension went out of the polka-dotted cloth, but the cups did not immediately fall away from her breasts. They clung for a moment, attached by heat or moisture or some more mysterious affinity, then fluttered down at last with the dreamy slowness of open parachutes. Tan lines appeared. Pale flesh billowed, swelling ripely before it tapered once again toward dark, emphatic nipples, which seemed to be the only part of Lydia that noticed the coldness of the room.

After a time she pulled the now-shapeless bit of cloth from underneath her tunic and dropped it on the coffee table. For a dizzy instant I was more fascinated by the empty garment than by her body. I stared at it with awe and terror, as though it were the hollowed pelt of an animal I had known when alive.

Struggling to hold my voice together, I said, "Listen, Lydia, you look great but it isn't going to work. I need to know what's in the pouch."

She reclaimed her drink, reclaimed, along with it, the goading tone. "Ask Mickey Veale."

"I'm asking you."

"Have you met him yet? Talked with him?"

"As a matter of fact I have. But—"

"And what'd you think of the fat bastard?"

I sighed. I did not want to be distracted by her boobs, and I did not want to be sidetracked by her relentless talk of Mickey Veale. Still, the question, her insistence on asking it, reminded me of a couple things. First, that there was something more than passingly sick in the relationship between the two of them, something that went beyond dislike to obsession; it suggested a case of adolescent thrall, in which miseries are linked, in which every wound is savored, every insult cataloged. Second, that I hadn't quite got around to sorting out my impressions of Veale. His largeness and his in-your-face manner made it difficult to see him in detail, to be confident of a few true things to say. But now, without really analyzing, I said, "Crude, crass, tries too hard. A buffoon." I surprised myself by adding, "And maybe sort of harmless in the end."

Did I really believe it? Or did I say it just to

tweak her? In any case, Lydia seemed genuinely affronted by the word. Her features all pushed forward on her face; a flush spread up her neck and down between her breasts. "Harmless! Pete, you just might be an idiot."

Very likely true, but neither here nor there. I sipped some scotch. I eased my shoulders and tried to make my voice more coaxing, less aggressive. "Lydia—why do you hate him so much?"

She stared at me. Her eyes seemed almost to throb, as though they were being pushed from behind. But the impulse toward candor, if that's what it was, didn't last long. Her mouth curled into a mordant and challenging smile; she tongued the edge of her glass. With a phony nonchalance she leaned far forward so that her breasts, diddled by gravity, seemed to float free of her torso, became separate from her, took on pendant and compelling lives of their own. She said, "You want to touch me?"

I chewed my lip. I said, "No. I mean yes. But I'm not going to. I need to know what's in the pouch."

She held my eyes. She pursed her lips into something between a pout and a sucking shape. She mimicked my tone. "You need to know what's in the pouch. You need to know why I hate Mickey Veale. I take it you've never been blackmailed."

This made me blink. It was a long deep blink that momentarily erased the world, and when my eyesight returned, nothing looked quite the way it had before. Blackmail? On top of murder, and smuggling, and Kenny Lukens' stupid larceny that had set all this in motion? The little universe in which I spent my days and nights seemed suddenly like one big ransacked room. Numbly, I said, "Mickey Veale is blackmailing you?"

Lydia reached up and cupped her breasts and gave them a little rub. "Did I say that, Pete? No, I didn't say that. Besides, you think he's harmless."

Like a drowning man I flailed after something to grab on to. "No," I said. "Blackmailing your father. It must go back that far."

Lydia pinched her nipples. They looked purple against her bright red fingernails. "Touch them, Pete. I want you to."

I said, "What's in the pouch, then—is it the payoff, or is it whatever it was Veale had on Lefty?"

Lydia sighed, and rustled her behind against the sofa, and abandoned her breasts, and went back to her drink. She took a reckless swallow then shot me a stare that was sardonic and desperate and held, perhaps, some shred of beaten hope.

"Ask your harmless friend," she said.

"For right now I'm asking you."

She ignored that. Her guard was up again and all she wanted was to taunt me. "Or are you too afraid?" she said. "Too afraid to touch me. Too afraid to ask your questions to anybody except a woman. Are you always such a coward, Pete?"

"I guess I am," I said, and rose to go.

Her insults dogged me as I went. I was gutless. I was sexless. I looked back once from the living room archway. Lydia's eyes were wide with fury and her body had hunched like she was throwing punches. All I could think of was a drowning swimmer who would flail and claw and fight off any chance of rescue.

27

If I'd been pale when I arrived at Lydia's, I was paler when I left.

Nothing was making sense to me. No, that's not true—certain things were beginning to fit together, I just didn't like where they were taking me. I'm basically lazy and I'm basically chicken—Lydia, damn her, had got that right. I'd wanted a quick and easy answer as to what the pouch contained, not another sordid wrinkle about blackmail. I'd been looking for a facile breakthrough that would get me out of danger, not some tangled hints that sucked me in still deeper. And the last thing I'd wanted was to be pushed into a confrontation with Mickey Veale.

Yet as I climbed onto my bike in the shadow of 2000 Atlantic, it was pretty clear that that's what needed to happen next.

Suddenly I had a bellyache. Maybe it was dread at the thought of sitting down with Veale, maybe it was the sludging up of little tubes and valves that occurs when sexual arousal goes too long unfulfilled. It seemed like twice a day I got sexed up and weirded out by Lydia, sexed up and shot down by Maggie. This could not be good for a guy's fragile plumbing.

I pedaled off, settling only gingerly on the hot and bouncing seat. I didn't know how to find Mickey Veale, but Paradise Watersports seemed the logical place to start. I headed across town toward the Hyatt.

Without really thinking about it, I took the shortcut through the cemetery. Once inside the fence, amid the croton bushes and the leaning headstones and the plastic flowers that the Cubans leave, I wished I hadn't. I couldn't help picturing Lefty Ortega, freshly cemented in his crypt. Morbidly I wondered how decomposed he'd be by now, what became of tumors when their victims had died. It was around five-thirty and still hot as hell; the slanting sun baked the unshaded walls of the mausoleums, and I wondered if bodies ever exploded in there. I pedaled faster till I was out the other side.

When I reached the harbor, I locked my bike and walked onto the dock where the Jet Ski concession was. I found the goofy kid with the lanyard around his neck. He went into his pitch like he'd never seen me before. To him I was just a tourist, after all, a wallet with a sunburn but no face.

"I was here yesterday," I reminded him.

He stalled at the part about how great sunset was. "Oh yeah," he lied. "I remember now. Ohio, right?"

"Jersey," I said. "Except I'm not. I'm from right here. And I need to speak with Mickey."

The kid stared at me. I couldn't tell if he was cautious or cagey or just plain dense. After a long moment I said, "So where is he?"

"I don't know."

"Where does he live? Does he have an office?"

"I don't know."

"He's your boss and he's a first-name kind of guy," I said. "I think you do."

The kid looked down at the water.

And then a strange thing happened. I found myself doing what a private eye does. Not posing, not pretending—doing it. I reached into a pocket and came up with a twenty. Folding it crisply, I slipped it to the kid between two fingers. When he took it I grabbed him by the wrist. Not real hard, just hard enough so that he'd pay attention. And sure enough, he told me that Mickey Veale mainly worked out of his condo at Harbor Watch.

So I pedaled off that way.

Harbor Watch was the fanciest of the developments crammed in recent years onto former navy property, and if it was true, as Ozzie Kimmel argued, that Key West had been divvied into fiefdoms, then it made perfect sense that Mickey Veale would live there. Cede the oceanfront to the Ortegas, keep the harbor side for himself. Fitting too was the reputation of Harbor Watch as the haunt of parvenus and millionaire snowbirds who didn't quite belong. Not more than six blocks from Duval Street, the place just didn't feel like part of the town; somehow the old grim military boundaries lived on in the imagination,

made the area feel more like a base than a neighborhood.

In any case, the Harbor Watch condos com-
manded drop-dead sunset views and, not surprisingly, as I learned from the rank of doorbells,
Mickey Veale had one of the primo top-floor
units. I rang and waited to be buzzed in.

Instead of a buzz I got the housekeeper, a
woman's voice with a heavy Spanish accent, asking who it was.

I announced myself.

"Who?" The tone made it clear I was nobody
to her.

I gave her my name again and said it was important.

"You wait one second please."

I waited. A schooner went by. Its sails turned
orange as they swiveled toward the sun.

"Meester Veale say he talk to you already."

"He's absolutely right. On that we agree. But I
need to talk with him again."

"Please, you wait."

Finally the buzzer buzzed. It sounded grudging
and resentful. I went upstairs and found the
condo door already open. The housekeeper was
standing in the doorway. She was wearing tight
pink shorts and had the tails of a lime-green shirt
tied against her midriff. Her high shoes gave a
pert tilt to her butt but didn't look ideal for vac-
uuming. She didn't say hello. She said, "Only a
few minutes, yes?"

I nodded and stepped past her. I hoped she had
other strengths than housekeeping, because the

place was basically a mess. Pictures, mostly nudes, hung crooked on the walls. Surfaces were littered with random stacks of paper. There was the oily smell of a stove that needed cleaning.

After a moment Mickey Veale emerged from a hallway. He was a bit of a mess himself. He was wearing enormous, tentlike khaki shorts and a black tank top that was not equal to the task of containing him. Flesh and tufts of hair overflowed the armholes; the crater of his navel could be discerned through the stretched cloth across his belly. He was barefoot; he left pale footprints on the blond wood floor, and the footprints were surrounded by misty auras like breath on glass. He said, "What is it, Amsterdam?"

I told him I had a few more questions.

He said, "I'm pretty busy."

I lied and said that I was too. "So let's not waste time."

He looked at me a moment and sucked his teeth. He was different today, but I couldn't pinpoint just how. Without the casino audience, he seemed less alert, less energized, less bent on performing. His legs were very pale, and this made him seem faintly pathetic. He seemed weary and burdened—but burdened by what? Guilt? Remorse? Or just the banal pressures of trying to run businesses in a town where hardly anybody cared? Resigned, he gestured for me to follow him.

We padded down a corridor, his damp feet sucking at the floor. He turned into a den that was chaotic but had a stunning view. He sat down heavily in a rolling chair behind a desk strewn with brochures and invoices and poker chips.

I got distracted by the sunset through the window. The sky was pulsing yellow and the water of the harbor was a copper color; boats trailed chevrons that foamed up white and then turned a patina green. Beyond the harbor and before the Gulf was Sunset Key. Its awnings gleamed and its yellow sand twinkled, and the truth was it didn't look like a Florida Key at all. Florida Keys are shallow domes of muck; the former Tank Island had been sculpted into a Caribbean fantasy of dunes and berms and bulkheads. It was fake but you couldn't say it wasn't pretty in the thick red light. I gestured toward the panorama. "Helluva spot, Mickey."

Dryly he said, "I thought we weren't wasting time."

The comment cut short my rhapsodizing, and I sat on the edge of a straight wooden chair. Wasting time or no, I took a moment to study my host. He had broken capillaries in his eyelids and a tense bulge at the hinge of his jaw. A man with an awful, gnawing secret. Unless it was only my impatience and my fear that made me think so. I said, "Okay, Mickey, then I'll get right to the point. Why were you blackmailing Lefty Ortega?"

He didn't answer immediately. First his neck seemed to thicken with a surge of rising blood, then his face darkened with a flush that was not red but bluish. It dawned on me that here was a

guy who would die of stroke. At last he said,
"What!"

"I think you heard the question."

He shook his head and tried to smile. The re-
sult was toothy and grotesque. He said, "That's
ridiculous."

"Maybe. But it would explain some things that
are sort of murky otherwise."

"Like what would it explain?" he challenged.

"Like, for instance, why Lefty, on his deathbed,
was paranoid that I'd been sent by somebody
named Mickey. Like, why Lydia hates your guts
and is always siccing me on you, but is too afraid
of you to ever make it clear just why."

Veale had folded his hands and was listening
carefully, as if he were his own jury. "It's my fault
Lydia's a scattered cokehead?"

Cokehead? She hadn't been hopped up when I
was there—or had she? That's not the kind of
thing I'm very good at noticing. I just marked it
down as one more case of Veale and the Ortegas
saying nasty things about each other at every opportunity.

"It's not your fault that Lydia's a nut," I said.
"But maybe it is your fault two guys are dead."

He squeezed his hands together then. I saw the
fingertips whiten. He said, "Be careful, Amsterdam. You're saying crazy things."

There was a pause. The sun must have hit the
horizon or a last low cloud because the light
dropped quickly in the room. It lost its ruddy
color and turned grainy. I realized now how reckless I was being. The feeling scared me but sud-

denly I liked it. I said, "Okay, then let's talk about something else."

Looking weary, put-upon, dyspeptic, Mickey Veale waited for what the something else would be.

I glanced at the now-lavender window and said, "Let's talk about smuggling."

"Smuggling?"

"Jet Skis at four in the morning," I said, and I told him what I'd witnessed from the deck of the *Lucky Duck*—the rooster tails, the warning flashes.

Veale was unimpressed. "Two lunatics out for a joyride," he said dismissively, "while a guy happens to be fumbling with the light switch in the head."

"Or," I countered, "two couriers bringing something small enough to carry on a Jet Ski. Which would probably make it small enough to fit into a bank-deposit pouch which, in turn, would fit in Lefty's safe."

Veale siowly shook his enormous, flubbery face. "You're reaching, Amsterdam. There's nothing there."

I glanced down at my lap, tried to juice up my momentum. "Last night I asked you what other businesses you had to give Lefty a piece of. You wouldn't tell me. You wouldn't tell me because it was this smuggling deal."

"Wrong, Amsterdam. Totally wrong."

Weary as he sounded, he also sounded cocky now, combative in a passive way, untouchable.

This made me mad, and I longed to punch at least a small hole in his serenity. I said, "Listen, Mickey, you feel pretty pleased that the local cops are in your pocket. That's obvious. But smuggling—that's federal. You think these clowns can protect you from the feds?"

There was a heartbeat's silence; then, to my surprise, Mickey Veale laughed. It was a bitter, snorting, percussive laugh without the smallest trace of amusement in it. He said, "You think the cops are in my pocket? Let me tell you something, Amsterdam. You don't know shit. You know worse than shit. You're the kind of half-smart guy who understands things just enough to get everything exactly wrong. So listen up. I'm not a blackmailer. I've never murdered anyone or had them murdered. So far. But you're getting to be more than an annoyance. So stay the fuck out of my face. Do we understand each other?"

It killed me to give him the last word, but a death threat is not an easy thing to answer, and the truth is, I couldn't speak just then. I forced myself to stare at him a moment. I wanted my eyes to tell him that, okay, I was through for right now but I wasn't backing down; I'm not sure how persuasively they conveyed the message. I drummed my fingers lightly on his desk, then stood up silently and turned to go.

I left his dimming office and walked down the corridor. Along the way I wondered why it was that in all these interviews—with Veale, with Lydia, even with the cops—I felt from moment to moment that I was doing fine, that I was winning, yet by the end it could not be clearer that I'd been outflanked, I'd lost.

I moved across the living room toward the door. The housekeeper with the bare midriff was leaning sultrily across a counter, her elbows spread around a magazine. There was a feather duster next to her, but as far as I could tell she hadn't dusted squat.

28

"He's lying," said Maggie. "Of course he's lying."

We were sitting on the deck of her trawler, speaking softly in the thickening dusk. I'd gone to Redmond's after leaving Mickey Veale's, and following a spasm of indecision in which I literally rode around in circles for a while, doing doughnuts around the grand horseshoe entrance to Harbor Watch. My mind was cluttered. I was afraid. But the vector of my fear had changed. For a while it had pointed, so to speak, at my chest, pushing me back and down into my chair, counseling retreat. Now it poked me from behind, goading me forward on feet that tingled. Make no mistake—it was still naked, selfish fear and I still felt like a coward. But it had somehow gotten through to me that it didn't matter how I felt, it mattered what I did.

I needed to talk with someone, air things out. The time just after sunset is a lonely hour anyway, and suddenly I felt very alone. Who could I talk to but Maggie? Even though, face it, I knew her only slightly. Such was the life I'd been living.

Still, I felt lighter with a destination, and pedaled almost jauntily to the boatyard. Straddling my bike, I called up to her, and she emerged from the companionway and out into the cockpit. It seemed she hadn't been home for very long. She was wearing the baggy pants she always pulled on after yoga class. Her leotard still seemed slightly damp with sweat; there was a faint zag of moisture like a lightning bolt between her breasts.

She unfurled the rope ladder for me. I climbed it and faced her. She looked at me and her eyes pulled down at the outside corners. "Pete," she said, "are you okay? You look terrible."

I tried to make a joke of it. I said, "You know, you're the second person who's told me that today."

Maggie didn't laugh, and I realized that it wasn't funny. Something let go around my solar plexus, and I felt that I could easily just sit down and cry. I did sit down, on a makeshift bench there in the cockpit, but instead of bawling I launched into a manic and probably none-too-clear account of all that had happened in the last day or so—in the time since Maggie had put her clothes back on and taken her much-desired self out of my backyard. I told her about my Jet Ski ride and the night aboard the *Lucky Duck*. About the rats in my pool and my most recent chat with Lydia. About my second sit-down with Mickey Veale.

At the end, Maggie blew out a long slow exhalation—what, in class, she called a cleansing breath. And that's when she said of course Veale was a liar. She said it with a matter-of-fact firmness that amazed me. The woman was a yoga teacher—spiritual, ethereal. And yet in that moment she seemed far tougher and more realistic than me. She'd embraced the simple, ugly truth that people lie, that lying was part of how the world proceeded. She said, "What's he going to do—say, Yeah, I'm a blackmailer? Yeah, I'm a smuggler? Yeah, I had those people killed?"

I blinked at her. She was backlit by the floodlights that were just coming on around the boatyard. Her short hair seemed downy in silhouette, but the outline of her shoulders and arms was very crisp and definite.

She said, "He's the one who had the rats thrown in your pool. Don't you think?"

"I don't know what I think."

She bit her upper lip, the nub of it I'd felt the time we kissed. Then she said, "We have to find out what he's smuggling."

It took a moment for this to register. Then I said, "We?"

"The Jet Skis—you said it was around four when they came around?"

"Maggie, listen—"

"I could borrow a skiff—"

"Forget about it, Maggie. I'm not getting you involved."

"I got *you* involved, remember?"

Weakly, I said, "Kenny Lukens got me involved. Besides, that's different."

"Why's it different, Pete? What's different about it?"

"Because it's my job to get involved," I said. I

said it without taking time to think; I was shocked to hear the words come from my mouth. They hung a moment in the muggy air.

Maggie started in again. "I'll borrow a skiff and a good pair of binoculars. We'll anchor near the gambling boat—"

"*You* borrow a skiff," I said. "*I'll* take it out and watch."

"I'm going too."

"No, you're not."

There was a standoff. In the midst of it we heard electricity buzzing in the nearby pylons, hulls chafing and squeaking against the wharves of Toxic Triangle. Stars got bolder as the gleam in the western sky finally gave up the ghost.

At last Maggie said, "I want to kiss you, Pete. Can I kiss you?"

Before I could answer, her lips were against mine, soft and parted and just slightly salty. I reached up and held her face. My palms cradled her cheeks, my fingers traced her jawline and the tender hollows beneath her ears. We ventured deeper into each other's mouths and at some point we were standing, pressed together at the thighs and the loins and the waist and the ribs. I felt the breath she pulled down deep into her belly. I felt the weight of her breasts as they squeezed against me, the moist and splendid channel between them. The kiss became a kind of trance, a small and perfect vacation, and in the midst of it I knew we would be lovers then and there, that we would waft down into Maggie's dollhouse of a cabin and find a cozy place to roll and join, to surge and sweat against each other as though on piles of hot leaves, to make the world stop if only for an hour.

Except it didn't happen.

Maggie pulled back from the kiss at last, her withdrawal slow but firm against the longing pressure of my arms. Our faces still close, she lifted an index finger and traced my lips. "There's a lot to do," she whispered.

I reached up and took her hand and nibbled the fleshy place beneath her thumb. "There's time," I whispered back.

She ignored that. "I've got to shower and change. Track down a skiff. Find binoculars. Can you meet me at the dinghy dock at midnight?"

I sighed and nodded, dreading another sleepless night out on the water. "But I'm going out there alone."

"We'll see."

"We won't see."

She shushed me with another kiss, a brief but fond and easy one such as longtime lovers give each other before climbing out of bed. Then she turned me by the shoulders, pointed me away from the salvation of her cabin and toward the rope ladder that overhung the transom.

Reluctantly, I moved to it and started climbing down. At the bottom I craned my neck and stared up for just one yearning moment, a suitor exiled to the shadows beneath the balcony. Then I climbed onto my bike and pedaled off.

As I went I reviewed the kiss, relived it. An extraordinary kiss, everything a kiss should be. But

I hadn't gone more than fifty feet when the memory of it grew clouded and ambiguous. Bumping over the coral gravel of the boatyard, my confused and thwarted loins ached worse than ever. Tendrils of pain climbed up toward my stomach, carrying with them an insidious question: Why had she kissed me *just then*?

It was an odd moment to embrace, after all. We'd been discussing blackmail, murder. Maggie had been not just tough-minded, but almost hard and cynical in her shrugging off of Mickey Veale's denials. And it had been her idea to send me out into the ocean in a tiny craft in the middle of the night. True, she volunteered to come along, pretended, even, to insist on it. But she must have known that I'd say no to that, that her clamoring to accompany me would only strengthen my resolve to go alone. Alone, where there was nowhere to hide and no witness to see, within easy reach of an enemy who'd just threatened me to my face.

I thought about the kiss, about the salt and raspberry flavor of Maggie's mouth, the texture of her flesh against me. If the kiss, and the promise of more to come, was, by some wild and appalling chance, part of a plan to set me up, I couldn't imagine how she might have done it better.

29

At home, I thought of napping but was far too wired even to imagine keeping my head down on the pillow.

So I cracked a bottle of old-growth zinfandel, laid out a plate of crackers and pâté, and settled into the music room. If I couldn't stop the world with lovemaking, at least maybe I could keep it at bay behind thick walls and a heavy door with felt-lined edges.

I put on some Schubert—the string quintet that has two cellos. There is nothing more serene than Schubert; he never fails to calm me. Or he never had until that evening, when the gorgeous melodies and effortless transitions were wasted on me. Worse than wasted—in some crazy way they pissed me off. How could he bushwhack through such complexity and emerge without a scratch, in a triumph of grace and balance? There was something smug about it, something of the African explorer returning from the heart of darkness with his mustache trimmed and the crisp crease still centered in his khakis. So I yanked that disc and switched to Brahms, who

oscillates between the poles of rage and heart-
break, with few punier or more resigned emo-
tions in between.

The wine was good, the music was great, but
still the time went slowly. Nine o'clock. Ten. I
corked what was left of the zin and made some
coffee. Then I thought of something that made
my fingers itch. I went into the living room and
moved a watercolor of a mangrove islet and
opened up the wall safe behind it. My unfired pistol was the only thing in the little metal box suspended between two studs.

A cup of coffee in one hand, I laid the other
across the gun. It was neither warm nor cold, but
there was something clammy in the way it felt. I
lifted it out into the light, felt its falsely reassuring weight. Stainless steel, it hadn't tarnished,
though there was a handsome gray patina on the
pebbled butt. The gun was loaded, and reloading
had at one time been explained to me—something about a magazine that snapped into the
handle. Then there was a sequence that you went
through to get the trigger ready. My tongue
poised at the corner of my mouth, I made a weak
try at remembering, at tracing the logic of levers
and springs. But my heart wasn't in it. I just
didn't like guns; I never would. Life or death, I'd
be the guy who froze and couldn't shoot, and felt
like a sucker for not shooting.

I put the pistol back into the safe. Spun the lock
and put the watercolor back in place. And felt,
once again, a compelling need to wash my hands.

By now it was eleven. The wine in my veins was breaking down to sugar, the caffeine was kicking in, and I was getting very jumpy. I took a lukewarm shower and got ready to go out for the night.

I put on fresh shorts and a clean shirt and a cotton sweater. I unlocked my bike from the palm I always chain it to, wiped the tiny beads of condensation from the seat, and climbed aboard.

I'd gone three or four blocks when I began to suspect that I was being followed.

The suspicion took shape only gradually, deriving from an oddly constant spray of headlights that fanned out from some vague but nearly steady point behind me. Their glow stuck to the shrubs on either side of the street I rode on; when I turned, the lights raked almost audibly against white picket fences, as though a child were dragging a stick along the planks.

I swallowed, and kept pedaling, and told myself not to speed up, not to panic. I'd only gone a little distance, after all, and I was on a not-untraveled route that led downtown. Then again, it was nearly midnight on a Tuesday out of season. Houses were dark. Locusts were the loudest sound. Little was moving except for cats, scratching their flanks against warm curbstones.

Vigilant now, I began to steer a more eccentric course. Down narrow vine-choked lanes that tourists wouldn't know. Along the curved perimeter of the west side of the cemetery. The headlights stayed with me, slicing through the vines, panning dully across the mausoleums. My mouth went dry. My churning knees got stiff, and I wrestled with the question of whether I should turn around and face my pursuer.

At a stop sign, I finally did—though without resolve, just peeking meekly back across my shoulder. All I saw was a dark generic car, a Chevy or a Chrysler or a Ford, discreetly crawling a block behind. I waited; it slowed still more. It slipped beneath a street lamp, revealing nothing but a windshield tinted a sinister purple. The car stopped altogether now, and idled, as though its driver would wait all night for me to carry on. Or as if he was taunting me, daring me to approach.

I didn't have the nerve. I sucked a breath and started pedaling again. Then, with guilt and horror, I realized that I was leading my pursuer straight to Redmond's Boatyard, straight to Maggie—who, if she wasn't part of some grotesque conspiracy, was an unselfish, almost saintly friend.

Needing badly to believe it, I told myself that no harm had yet been done. So far, I could have been headed almost anywhere—Duval Street for a beer, Mallory Square to hear some old songs badly played. Toxic Triangle was only one of many destinations in the extended arc of my meandering. Still, at the next corner I turned away from the harbor. I started making random lefts and rights, launched upon an itinerary as aimless as Key West life itself. The dark car stayed with me, harassing, although its driver had to know by now that I was leading him to nowhere.

Finally I lost him in a lane behind the library, a stanchioned dead end for cars but with a narrow rocky path that bicycles could slip through. I clunked along the coral knobs for a hundred yards or so, then stopped in the still and fragrant no-man's-land between two streets, a tiny patch of jungle in the midst of town.

Overgrown, it was primordially dark in there. Straddling my bike, I caught my breath and listened to the crickets and the toads, heard lizards and small snakes slithering under brittle leaves. For a moment I was pleased with my resourcefulness in finding this haven; then all at once I realized it was the dumbest place I could have stopped. It was visible from nowhere. The going was slow and essentially blind; a killer on foot had every chance of overtaking a bike that had skidded on a root or crashed against a stump. I'd cornered myself. My heart began to pound. Did I only imagine that I heard the dry click of a car door, the crunch of hard shoes on gravel, the swipe of undergrowth at pants legs?

I jumped on my pedals and took off. Straining to see the thin and rugged coral swath between the vines and shrubs, I bounced and leaned and fishtailed. Thorns slashed at my arms and shins; spiderwebs stuck to my face; my scalp was grazed by an overhanging limb. I humped till I reached the alley that gave onto Elizabeth Street, then slowed just enough to pluck the burrs out of my sweater and shake the bugs out of my hair.

Mostly confident that I'd shaken my pursuer, I still took a long and circumspect meander to Redmond's Boatyard.

It was nearly twelve-thirty by the time I'd locked my bike and was jogging toward the dinghy dock. I didn't see Maggie right away. That's because she wasn't standing on the dock, but sitting in a dinghy. Waving up to me, she said, "I was getting worried."

Worried. The word seemed oddly mild. How about scared shitless? "Sorry," I said, "I was followed."

"Followed?" She narrowed her eyes and looked at me more closely in the ugly pink light from the security floods. "Your wrists," she said, "your legs. You're bleeding."

It was true. The thorns and sedges had got me pretty good. I was crosshatched with long and shallow cuts, the kind that bulge and pucker with lines of blood that stop just shy of overflowing. They didn't hurt, just itched. I shrugged them off and pretended to be calm. I don't think I pretended very well. I couldn't stop my feet from shuffling. My throat felt constricted, and my voice didn't sound exactly right.

"Who followed you?" she said.

My shoulders lifted to my ears. "Veale's people? Lydia's people? I don't know."

We looked at each other. It was a caring, comradely look and I guess it should have bucked me up. In fact it only multiplied my misgivings, reminded me how out of my depth I was, how trapped. Too late, I realized that of course I should have brought my gun—what kind of idiot liberal does this sort of thing unarmed? Not bringing it was the fundamental blunder of a person simply not up to the job. I was inadequate, and inadequacy now cast a sickly pall on everything.

I frowned down at the boat Maggie was sitting in, the boat in which I was supposed to track down smugglers. A pitiably inadequate craft. Maybe ten feet long, made of the same cheap galvanized aluminum as garbage cans. The seats were metal slabs with neither backs nor cushions. There was no steering wheel, just a stem on the ancient, sun-beaten engine. The tub's forlornness seemed to match my own. Masking desperation with wryness, I said, "On television they use speedboats."

"We're a cheap boatyard, not a yacht club," Maggie said. "Climb aboard."

"I'll wait till you get out."

"I'm not getting out," she said.

"Maggie—" I began, though I understood by now that I would lose this argument, that I'd already lost it hours before. Secretly, I was thrilled, of course. My nerves were shot. I wanted company. Still, I launched into some mumbled protests.

Maggie didn't wait to hear them. She swiveled toward the stern, vented the gas tank, and squeezed the priming ball. After three hard pulls on the starter cord, the motor grudgingly turned over.

Gratefully defeated, my small wounds stretching and throbbing as I bent, I clambered down into the skiff and uncleated the skinny line that held us to the dock. I pushed us back; we lightly clunked against the other dinghies. Maggie pointed us toward the broad entrance of the Bight at Toxic Triangle, and, preposterously, we headed out to spy on the presumptive killers aboard the *Lucky Duck*.

30

Night on the water with Maggie.

Hard to imagine anything sexier. I could envision whispered confidences and languid kisses beneath a spray of shooting stars that mirrored the mystic flash of ocean phosphorescence. The dampness of the predawn air rendered incubator-warm by the mingled heat of limbs and hollows . . .

But in the actual event, circumstances challenged sensuality. I was bleeding and afraid. Maggie seemed solemn. As we scudded across the resting harbor, our motor sent up a hideous whine that jangled the nerves and obliterated conversation. The dinghy vibrated like a beaten gong; my backside soon went numb against the trembling of the metal seat. At the harbor mouth, currents collided, setting up a small but steep and surging chop that rocked the skiff and made the engine labor. I gripped the gunwales and watched Maggie steer. She was wearing roomy drawstring pants, a loose sweater with billowing sleeves. A small muscle was twitching in her neck.

Beyond the harbor the currents diffused and the ocean went improbably flat. With the growing distance, Key West, already small, seemed ever dinkier and more insignificant, its buildings thin and frail as matchbooks, its street lamps faint as dying candles. Back to the east, a red smudge on the horizon marked the place where a waning moon would soon be rising. Huge in the south, Scorpio crawled across the sky, dragging its fearsome tail.

We putted along for what must have been an hour. A pink moon came up, pocked and gauzy, more than a crescent, less than a half. My mind went as numb as my rear end.

Finally Maggie brought the engine down to idle and pointed beyond our bow. I swiveled and saw the *Lucky Duck*, perhaps a third of a mile farther out. A chartreuse gleam came from its portholes. "I don't think we should go closer," Maggie said. "Go ahead and drop the anchor. Don't throw it— ease it down."

Her tone, its certainty, made me careful to do as I was told. The anchor settled slowly, as though falling through Jell-O. Maggie cut the motor.

The skiff stopped vibrating and the night went magnificently quiet. Quieter than silence. Wavelets licked at the hull. Now and then a faint laugh or a cough or the ring of coins came across the water from the *Lucky Duck*. But somehow these ghostly sounds did not disturb the quiet; rather, they pointed up the vastness and the texture of it. It was a velvet quiet, an embracing quiet. It muffled everything except the present moment in the present place. Things finally felt sexy after all.

Maggie scuttled forward and sat down next to me. The boat rocked with every lean and gesture; we realized that we couldn't move much. But our bodies touched at the hip and at the outsides of our thighs. I put my arm around her back. She rested her head against my shoulder. Her hair had taken on the salt tang of the ocean.

For a long while we just sat there, sharing warmth along our flanks, not speaking. We vaguely watched the gambling boat. Through our fatigued eyes and with the limitless expanse behind it, it seemed at moments insubstantial, painted on a backdrop. I felt time passing, and was reminded that time isn't just an empty bowl in which events are mixed. It's a thing unto itself, has a flavor and a weight, and as it passes it drags a breeze as soft and melancholy as the memory of everything you've ever lost.

Maggie nestled closer up against me, whispered, "Wonderful out here."

I squeezed her waist and nodded.

The late moon climbed and whitened. A jackpot on the *Lucky Duck* was announced by a flat and trivial tinkling.

A while later Maggie turned her face up toward me, kissed me underneath my jaw. "Why do I like you, Pete?" she said. "I don't know anything about you."

I ran my fingers up and down her amazing spine. "Maybe that's exactly why," I said. Then I added, "But hey, you know some things. You know I'm the worst detective in the world. You know I hate to get mixed up in other people's problems."

"That's what you say, but here you are. I can't figure it out."

"I can't either."

Stars wheeled. A big fish or a manta ray trailed green-gold streamers just beneath the surface.

Time breathed in and out. Maggie gently touched the dry cuts on my hands. I found this wildly intimate and maybe just a little bit perverse.

"Tell me about your life before," she said.

"Before?"

"Before Key West."

I sighed. I stalled. I didn't want to talk about it. Not that I was being strong and silent. Just the opposite. I was afraid that if I started talking I wouldn't stop, that I'd be sucked into a whirlpool of whining and regretting, launched upon a litany of rancid old frustrations and ill-digested disappointments. "What's to tell?" I dodged. "It was a pretty standard life."

"Always lived alone?" she prompted.

I felt the rasping birth of a laugh I knew would come out bitter. It would have been rudely out of place in the empty and accepting night, and I tried my best to choke it back. "Basically," I said. "Especially for the six years I was married."

"That bad?"

"Not all of it, no," I said. "For a while it was pretty nice, in fact. But it got kind of uncomfortable once my wife made up her mind I was a failure."

Maggie straightened up a bit. I felt sympathy

and indignation in her posture. "Why'd she think that?"

"Because I was."

"I don't believe you."

I looked down at the water. I wiped mist off the gunwale. Then I said, "You know what? I didn't believe it either. I thought I was a success that hadn't happened yet. I really believed that. Slow learner. Late bloomer. But I'd get there. I knew I would. I believed it for years. I really thought I'd do it."

Maggie's eyes were wide, her face a pattern of gleam and shadow in the moonlight. She said, "Do what?"

Right. I hadn't explained, had I? But Maggie's simple question made me shy. A nervous laugh escaped me. To my great surprise, the laugh did not sound bitter. Baleful and nostalgic, maybe, but almost peaceful, almost resigned. Was it possible that old poisons were dissipating, old defeats losing their sting? How did that happen? Was it the velvet quiet of the ocean, or the sweeping breeze that time trailed like a gown? Or was it Maggie? Was it possible that this woman was not just lithe and supple but could be really good for me? "You know," I said, "it's so typical, such a cliché, I feel silly telling you."

"Nothing wrong with feeling silly."

For an instant I thought this was just a quip, then I realized it was far more than that. It was a credo, a statement of a kind of wiggy and unjudging faith. *Nothing wrong with feeling silly.* A giddy sense of freedom made my hairline crawl. Relief flowed in the form of a flushed heat that came streaming past my collar. I belched out a pure ecstatic childish laugh and decided, what the hell, I'd go on with my silly tale.

Except I didn't get to.

By the time I was ready to speak again, a new sound had started scratching at the quiet. It was a high nattering buzz, faint and distant but becoming less so.

Maggie and I stiffened like hunting dogs. Scanning the ocean, we saw nothing but wreaths of vapor doing a weird slow boil on the surface, rising up to meet faint damp curtains that weren't quite clouds. But small craft were approaching; there was no doubt of it. We felt more than heard them as they thumped and whined, tugging at and wrinkling the carpet of the sea.

A minute passed, two minutes, then finally we saw the rooster tails, tinselly silver in the moonlight, cresting and dissolving like the spray from city fountains. There was a pair of them, as I thought there'd been the night before. They were approaching from the east—from the direction of Key Largo, Miami, the Bahamas, a million other places. Maggie reached down and grabbed the binoculars she'd borrowed.

I watched the *Lucky Duck* to see if there would be some signal, a flash of warning or of welcome. But tonight there was no beacon, and the Jet Skis kept approaching. Two hundred yards or so from the mother ship, they slowed to idle speed. The rooster tails subsided; the craft rocked with the last of their momentum. The drivers, as far as I could tell, were wearing short-sleeved and short-legged wet suits; the big plastic zippers glinted in the moonlight. Their goggles did too, and made them look unearthly.

The Jet Skis edged around the stern of the gambling boat and floundered there a moment, motors softly burping. I realized I was squeezing the gunwale of the skiff, sharp aluminum biting deep into my fingers. They were about to pass off the smuggled goods. I was about to witness it.

Maggie handed me the binoculars; I pressed them to my exhausted eyes. The glasses brought me closer but also exaggerated motion—every wavelet, every lean. The image blurred and bounced; I struggled to hold steady, expecting to see . . . what? I guess I expected pouches. Pouches like the one that Kenny Lukens died for, produced from mysterious compartments in the innards of the Jet Skis.

But in fact there were no pouches. In fact there was no handoff. What actually happened was something altogether different and totally befuddling.

The Jet Skis idled until a hinged panel was lowered from the transom of the *Lucky Duck*. The panel became a platform hovering barely above the surface of the water. One at a time the Jet Skis bumped up against the platform and were yanked aboard by a thick silhouette, a figure shorter and more muscular than that of Mickey Veale. The Jet Skis, their drivers—everything vanished into the belly of the gambling ship. All that was left was a faintly roiled piece of ocean with some dying eddies in it.

Baffled, disbelieving, I kept on watching. After a moment some boards creaked faintly; a winch groaned as chain links grated. The platform lifted once again, the transom of the boat sealed off, and it was as if nothing whatsoever had transpired.

I lowered the binoculars, let out the breath I'd been holding.

I looked at Maggie. Maggie looked at me. The letdown and bewilderment were all there in the glance we shared. We didn't even need to shrug.

31

We sat there awhile longer, unwilling to accept that nothing more would happen, that there'd be no bigger payoff for our numb butts and our cramped legs and our sleeplessness. But time breathed by, and nothing happened, and there was no bigger payoff.

Eventually Maggie said, "Head in?" But it wasn't really a question and she was already moving back to start the engine when she said it.

The skiff rocked as she yanked the starter cord. The flywheel clattered, gas exploded in the cylinder, but the motor didn't catch. She pulled again, and then again. The groaning of the piston and the splutter of exhaust grew louder with each try, and I started getting paranoid that we were making too much noise. I could not afford to be seen out here; I could not afford to get caught annoying Mickey Veale again. True, our dinghy was a mere speck on the water, with a low profile and no lights whatsoever. But we'd found the Jet Skis in the moon glow; anybody with binoculars could easily find us if he had a reason to look in our direction. I felt my stomach tightening with each abortive grind and pop; I kept expecting to be raked with a searchlight from the gambling boat.

But the light didn't come, and at last the old engine turned over. With my back stiff and arms weak from fatigue and inactivity, I raised the anchor, and we veered away from the *Lucky Duck* and slowly headed back toward land.

Subdued by disappointment, we stayed silent for a time. Then, apropos of nothing, Maggie said, "Wet suits. Goggles."

"What about 'em?"

"Not necessary," she said, "unless they were really covering some distance."

"Like how much distance?"

Maggie couldn't specify, and I think we both knew we were grasping, pretending to some insight that would make this errand seem to have been worthwhile. But in truth the errand was a washout. We were supposed to learn what Mickey Veale was smuggling. We were supposed to figure out if it could somehow be connected to a blackmail scheme aimed at the Ortegas. But we'd sat there all night and figured out zilch. How could we learn what Veale was smuggling on the Jet Skis if he swallowed up the whole damn Jet Ski?

Sulking, we continued in. The first hint of day appeared in the east. It was extremely undramatic. The black sky turned purple and pushed up from the horizon like a fat man struggling to lift himself from bed. Stars flickered and went out. Off in the distance, Key West slept under the powdery orange blanket of its streetlights.

As the purple was taking on its first tinge of dark red, Maggie said above the clatter of the motor, "But you never finished your story."

"Hm?"

"Your life before," she said. "What you were almost a success at."

I puckered up my face and shook my head. I didn't see the point of resuming that conversation. I half regretted having started it, though I couldn't say exactly why.

"Oh come on," coaxed Maggie, "don't get all tight and cool again."

Tight and cool? I'd never thought of myself as tight and cool. I was just plain tired. Tired and gloomy and afraid. Besides, there are things you can whisper into a velvet quiet that you wouldn't shout above the ugly whining of an outboard engine.

Was that enough excuses?

"Pete," she said, "it isn't fair. You can't just break off in the middle."

I had to laugh at that. She puts her clothes back on after sitting naked by my pool and showing me her breasts, and *I* can't break off in the middle? Plus there was another reason that the comment struck me bleakly funny. I said, "I *always* broke off in the middle. Why do you think I failed?"

"Stop saying you failed." Then she added, "Failed at what?"

I squeezed my knees. I blinked toward the sky. Mauve seams showed now between steely slabs of cloud; even their wan light was enough to hurt my eyes. I was worn down, nerves abraded, slaphappy. Finally I said, "Okay, okay, what I failed at, what I was trying to do . . . I was trying to be a writer."

"What?"

Had I choked on the humiliating word, or was Maggie forcing me, for some therapeutic or sadistic reason, to repeat the galling and preposterous admission? I said it again. It sounded brassy and mocking in the vacant twilight.

Maggie said, "I knew it!"

"Then why'd you have to ask?"

She didn't answer that. She said, "Were you already rich by then?"

"I'm not rich," I said. "And that's a really gauche question."

"It's not gauche. It's direct."

"Well, the direct answer is that I was basically broke. The money I made, that happened later."

"So you were living off your wife?"

"Christ, Maggie—"

"No value judgment," she said. "I'm just trying to understand. She supported you?"

I blew air past my gums and vaguely wondered how I'd fallen into this ambush of a chat. Resigned, I said, "She was a lawyer. Made good money, liked the idea of having an artsy type in the family. Made her feel unconventional, I guess. But the novelty wore off."

"So she left?"

I nodded. I hadn't blamed her then and I didn't blame her now. True, her leaving stung me, shook me, but that had more to do with pride than love.

Maggie paused but wouldn't quit. She said, "So what kind of writer are you?"

"*Was* I." I scratched behind my ear. "I guess I'd have to say I was the kind of writer who never quite finished anything. Clever beginnings, interesting middles, then nothing."

"Couldn't figure out the ending?"

"Nah, it wasn't that. Maybe some days I told myself it was—but it wasn't. Any idiot can figure out an ending. Finishing is something else."

"What else?"

"Finishing takes . . . what does it take? Conviction. Confidence. Takes believing that you've earned it."

"And you didn't think you'd earned it?"

I just shrugged to that.

"How come?"

"If I knew that . . ." I began, then abruptly broke off. If I knew that, *what*?

I pushed out my lips and looked across the water. We were nearing the jetty at Fort Zack. Currents lifted a magenta chop. Channel markers flashed red and green. After a moment Maggie said, "Maybe finishing is just a habit."

"I wouldn't know."

"The conviction," she said. "The confidence. Maybe they come after. You finish something, *then* they're there."

I gave a noncommittal shrug. I wasn't sure I got it. The paradox struck me as a little glib, a little yogalike. Frankly, I found myself irritated. In some perverse way, I cherished my failings; I'd lived with them a long time, was used to them in the way people get used to pets that smell. I sort of resented the idea of someone blithely stepping in and disinfecting them.

I didn't have long to brood on this, because as we scudded through the harbor entrance, the shock of tropical daybreak made everything start over. Low clouds sundered like a cracking egg, and all at once the naked sun was there, orange yellow, flinging spiky rays up toward the zenith and out across the water, so bright, hot, and instantly sovereign that in a heartbeat it became hard to remember that night had ever been. A puff of breeze that seemed to be the sun's own breath bumped the sailboats on their moorings. On land, blank windows flashed suddenly silver; flat black palms turned green and animate and shook their heads.

We were opposite Tank Island—excuse me, Sunset Key. Virgin daylight put a sharp gleam on the enclave's stamped tin roofs, and a jewellike sparkle in its creamy yellow sand. Cool blue shadows stretched back from its contrived, imported dunes—and all at once I noticed something; or, to put it more precisely, something I'd been noticing for days finally ripened into meaning. I'd noticed it when I'd pulled my rented Jet Ski up onto the extended foreshore; I'd noticed it as I took in the view from Mickey Veale's study. Now, in the sharp and probing light of daybreak, it could hardly have been clearer: This was nothing like a natural Florida shoreline. True, Tank Island had been man-made to begin with, but it had been piled up from what was *there* and then been left alone. Whereas the real estate of Sunset Key had been designed, invented, tampered with, reshaped.

Pointing, voice pinched, I said to Maggie, "That whole damn beach has been moved."

I said it in the tone reserved for deep, original discovery. Maggie's response was deflatingly matter-of-fact. "Sure it has," she said. "Remember when the cranes were here, the barges? A year or so ago? They dredged and filled and planted for a solid week."

Well, no, I hadn't remembered the cranes and barges. Maybe I was out of town. More likely, more characteristically, I just hadn't paid attention. Now I said to Maggie, "Go in closer."

She nosed the dinghy toward the phony shore. I leaned forward and squinted at palms. I was struck by several things about them. Palms rustled softly and they threw long shadows. Alone or in small clusters, they backbent with the prevailing winds. And they basically all looked alike.

I found the trees that Kenny Lukens had been scrabbling under when he died, the ones that butted up against the fence. They were a pair, their bases perhaps four feet apart. For maybe ten feet up, their trunks diverged, then gradually leaned together in an inevitable parallel.

I looked beyond the steel enclosure. Three, four yards inside it, there was a virtually identical pair of palms. The same distance apart. The same raised and stringy roots. The same windswept geometry.

I rubbed my stinging eyes. Kenny Lukens had

memorized the trees under which he'd stashed his
treasure. Probably he'd counted steps up from the
water's edge. He'd counted right, he'd remembered right, but new trees had been put in and the
shoreline itself had been moved, widened as a sta-
bilizing buffer for the private lots beyond. A final
insult to poor strange Kenny: He'd died digging
the wrong hole.

I pointed past the fence to the farther set of
trees. "The cranes," I said. "The barges."

Maggie measured distance with her eyes. She
understood. "Oh my God," she said.

"Wanna bet that's where the pouches are?"

She didn't take the wager. Instead, she blinked
and panned across as much of the island as we
could see from where we sat. She said, "I know a
little bit about the setup here. It's a pain getting
past that fence."

Getting past the fence? Until she said it, I
hadn't really thought of getting past the fence. I
kept thinking that I'd done enough. Like figuring
out where the pouches were, why no one had
found them so far. Wasn't that enough?

"Just one entrance," she went on. "By the dock
where the island's own launch comes in. There's a
guard there. You have to be a resident or an invited guest to be let in."

I frowned up at the private island. It was elab-
orately landscaped. Manicured. Hibiscus shrubs
had been sculpted into hedges; patches of coarse
Bahama grass gave neatly onto beds of vinca and
bird-of-paradise. This was a version of nature

that took a ton of work. "How about if you're a gardener?" I said.

Maggie lifted an approving eyebrow.

Too bad, though, that the idea hadn't come a couple minutes sooner, and we'd gotten out of there by now. Because as I was speaking, the *Lucky Duck*—its bow wave pink, its windscreens glinting—roared by in its early morning return trip to its berth.

The gambling boat stayed in the main channel, perhaps forty yards from where our dinghy lightly bobbed; and maybe I only imagined that it slowed as it was pulling even with us. But no— the drop in pitch of its engine was hard to deny. We turned our backs, whether soon enough or not we couldn't tell. We had no idea if we'd been noticed, if there was anyone to find it strange that we were reconnoitering at daybreak. But there was something slightly sickening in the way that Mickey Veale's spreading wake crawled beneath our little craft, slithering and undermining.

The big boat lumbered past; the skiff eased off in its rocking. We swallowed fear and Maggie feistily picked up where we'd left off.

"Gardeners," she said. "That could get us in."

Us again. I didn't have the energy to argue. Even though my gut was telling me the whole thing was a really bad idea. Still, I said, "I think I know a way. I've got to talk to someone."

The sun was already bleaching out to white, and the dark water had turned emerald. We sat there for a moment, letting the gambling boat get

well clear of our path. Maggie seemed about to
speak, then caught herself, then gestured toward
the island and spoke up anyway. "Pete," she said,
"you're going to finish this. I know you are."

I didn't answer. I had my doubts. I yawned.

"It's just a habit," she said, as she turned the
skiff and motored slowly to the dinghy dock at
Redmond's Boatyard.

32

Potatoes were frying at Raul's; coffee had just been brewed.

We were among the very first customers, and we grabbed the choicest table—in the corner, next to a wall that dripped purple bougainvillea, under a mahogany tree. I suddenly realized I was famished. I ordered steak and eggs. Maggie laughed, but then she did too. You can't do this kind of stuff on oatmeal.

Waiting for the food, I looked at her. I was so tired that my drooping eyelids started twitching. It occurred to me that we'd just spent the night together. We hadn't done what was usually suggested by the phrase, but it was plenty intimate nevertheless. I'd had time alone with her eyes, her mouth. We'd leaned against each other, our flanks making a hot seam against the misty coolness of the night. I'd seen her yawn and stretch.

Now I watched her eat. I loved the way her loose blouse moved each time she raised her fork. I admired the little muscles in her forearm, which rippled slightly when she used her knife. She pressed her napkin to her lips and I felt their texture once again.

After breakfast I walked her back to her brightly painted trawler. Then, some time after eight, I reclaimed my bike and rode to Bayview Park.

I pulled into the shade of the players' enclosure. Ozzie Kimmel was sitting there, shirtless, in his perennial puke-green bathing suit. He was wrapping gauze around the handle of his racquet, concentrating so hard that his tongue stuck out from the corner of his mouth. He looked up as I approached and, tactful as ever, said, "You look like shit. Where's your stuff? You here to play?"

I told him that I wasn't there to play.

"Not here to play!" he parroted disgustedly. "What is with you, man? Look at you. Fuck has happened to bright-eyed Pete, here at eight and hot to—?"

"Oz," I said. "I need a favor. It's important."

"Important? Uh-oh. Guy starts thinking something's important, you know he's going down the—"

"You know who does the gardening for Sunset Key?"

"You mean Tank Island? That abortion? That pimple on—"

"Oz—who's got the contract for the landscaping?"

He pursed his lips and rubbed his chin. "Why you wanna know?"

"I can't tell you why I want to know."

"Then I can't remember who has the gig."

I said, "Oz, please don't be an asshole."

He said, "*I'm* an asshole? 'Cause a you I'm getting really shitty tennis lately. When we gonna start playing again?"

"When this is done," I said. "Few more days. I hope."

He pouted, went back to gauzing up his racquet. "Okay," he said, "okay. I'm pretty sure it's Cayo Hueso Landscaping. Eddie Baskin."

"You know him?"

" 'Course I know him. Poor bastard's been rotting here almost as long as I have."

"Take me to meet him."

"Now? I'm here for tennis!"

I just stared at him with tired pleading eyes.

"Awright, awright," he said. "We'll take the cab."

"The cab?"

"It's a workday for me. I'm working—can't you tell? Christ, you don't even remember what days I work."

"No way," said Eddie Baskin. "Could cost me the whole damn contract."

We were standing in his backyard at the end of Elgin Lane. The yard was part nursery, part jungle, part alfresco toolshed. Giant tree trimmers leaned on top of sky-flower shrubs; weed whackers stood like golf clubs in a row. Baskin himself was tall and skinny, but with huge gnarly hands and forearms. He had a ponytail and a torn shirt and some kind of funky coral necklace on a leather string. He also, according to Ozzie, had three trucks, a crew of twelve or so, and most of the town's high-end gardening work. A Key West type—the hippie bum with an embarrassing knack for making money.

"Look," I begged, "we'll be on the island half an hour. Anything goes wrong, I stole the shirts, I stole the tools, this meeting never happened."

"Why should I risk it?" Baskin said. "There's no reason I should risk it."

"Yes, there is. It's real important."

"To you maybe."

"Not just to me. To a lot of people."

"Like who?"

"I can't explain right now."

Baskin lit a cigarette, squinted past smoke at Ozzie. "Oz," he said, "I don't know this guy from Adam. Gimme one good reason I should trust him."

My tennis buddy thought that over, a little longer than was flattering or reassuring. Finally he said, "He's very fair on line calls."

The gardener said, "Line calls?"

"All the times I've played him," Ozzie said, "I've gotten maybe two bad calls."

Over several years and a hundred matches, he remembered two bad calls? What kind of lunatics was I recruiting as my allies?

Baskin took a deep drag, slowly exhaled, and waved away the smoke. He frowned at Ozzie. He frowned at me. Finally he said, "Fuck it. Grab some rakes. Grab some shovels. I'll go inside and get a couple shirts." He headed for the house, looked back across his shoulder. "You get snagged out there, you're on your own."

The tools did not quite fit in the trunk of Ozzie's cab. No matter how he laid them in, the handles stuck out past the fender. Finally he found a piece of fraying twine and tied the trunk lid down. I rolled up the borrowed shirts and held them on my lap.

As we drove away from Elgin Lane, I asked him if we could drop the gear off at my house before returning to the park so I could get my bike. He surprised me then.

He said, "I'll bring you down to where you get the launch. What time you wanna go?"

I said, "You don't need to do that, Oz."

"No problem. I wanna do it."

"How come?"

"How come?" He gave the steering wheel a little slap. He didn't look at me. He said, "You don't think I pay attention, do you? You don't think I notice things. *How come?* Because this is a big deal to you. That's how come."

That put me at a loss. I swallowed. I said, "We'll be picking up another person."

"The woman you hide in the backyard?" said Oz. "The one who makes your little thing stand up?"

What could you do with a guy like this? I just looked at him and gave a cockeyed nod.

"Very nice. Just say what time you want to be picked up."

"Let's make it three." I thought about bed, how much I longed to be racked out, curled up beneath a steamy sheet. "No, let's make it four."

"Whatever."

He brought me back to Bayview. I said, "Thanks, Oz. Thanks a lot."

He got shy and waved it off.

I said, "Soon we're back to tennis. Really soon."

"I'll kick your ass," he said.

I locked my bike to the palm I always lock it to, and trudged up the three porch stairs.

It was around ten o'clock by now. Ten, in late April, is just about the time that the freshness of the morning has been all used up, and it starts feeling very hot, and somehow parched in spite of the humidity. The plants have given up the little dribs and veins of moisture they'd hoarded through the night; their leaves begin to curl. Shadows shrink inward like evaporating puddles; collected sun throbs upward from the pavements. I was glad to be going inside.

I opened my front door. A wedge of sunlight slipped in with me, and in its yellow glare I saw a piece of paper on the floor. The paper was around four inches square—a torn-off sheet from a desk pad of some sort. I bent to lift it up. It had three words printed on it. The words were *Stop Right Now.*

I read them with an odd dispassion. They reminded me of my fear but did not increase it. I found this strange. Fear had invaded my life only a day or two before, yet already it had become a

given, like a chronic ache or a background hum
of pipes. With a numbness that stood as a fair
approximation of real calm, I read the threatening note again.

Then I thought of something. I tracked down
the matchbook that I'd found in Kenny Lukens'
duffel and compared its writing with the note. It
was hard to tell if they came from the same hand.
Two different pens, two different thicknesses of
paper. The matchbook had only numbers, and the
person who scrawled on it had been drunk; the
note had only letters, and was stone sober in its
terseness. Still, there were definite resemblances: a
certain impatient leaning of the characters, a
jumpy tendency to lift the pen where other people
might have made a curve.

I concluded that the samples matched, then
was unsure what, if anything, I'd proved. If nothing else, I became persuaded that the person I was
most annoying was the right person to annoy. I
wasn't sure I found this comforting.

I went upstairs and had a shower. I didn't want
the water to be hot; I didn't want it cold. I wanted
it the same temperature as my skin so that it
would lull me with the deliciousness of feeling
like nothing at all.

I fell into bed with my hair still soaking wet,
and slept until midafternoon.

I woke up nervous, suspecting that my earlier
calm had in fact been nothing but exhaustion, a
brief depletion of adrenaline.

I went downstairs and put on a pot of coffee. While it was brewing, I jumped into the pool. It was slightly creepy, wading where the rats had floated; I couldn't yet bring myself to put my face in. Still, the pool was all in all a pleasure. I twirled in it, bent my knees so I was submerged up to the chin. Sunlight twinkled as I looked around my little yard. At the hot tub, the thatch palm, the table where I'd opened Maggie's robe.

Bobbing, slowly turning, I suddenly felt a wistful, almost maudlin affection for my life, as if that life were a thing unto itself, a thing outside of me. It seemed insignificant and precious; it required no grandeur or meaning to give it worth; its value had to do with nothing large. The idea broke through to me, less with fear than sorrow now, that I might die before this thing was finished. But I would try to finish anyway. I no longer had any doubt of it. I would try my best to see it through, and I would find out if Maggie's notion made any sense at all—if finishing would somehow backflow into me and teach me how to finish, or if this would prove to be just some isolated episode, a detour leading nowhere.

I climbed out of the pool, dried myself, had some coffee and some food. And waited for four o'clock to come.

Waited with no patience whatsoever. Suddenly I was eager, almost crazed to power through to a conclusion. I couldn't pinpoint when or how my reluctance had been transformed into avidity, but this much I knew: What I was feeling wasn't courage—unless courage is nothing more than fear stood on its head. What I was feeling was the same dread that had been urging me to flee, except that now it made me itch to charge, to take my shot and get it over with.

At ten till four I was on my porch, wearing a work shirt that bore the logo of Cayo Hueso Landscaping, waiting for Ozzie to come by and pick me up.

I sat up front with him as we drove to Redmond's Boatyard.

Amazingly, he hardly talked along the way. I could think of just one other circumstance in which Ozzie Kimmel didn't yammer. That was late in a tennis match, and only on those rare occasions when the outcome was in doubt. He was a spaceshot but he could focus when he wanted to.

Now he pulled up alongside the chain-link fence at Redmond's. Carrying the extra gardener's shirt, I got out and crunched along the coral gravel toward Maggie's trawler. I walked right past *Dream Chaser*. The stanchions that had held the crime-scene tape were still in place, but the tape itself had already gotten cracked and tattered by the sun. I vaguely wondered who would get the job of cleaning up the blood and who the next owner of the cursed craft would be.

I reached Maggie's boat and called up to her. She came out on deck and lowered the rope ladder. I climbed up. She kissed me on the cheek and we went down into the cabin.

I told her about the note that had been slid under my door. "Look," I said, "you really don't need to do this part."

With no hesitation, she said, "Then why'd you bring the shirt?" She reached out and took it from me.

She turned her back and pulled off the blouse that she'd been wearing. I watched her naked shoulders, sturdy and just lightly freckled. I watched the clean cleft of that enviable spine. She poked her arms into sleeves and I sensed the lifting of her breasts, saw their slight tug on the skin of her sides.

She buttoned up and faced me. There was something antic in the way she looked. The sleeves were much too long for her. The placket hung down to the middle of her thighs. She looked like a child dressing up. Except for her face, which was utterly composed and serious, the forehead intent but smooth. Efficient, she grabbed a canvas tote to put the pouches in.

We left her trawler and walked back to the cab. Ozzie seemed distracted when we got there. At first he didn't say a word as we climbed into the backseat. When I made the introductions, he said only a perfunctory hello. I noticed that his eyes kept flicking toward the rear- and side-view mirrors. At first I thought that, in his adolescent way, he was checking Maggie out. But that didn't seem to be the vector of his gaze. I began to have misgivings. I kept them to myself.

He put the cab in gear and we continued on

our way downtown. The Sunset Key launch left
from a private dock right next to the Hilton. The
location was prestigious and wildly inconvenient.
The only way to get there was to join the crush of
traffic funneling toward Duval Street, then to
crawl along the overburdened cobblestone lanes
beyond it. With Ozzie drumming on the steering
wheel, we idled past the tourist bars and T-shirt
shops, braking now and then for oblivious pedes-
trians. The streets got narrower and narrower;
Ozzie's eyes kept blinking toward the mirrors.
My stomach tightened and began to burn; I
wasn't sure if it was dread or just the traffic.

At last we picked our way across the parking
lot that led to the foot of the pier. Ozzie stopped
the car. I reached for the door handle; he gestured
for me to wait. We sat a moment.

Then he said, "That's weird."

"What's weird?"

He studied the mirror some more. "When I
stopped at Redmond's there was a black car tail-
ing us. Now there's a dark blue one."

"You sure?" I said.

"I'm sure."

"Two different cars?"

"Two different cars. That's the part that's
weird."

I scratched my ear, pulled on my face. "Jesus,
Oz, you could've said something sooner."

"I didn't wanna worry you," he said. "You
have enough on your mind." He paused then
added sheepishly, "I can try and lose 'em. You
want I try and lose 'em?"

"A little late for that," I said.

We sat in silence for a while, baking in the sun-shot cab.

I mumbled, "Why the hell two cars?"

Ozzie, backpedaling, trying to make amends, said, "I can lose 'em, we can come back later. Or tomorrow."

We stalled some more. The cab was getting very hot and close.

Finally Maggie said, "Look, we've come this far, let's just go and get the pouch."

I said, "But if they're following—"

She said, "What's the difference? Face it, we're not fooling anybody. Whoever's following—they've seen where we came from and they've seen where we're going. We've got shovels sticking out the trunk, for God's sake! So let's just go ahead and force their hand."

Her vehemence embarrassed, impressed, and unsettled me. Something about it did not seem right. She was almost too determined, too unshakable. Either she was very brave . . . or she had nothing to be afraid of. She was in cahoots with someone, after all. Someone who would appreciate her recovering the pouch. And would deal with the gullible idiot who'd helped to dig it up.

Was it possible? After the kisses and the confidences? Not knowing seemed as unbearable as anything else that could possibly happen. I chewed my lip, and blew air out through my teeth, and reached once again for the door handle. I said to Ozzie, "Can you come back for us in an hour and a half?"

He looked down at his watch. "Call it six-fifteen?"

"Fine. And Oz—try not to get followed."

We climbed out of the cab, and got the tools out of the trunk, and walked down the pier to get the launch to Sunset Key.

34

The launch ride was a somber one.

Boarding with us were half a dozen residents of the private island. They wore seersucker shirts and beautiful belts. The women carried straw bags and the men had fancy loafers. They didn't sit near us, didn't even look at us. A class thing, I guess. We hunkered near the stern, and didn't talk, and tried to keep our rakes and shovels from chattering as the launch bounced in the harbor chop.

On Sunset Key we walked up a floating ramp, then checked in with the security guard. The poor guy was around sixty, and they made him wear a mock-Colonial getup, with knee socks and a shirt with epaulettes. He pushed a sign-in sheet in our direction and said, "Funny time to be starting work."

I scrawled a phony name and said, "No sense digging in the heat of the day."

He said, "You got that right, Bubba."

Fraudulent and nervous, I blathered on. "Gotta dig around some palms. Check out if they got a root dis—"

Maggie kicked me in the ankle then. She was right to shut me up. We had the Cayo Hueso shirts, we'd signed the sign-in sheet; no one cared why we were digging. We stepped past the guard and moved coyly, indirectly toward the pair of palms that grew apart awhile then leaned together once again.

Along the way, we passed a clubhouse, in front of which a few people were sitting on a patio and sipping gin and tonics. We passed a couple brand-new houses trying to look old, with prefab picket fences and sash windows whose sills had never been leaned on by a human elbow. Here and there the ersatz paradise was littered with building materials waiting to be slapped up before the new development lost its cachet or was blown to pieces by the first good storm. We edged around a half-framed dwelling then cut across grass and sand to the trees that were our destination.

Stopping before them, we dropped our rakes and shovels. I could not resist an impulse to look back across my shoulder. But we were gardeners, there to do a grimy, sweaty job; we were being totally ignored.

I turned my attention to the pair of palms. Suddenly I was far less confident than I'd been at daybreak that they were the right trees, after all. They *mostly* looked like the pair that was closer to the fence. It was *plausible* that Kenny had been fooled by the reengineering of the coastline. But none of this was definite, and if it wasn't right, we'd accomplished zero. The thought made my shoulders slump.

I hid my doubts behind a tight little smile at
Maggie. I picked up my shovel and started digging.

It was nasty work. The sun was low but hot; it
hit us broadside, the whole length of our bodies.
The sand was heavy, and grains cascaded from
the edges of the shovel, undoing part of every
heave. Then there were the roots; palms have lots
and lots of them. They're woody as bamboo, and
they arc down in thick tangled bunches. Those
bunches stopped the shovel blade with an abruptness that bruised the hand and jarred the wrist.

I was quickly soaked with sweat. I stopped a
moment to dry my face. I looked at Maggie, who
dug with compact and rhythmic strokes. She glistened at the hairline and there were damp spots
on her shirt. I went back to digging.

Nasty work—but with a primitive excitement
in it too. Digging for treasure. Digging for *anything*. Scratching and clawing so that something
hidden might be brought to light. Having a goal
that could be reached at any moment.

But how deep did we have to dig? Kenny
Lukens, in a hurry and probably without tools,
would have dug a shallow hole. But what thick-
ness of imported sand had been heaped on in the
meantime? Two feet? Six feet? Did we have to dig
deep as a mainland grave?

The sand got wetter and heavier as we went. It
got more like cement. We couldn't dig straight
through it anymore; we had to shave it from the
edges of the hole. The hole got deep enough to fill
with shadow; the shadow was dank and chilled

our legs. The lip of the hole was at the level of our chests.

Then Maggie's shovel scraped against something that wasn't sand and wasn't root. We knew this because it made a foreign sound, a little squeak. With another bite of the shovel, a corner of wet vinyl was exposed—the vinyl of a bank-deposit pouch. It wasn't quite at the bottom of the hole, but in, so to speak, the wall. She scraped at it like a terrier until it fell.

I stepped across to help. Poking and twisting, I excavated a small niche. A second pouch came free.

Maybe it was only the coolness of the shaded hollow, but as I stared down at the pouches, a chill seized my back and lifted the hair at the base of my skull. I looked at Maggie, to see if she was sharing my freaked and unhappy awe. There was a stolid satisfaction in her face, but it hardly seemed like gladness. We'd done what we set out to do. I guess this was a victory, but a baleful one. We were in possession of what everybody seemed to want; what certain people had shown that they would kill for.

It occurred to me that wisdom would have been to leave the pouches where they lay and to bury them again. Instead, I bent to lift them. The first pouch I touched was swollen but soft, stuffed with what must have been a stack of mildewed cash, the take from Lefty's bar. But the second pouch had something hard inside. It had firm edges and sharp corners—a box of some sort.

Again I glanced at Maggie but couldn't say a

word. She climbed up from the hole and handed me the canvas tote. Without ever lifting the pouches out into the daylight, I slipped them into the bag. Then, on legs that quivered with a mix of edginess and plain fatigue, I scrabbled up from the hole as well.

Quick and silent, we replaced the piled sand. We tamped it down; we raked it. Soon, light breezes and burrowing crabs and bugs would ripple through and make the place look as natural as it ever would. No one would know this sand had been disturbed.

It was getting close to sunset now. Tatters of cloud hung near to the horizon and made the red rays intermittent. Music wafted across the water from the downtown bars. Reggae. Probably it had been playing for a while, but only now did it register. Other people were having a pleasant afternoon, normal for Key West if not for other places, lazy, aimless, sensual. Music and a margarita as the sun dived into the Gulf. God, I missed my life.

We mopped our faces and our necks, and gathered up our tools, and strolled back to get the launch.

35

"*Were you* followed?" I asked Ozzie.

We were somewhat late and he'd been sitting in the parking lot awhile. We found him leaning up against his cab, arms crossed, staring at the water and the streaky sky.

"Yeah," he said.

I chewed my lip.

"I was followed to the Pier House, where I picked up a fare; followed to the airport; followed to the Casa, where I dropped off the next asshole. By then I think they realized I was just some jerk trying to make a living. After that I wasn't followed." He lifted his chin toward Sunset Key. "How'd it go out there?"

"Went okay," I said. "Followed by one car or two?"

"Hard to tell," he said. "The glare, the traffic. But anyway, I lost 'em."

I tried to feel reassured by this. I couldn't quite manage it. We were on a tiny island, after all, a place where it was no great trick to find someone again. But there was nothing to be done about it now. We put the tools back in the trunk and got into the taxi.

My nervousness made everything annoying. Our hot wet shirts had cooled and gotten clammy. My back itched. My bare legs stuck to the seat.

We entered the maze of tiny downtown lanes and crawled. Rental cars, pink mopeds, crazy bicycles—a tidal wave of vehicles streamed against us as they swarmed toward the Sunset Celebration, blocking our path, keeping us trapped. Drunks weaved. Kids swaggered. The bag that held the pouches was on the floor between my ankles. I hated having it there. I felt like I was handcuffed to a bomb.

Beyond Duval the traffic finally relented. In fact, with a macabre abruptness, the streets seemed all at once deserted. No cars moved now; nobody was walking. The lemmings had all massed at the water's edge; the land side was lifeless and bereft.

If the traffic had been frustrating, this sudden abandonment felt sinister and jarring. It was as if the town had been evacuated in a panic, emptied by a tragedy. Here among the unpeopled houses and the clustered trees it was already dusk. Light refused to come down from the sky; shadow spread and conquered. Quiet reigned, but it was not a peaceful quiet. It was the hissing silence of conspiracy, the silence that went with an absence of witnesses.

Uncannily, we went eight blocks, ten, without seeing a single person. Then Ozzie pulled up to my house.

My haven and my retreat. I just stared at it through the taxi window for a moment—at my bicycle chained to its accustomed tree; at my shady porch, where I could rock and peek out through the lacy foliage. Everything seemed as it should be—it was all right there in front of me— yet I looked at it nostalgically, as if it had already long been lost or ruined. I'd made this house exactly what I wanted it to be; it was the perfect container for the life I'd chosen. I'd always felt safe here. Now this house seemed less safe than the open streets. It was where my enemies could find me. It was where I had the most to lose.

I sighed and reached out for the car door handle. I thanked Ozzie for his help.

He swiveled back and looked at me across the seat. "Want me to hang around?"

I shook my head. I didn't see what it would accomplish.

"I'll bring the tools back in the morning," he said.

I nodded. It was nice of him to remember the tools. I'd already forgotten all about them.

"Nice meeting you," he said to Maggie, and extended a hand to shake.

This unexpected bit of gentility from Ozzie only made the moment more bizarre. I stalled in my leaning out the door.

"You okay?" he said to me.

I nodded that I was, but I was lying. I was terrified in a way that seemed to be making me slow and stupid. My joints felt stiff, my arms and legs were heavy. My field of vision shrank and glared a sickly yellow at the edges. But I climbed out of the taxi, reached back in to grab the canvas bag. Maggie got out from the other side, and together we went up the porch steps to the house.

I opened the door, expecting . . . what? A knife at my throat? A sap to the base of my skull?

I pressed myself against the door frame then sprang in like I knew karate. Nothing happened, and I felt ridiculous. A ceiling fan murmured. The refrigerator hummed.

I made sure the curtains were snugly drawn before I switched on a light. I dropped the tote bag on the sofa. Then I said to Maggie, "I need a drink. Some grappa?"

Grappa was the first thing we'd ever drunk together, but I wasn't being sentimental; I wanted the strongest liquor I could think of.

"Love some," she said.

I went to the freezer to fetch the bottle. A puff of frost reminded me I couldn't bear my clammy shirt for one more minute. I poured drinks then ran upstairs and grabbed a couple sweatshirts. Bashful away from her own place, Maggie slipped into the bathroom to put hers on.

During her brief absence I sipped my drink and wandered back into the living room. Pacing slowly, my eyes drawn irresistibly to the bag that held the pouches, I was suddenly seized by an appalling thought: I needed to get out my gun. This did not seem like a choice, but rather a compulsion, an imperative. Did I believe that, in a crisis, the gun would save me, that I'd somehow in-

stantly take on the nerve and skill to use it? No, I
don't think I believed that for a second. What I
was feeling was unreasonable, primitive. Galled
at my own fragility, I was reaching blindly for
strong magic.

I lifted the watercolor of the mangrove islet
from its hook; I started fiddling with the lock on
the wall safe.

Maggie came into the room.

The gun was in my hand, and shoulder high by
the time I turned to face her. She saw it and
flinched; she suddenly stopped moving and let out
a tiny gasp. She looked at me as though I'd been
monstrously transformed, as though, suddenly, it
was me she was afraid of. Mortified at having
frightened her, I let the hand that held the pistol
fall limply to my side. But for some fraction of a
second, a question nagged at me: How could she
imagine I would hurt her? There was nothing that
could make me turn against her—was there?

There was a moment of supreme awkwardness.
I struggled to produce a reassuring smile. It didn't
work; I could feel in my cheeks that the smile
came out grotesque.

Maggie's hand was at her throat. A little
breathlessly, she said, "I've never been so close to
a gun before."

Maybe there was nothing more to it than that.
Guns were unsettling, after all. I nodded, sipped
some grappa. My voice pinched, unnatural, I
said, "Shall we see what's in the pouches?"

Stiffly, we sat down on the edge of the settee.
The canvas tote was between us, a ghoulish chap-

erone. I put the pistol on the coffee table and
reached into the bag. I grabbed the swollen
pouch, the one that seemed to hold money. I offered Maggie the chance to open it. She declined
with a shake of her head. So I opened it myself. It
wasn't so easy. The zipper was plastic but fouled
with sand. The slide hit roadblocks with every
tug. I tried to finesse it for a bit, then quickly lost
my patience and tore the rotting fabric where it
was seamed into the vinyl.

I dumped the contents onto the coffee table.
No surprises—it was cash. Tens and twenties
mostly, with bent corners, the bills gone grayish
and greasy with mold. We didn't bother counting
it, though I guessed it was five, six hundred dollars. Not a bad take for a weeknight late shift at
a bar; then again, a pretty paltry sum to die for.

I guess that's what Maggie was thinking too.
She looked at the money and bit her lip. I thought
she might start to cry. I guess she and Kenny had
been pretty good friends.

I reached into the bag and seized the other
pouch. With her eyes alone, Maggie made it clear
that she didn't want to touch it. So once again I
tried the zipper, then, with clumsy and unsteady
fingers, tore the wretched thing open. Tiny sand
grains bounced onto my legs. A dank smell
wafted up. Probing past the sundered closure, I
felt something hard but flimsy, damp but not
porous, sharp-edged yet nearly weightless.

I pulled out a videocassette. There was no label
on it. It had a superficial crack in the black plastic
of its casing, though it seemed like it would play.

I held it up and stared at Maggie. She took my free hand and placed it on her chest. Her heart was jumping. We both knew there was something on that tape it would be better not to see. We both knew we had to finish. We got up from the sofa. I took my pistol and my drink and we went toward the music room to watch the video.

36

I switched on the dimmered lights but kept them low. The heavy insulated door swung closed behind us, blocking out the deepening dusk and the memory of the weirdly empty streets. I put my gun and grappa on the small table between the room's two cushy chairs, then crouched before the VCR and slipped in the cassette. I sat down next to Maggie and picked up the remote. Squeezing it way harder than I had to, I turned on the TV and started the tape.

The screen stayed black a moment, then brightened to an image that was only gravel. I found myself both hoping and fearing that perhaps the long-buried cassette had been spoiled, its secrets leached into the sand of Sunset Key.

Abruptly, though, the gravel resolved into a picture. It was a picture of a room that looked familiar, but which I couldn't place at first. Heavy lamps stood in thick carpeting. Another decade's furniture was arrayed around a space with many mirrors. I realized it was Lydia Ortega's condo. The camera shakily panned . . . and there was Lydia herself, sitting on her sectional. Her eyes were

much too wide and much too black, and even I
could tell that she was wigged on coke. She was
wearing a bizarre half-bra that pushed her breasts
up but stopped short of covering her nipples, and
a G-string that drew the eye to the cleft of her sex.

For an instant, plain embarrassment overwhelmed fear and curiosity. I said to Maggie,
"We don't have to watch this."

She didn't answer. The tape ran. Lydia mas-
saged herself, did lewd things with her tongue.
There was a wine bottle on the coffee table in
front of her. She slid her hips down toward it.

My head swam. Arousal and bewilderment.
Lefty had said his daughter had a problem. That
a woman had put the pouch into the safe. Lydia
had claimed that she was being blackmailed. Had
hinted that the blackmailer was Mickey Veale . . .

On the TV screen, she writhed, she cooed, she
pulled away the G-string with her red-nailed fingers. My eyes went where her fingers did.

Then something happened in the upper left-
hand corner of the screen, something all but
unimaginable. An electronic stamp suddenly
flashed on. It hung there for a second, maybe
two, and then switched off again. The stamp read
KWPD.

I blinked. I forgot to breathe. I thought, But
wait—if Lefty owned the cops . . . ?

The tape was running. Lydia had grabbed the
wine bottle, was bringing it up between her legs.

I was thinking, and if Veale owned the cops . . . ?

That was as far as I got. Because that was when
the heavy door of my silent room slammed open,

came crashing in as though the hot and urgent breath of the entire outside world had been aimed at it. Barreling behind the crash were Officer Cruz and Officer Corallo. Their guns were drawn and they held them the way real shooters do, with a hand braced on the wrist.

Time froze as thoughts trampled one another. Affront kicked in even quicker than terror—how dare these bastards violate my haven? I glanced at my pistol on the little table, useless, unready, as I always knew it would be. I saw Maggie out of the corner of my eye, pasted back into her chair; sinews stood out in her neck.

Cruz bulled into the middle of the room. Corallo held his ground and blocked the doorway. Cruz's crazy hairline crawled as he gestured toward the filthy video. "So," he said, "the amateur gets lucky."

I didn't feel that lucky. I said nothing. The tape ran. Lydia Ortega had gotten down onto her knees. The electronic stamp flashed once again. This seemed to embarrass Cruz—not too bright, after all, to use the department videocam—and so he shot the television. Vaporized colors seemed to waft from the obliterated screen, a wisp of pink, a fog of sickly yellow. The sound of the gun went on and on; first the explosion, and then a shattering, and then an echoing whine.

The noise was so persistent that we barely heard the second shot—the one that entered Corallo's thickly muscled back and tore through his heart and sent him sprawling facedown dead on the floor behind our chairs.

An instant's complete incomprehension then erupted into mayhem.

Cruz wheeled and fired toward the doorway. His bullet lodged in heavy lumber and bundled insulation.

A slender arm poked into the room. Red fingernails wrapped around a trigger. Another shot rang out. It missed Cruz and knocked my amplifier off its shelf. By reflex, Maggie and I slithered from our chairs and hunkered on the floor, our bodies close and quaking. Embarrassingly but not surprisingly, I'd blown the chance to grab my own weapon and enter the fray.

Blast now followed blast. There were three exchanges, four. A stack of CDs toppled; a speaker grille was gashed.

Cruz moved in our direction; maybe—probably—he had in mind to use us as a shield. But the motion made him more exposed, and before he reached us, a bullet caught him just above his trigger hand; his revolver flew out of his fingers. He shook the wounded arm and dropped low to scramble after it.

Lydia Ortega took the opportunity to stride into the room on high-heel shoes. Her makeup was tidy; her face had taken on a deranged and fatal clarity of mission. She stepped close to Cruz and shot him in the knee; we could hear the crack of bone. He rolled and writhed and kept on crawling. Standing over him, she shot him in the other leg and he finally kept still. A lot of blood was coming out of him, but his eyes were open and he looked more pissed off than frightened.

I cowered on the floor. Strangely, perhaps, I felt no threat from Lydia. She was there to settle scores, to avenge old torments, not to kill outsiders, and not to save herself. But I was still afraid of Cruz. He was desperate and I didn't trust that he was finished. I stared at him; his eyes and my eyes were on a level. Belatedly, I thought to reach up to the little table and grab my own unfired gun. Never taking my gaze off his, I seized my weapon, braced my elbow on the floor, and pointed it at his face. Too late I realized that what I'd picked up was the remote control.

Shot three times, the rogue cop still managed a sarcastic snarl. Just before losing consciousness, he said, "You're pathetic, Amsterdam." Then his eyeballs rolled and his head thumped lightly on the floor.

Maggie scuttled over and knocked his weapon farther away.

Slowly, I sat up and looked at Lefty's daughter. Her eyes were dazed and distant. I took a deep breath. The air was acrid with gunpowder; it caught at the back of my throat. As steadily as I could manage, I said, "It's over now, Lydia. Can I have the gun, please?"

She blinked, then gazed down at me as if she'd only at that moment noticed I was there. Suddenly she seemed confused, and, I thought, a little piqued, like her revenge was not quite perfect. She said to me, "Where's Veale?"

I said I didn't know.

"Where's the tape?" she said.

I nodded toward the VCR. She shot it. Then she handed me her gun. It was very hot.

She sat down in the chair where Maggie had been sitting, and crossed her legs with a rustle of silk, and helped herself to the last of my grappa while she waited to be taken away.

27

"*When did you* know it was the cops?" asked Maggie.

This was a couple days later, and we were sitting in the hot tub. We had a lot to talk about, and it was hard to talk above the rumble of the jets, so we hadn't turned them on. This meant we had no bubbles to disguise our nakedness. I looked at Maggie's lightly freckled breasts, her tan and tapering midriff.

Sheepishly I said, "I didn't realize it until that stupid stamp came on the tape. Being honest, I didn't totally get it even then. I got it when they stormed into the room."

She nodded, fixed me with the limpid and sincere gray eyes that, to my secret shame, I had at moments doubted. "And now it seems so clear."

"Now it does," I said. "But I made the same mistake that Kenny made. An understandable mistake, I guess. I assumed that Lefty owned the cops, rather than vice versa."

Sweetly, Maggie said, "Those bastards."

I reached over and grabbed my glass of *prosecco*. One should never drink in the hot tub, of course, but if one must, this off-dry Venetian sparkler is the way to go. I rolled some over my gums and said, "And it never even dawned on me they owned Veale too."

"And played them off against each other," Maggie added.

"For *years*," I said. I leaned back and glanced up at the poinciana tree that hung over the spa, and thought back to the chat I'd had with Veale the day before.

I'd gone to him to try to help out Lydia, who was in custody, being held without bail. She'd killed a cop and badly wounded another. Forget that Cruz and Corallo were murderers themselves—the brutal men in snorkels, who'd killed Kenny and Andrus, and would surely have killed Maggie and me, had things gone a little differently. The fact was, Lydia had shot Corallo in the back; so much for self-defense. I hoped to show, at least, that there were extraordinary circumstances that should allow her to finesse a plea and ask for clemency.

The Mickey Veale I'd found that day, almost catatonic in his office, with its shades drawn against the brilliant light and the view of Sunset Key, was shaken, self-pitying, but surprisingly forthcoming. "A cheeseball but not an evil guy."

"Who?" said Maggie.

I hadn't quite realized I'd spoken aloud; I was still catching up on my sleep. "Veale," I said. "He told me he was being blackmailed too. Cruz and Corallo figured out exactly how to set him up, practically from the minute he hit town. Motel room with an underage girl. Procured by them, of course. They got Polaroids, a statement from the girl, the works. If the paperwork got turned in, maybe he'd do time. At the very least, there went his chance of ever getting a license for the gambling boat. They owned him from then on."

Maggie pretzeled up her legs, twisted onto her side to stretch her hips. She said, "But if Veale was a victim too—"

"Then why did the Ortegas hate him?" I said. "Because they didn't know. The cops used him as their point man. When they'd made the tape of Lydia, it was Veale they sent to put the squeeze on Lefty. Veale had to fake being involved. Lefty believed him. Lydia still thought it came down to Veale when she walked into the house and started shooting."

Even in the hot water under the hot sun, Maggie gave a little shiver. "And a good thing she showed up."

"A good thing *two* cars followed Ozzie," I said. "When Lydia's flunkies reported that we were heading off with shovels, it was a pretty good bet that she'd visit."

Maggie sipped some wine, then went into another yoga stretch, one that arched her back. The effect was pretty stunning. She said, "And the water-sports business—as much as they hated each other, Ortega and Veale really shared it?"

"Ortega and Veale," I said, "were names on paper. Probably they'd been hit up for some seed money. But the business belonged to Cruz and Corallo. And I'll bet it was quite profitable, since most of the Jet Skis had been stolen."

"Stolen?"

I sipped some more *prosecco*. It was tasting fabulous. I said, "That's why we couldn't figure out what they were smuggling with the Jet Skis. What they were smuggling *was* Jet Skis. Associates would grab them from other operations all up and down the Keys, from as far away as Lauderdale. They'd disappear into the *Lucky Duck* and come out with new serial numbers. Handy too if the cops needed an untraceable craft for when they put their snorkels on and went off to kill somebody. Or even for making little jaunts to the Bahamas."

"So you think it was one of them who found Kenny on Green Turtle?"

I shrugged. "Seems reasonable," I said. "The handwriting on the matchbook seems to be the same as on the note that was pushed under my door. Plus, what the guy told Kenny happened to be true: The pouch was worth nothing—except to the people it incriminated."

There was a pause. Maggie slipped down lower in the water, made it look as though her chin was floating. The wispy hair at the nape of her neck was plastered down. Her smooth face darkened, and in completion of some unspoken train of thought, she said, "Poor Lydia."

"Poor Lydia," I agreed. The mention of her name sent me reaching for my wineglass once again. "A victim of good old-fashioned hypocrisy and family craziness."

"How so?"

"Here's what I think. Take it for what it's worth. Lefty was a macho papa. I think he wanted a son, and Lydia felt that every day. Lefty would have wanted his boy to be a hell-raiser and an ass-kicker and a stud. Lydia got even by trying her best to be exactly those things—even to the extent of snorting coke and doing sex shows for the cops. Here's your ideal, Dad—in your face."

Maggie thought that over. "A little pat," she said.

I admitted that it was. "But pat doesn't mean wrong. Look, Lydia found the perfect way to humiliate herself *and* to hold an unbearable mirror up to Lefty. So of course he'd do anything to keep that tape from being shown around. He gave Lydia the money to buy it back, then she rubbed his face in it still more by putting the dirty prize in his safe."

Maggie shook her head. "On the night that Kenny pulled his robbery."

"Which was just Kenny's lousy timing and piss-poor luck."

She bit the delectable nub at the center of her upper lip. "Very sad," she said, and then she tried to brighten. She lifted an arm from the tub, and shook it off, and grabbed a soggy paper folded on the edge. Snapping it open, she said, "But hey, according to the *Sentinel,* at least you solved the whole thing brilliantly."

According to the *Sentinel*, yes. But of course, the *Sentinel* was seldom accurate. From the banner headline on—LOCAL P.I. CRACKS LINKED MURDERS—the paper gave me entirely too much credit. It hinted at expert detection, when in fact I'd only blundered into information here and there. It suggested deep commitment, when the truth was that I'd fought involvement at every turn. It conjured for the reader a climactic and heroic shootout, but the reality of that confrontation was that I'd been sitting there watching a porno flick when all hell broke loose, at which point I trembled on the floor till it was over.

Still, I was glad to have this single flashy item for my scrapbook. It would preempt any hassles I might have with the IRS. Not a real private eye? Oh yeah? Well, suck on *this*! Then again, my music room had been destroyed. Speakers shot out, carpet stained with gore. Repairs would just about erase what I'd saved in taxes. Some might call that justice.

Rather goadingly, I thought, Maggie waved the paper in my face. "You're going to get a lot more work from this," she said.

"Oh no, I'm not," I vowed.

She raised an eyebrow, then refolded the paper and put it aside. Something in the gesture made me sad; for a moment I didn't know why. Then I did. It somehow made me think of Kenny Lukens, with his mildewed clipping from a long-forgotten paper; his clipping and his desperation and his tattered dream. Dreams sometimes made people reckless. Things got out of hand and people

needed help. And you weren't immune from being asked for help just because you happened to
be naked in the hot tub. Would Kenny Lukens be
alive if I had helped him sooner? Would I?

I looked up at the poinciana tree. It was coming into leaf just as its shade was needed most.
Sometimes things worked out, happened in their
proper season.

Distracted, I didn't notice Maggie moving until
she was nestled up against me. I felt her arm, her
flank. Under water, her body had no temperature,
just a smoothness and an almost fluffy buoyancy.
She threw a leg across my thighs. I leaned my
cheek against her short damp hair. She'd told me
that you learned to see things through by seeing
them through, that finishing was just a habit. I
wanted to believe it. She and I had something left
to finish, after all. Though at that moment, for
the first time in what felt like many days, there
seemed to be no hurry.

MANGROVE SQUEEZE

by Laurence Shames

Key West seduces people—then asks them to leave in the morning. When one opportunity seeker stumbles upon a nefarious plot revolving around a handsome Russian and his string of T-shirt shops, she finds the Russian mafia on her trail. As dead bodies sully the Key West scenery, a secret society of killers puts on the squeeze—and conspires to turn an island paradise into a tropical death-trap. . . .

* * *

"Laurence Shames has carved out his own piece of turf in South Florida. *Mangrove Squeeze* is his sixth book set in torpid, unpredictable Key West. Shames' sense of place is unerring, but it is his people that make his books unforgettable."

—*The Hartford Courant*

Published by Ballantine Books.
Available at your local bookstore.

WELCOME TO PARADISE

by Laurence Shames

Before mild-mannered furniture salesman Al Tuschman left New Jersey for a week in Key West, he hadn't an enemy in the world. But a series of puzzling assaults on his privacy, his sanity, and his life has turned his stay at the Paradise Hotel into Tropical Hell. Now, if Tuschman doesn't watch his back, somebody's going to be reporting the death of another salesman.

* * *

"Zany humor. . .Shames mixes sun and fun, wise guys and dumb guys, smart gals and bad gals with such wit and style it makes you want to head straight to Key West and join the party."

—*The Orlando Sentinel*

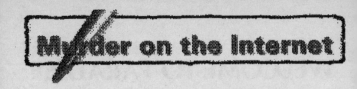